Murder in Half Moon Street

A Redmond and Haze Mystery

Book 8

By Irina Shapiro

Copyright

© 2022 by Irina Shapiro

All rights reserved. No part of this book may be reproduced in any form, except for quotations in printed reviews, without permission in writing from the author.

All characters are fictional. Any resemblances to actual people (except those who are actual historical figures) are purely coincidental.

Cover created by MiblArt.

Table of Contents

Prologue 5
Chapter 1 6
Chapter 2 16
Chapter 3 23
Chapter 4 31
Chapter 5 41
Chapter 6 46
Chapter 7 53
Chapter 8 59
Chapter 9 65
Chapter 10 68
Chapter 11 72
Chapter 12 80
Chapter 13 87
Chapter 14 95
Chapter 15 102
Chapter 16 106
Chapter 17 112
Chapter 18 120
Chapter 19 128
Chapter 20 135
Chapter 21 142
Chapter 22 145
Chapter 23 150
Chapter 24 156

Chapter 25 160

Chapter 26 169

Chapter 27 175

Chapter 28 180

Chapter 29 184

Chapter 30 188

Chapter 31 194

Chapter 32 197

Chapter 33 210

Chapter 34 221

Chapter 35 226

Chapter 36 229

Epilogue 232

Notes 234

Prologue 235

Chapter 1 237

Chapter 2 242

Chapter 3 245

Prologue

Valerie Shaw balanced the tray in her hands as she walked up the stairs, careful not to spill the scalding tea. The only item on the tray besides the cup and saucer was a plate of lightly buttered toast spread with orange marmalade. Her mistress requested the same thing every morning and usually left half her breakfast untouched, mindful of preserving her figure. Valerie was all for keeping a trim waist, but if she were ever served breakfast in bed, she'd ask for soft-boiled eggs, toast smothered in butter, strawberry jam, and a pot of chocolate, which she would drink down to the last drop. She was sick of the milky tea and porridge Mrs. Taft served below stairs.

Dragging her mind away from food, Valerie set the tray on the hall table and knocked on her mistress's door before turning the handle. The door failed to open. Puzzled, Valerie tried again. Miss Grant never locked her door at night. Valerie called out, asking Miss Grant if she was all right, but received no answer. In fact, the silence inside the room was ominous. Valerie looked around to make sure no one was about and pressed her face to the door, peering into the keyhole. She wasn't one to listen at doors or spy on her mistress, but this was unusual, and she was concerned. In place of light, Valerie saw impenetrable darkness. The key was still in the lock.

As Valerie straightened, she thought she smelled something wafting from beneath the closed door. She inhaled deeper, taking an involuntary step back as her nose registered what her mind had already acknowledged. She'd grown up above a butcher's shop and recognized the odor instantly.

What she smelled was blood. And death.

Chapter 1

Monday, June 8, 1868

Gentle rays of summer sunlight bathed the city of London in a golden glow, the wide ribbon of the Thames glittering playfully as it wound its way through the sprawling metropolis. On mornings like this, London looked magical, a fairytale place where nothing ugly ever happened and everyone lived a life filled with meaning and purpose, but Lord Jason Redmond was on his way to examine a body, a task he performed all too frequently, and only when the deceased was a victim of sudden and violent death.

Alighting from the hansom, Jason followed Constable Napier, who'd been sent to fetch him from the hospital where Jason volunteered his services several days a week and instructed a new generation of surgeons, into the house in Half Moon Street. Inspector Haze was waiting for him in one of the upstairs bedrooms, his continued presence necessary to preserve the crime scene until Jason arrived. Jason and Constable Napier were greeted by a churchlike hush, the sort of silence that was often the result of shock and disbelief. There wasn't a servant in sight, the staff most likely too unsettled to do anything but congregate in the servants' hall and talk in soft tones over cups of strong tea, their morbid curiosity outweighing their grief for the dead.

Jason glimpsed the master of the house. He was in the library, sitting by the cold hearth, a glass in his shaking hand. They'd speak later, once Jason had completed his examination and left the body to the tender mercies of the undertakers. Constable Napier led him upstairs, toward a room at the end of the carpeted corridor. The door was ajar, hanging askew off the frame. Daniel Haze was inside, his hands clasped behind his back as he gazed out the window, his face set in grim lines, the wire-rimmed spectacles reflecting the shimmering morning light. He turned as soon as he heard them enter, relief clearly showing in his face.

"At last!" he exclaimed when he saw Jason. "What took you so long?"

"My apologies. I was in the operating theater," Jason replied, wondering exactly how long Constable Napier had been forced to wait for him. "I came as soon as I could. Tell me what happened," he invited.

"Miss Sybil Grant was found dead this morning. The room was locked from the inside, and there's no sign of the murder weapon."

Jason nodded. This promised to be another corker of a case. "Let's have a look," he said as he set his medical bag on a chair and approached the bed.

"Miss Grant's brother has forbidden an autopsy, so you will have to base your conclusions on an external examination," Daniel said. He was clearly displeased but could hardly override the wishes of the next of kin without a court order.

Jason sighed heavily as he took in the woman on the bed. She was young, probably still in her twenties. Her face was pale where it wasn't streaked with blood, her dark hair in disarray, the curls fanned out on the pillow like Medusa's snakes, and her eyes closed as if she were still asleep. She was clad in an expensive nightgown, silk or satin, with delicate embroidery at the neckline and hem. Trim ankles peeked from beneath the fabric, the woman's bare feet no bigger than those of a child.

To say that someone had slashed her throat would have been a gross understatement. At first glance, it looked as if her throat had been ripped out by a savage beast, not by any weapon known to man. The wound looked like a grotesque smile, the jagged lips pulled wide to reveal the gleam of bone. The woman's bloody hands were folded on her chest, her eyes shut.

"Did anyone touch her?" he asked Daniel.

"I don't believe so."

"Shut the door," Jason said before taking off his coat and rolling up his shirtsleeves.

He feared Mr. Grant might burst in during the examination to express his outrage at Jason's handling of the body. The cause of death was obvious, but there were many things a dead body could tell a knowledgeable surgeon, and Jason meant to hear what the victim had to say before her earthly remains were turned over to an undertaker, who would do his utmost to hide any trace of trauma for the benefit of the family.

Daniel approached the door and pushed it shut, but the panel wouldn't fit properly into the frame due to its twisted hinges.

"I'll make sure you're not disturbed," Daniel said, pulling up a chair and setting it by the door. He lowered himself into it, clearly relieved not to have to watch Jason probe the body. For a police inspector, Daniel was a bit squeamish and preferred to leave the corpse to the expert.

Jason spent the next half hour carefully studying every inch of Miss Grant's remains. He examined the wound carefully, probed her every orifice, and then performed a pelvic exam before finally covering her with a sheet and pouring water into the pretty basin positioned on the washstand in the corner.

"Well?" Daniel demanded impatiently as Jason washed his hands, the water blooming red with the victim's blood.

"Miss Grant appears to have been in fine health prior to her death. She was well nourished, had excellent teeth, her skin was clear, and her hair lustrous."

"What's the cause of death?" Daniel asked, pulling his gaze away from the figure on the bed.

"There's considerable bruising to the neck. I think the killer tried to strangle her first, then used a long, narrow object, possibly a dull knife, to stab her in the neck. I believe the hyoid bone is fractured and the larynx is crushed, but I would need to perform a postmortem to be certain of the extent of the damage."

"Can you explain that in layman's terms?" Daniel asked. He wasn't familiar with the inner workings of the body or the nomenclature.

"Sorry. Of course. The hyoid bone is situated right here," Jason said, pointing to an area just above his Adam's apple. "And the larynx is the voice box, which is a bit lower. Whoever strangled her had powerful hands and pressed down hard with the thumbs to inflict the maximum amount of damage. I'm not sure why they felt the need to stab her as well, since they could have easily finished the job without resorting to such violence. Given the amount of blood on the victim's hands and beneath the fingernails, I think she fought for her life, but once the carotid artery was severed, death would have come almost instantly."

Jason exhaled deeply and continued. "There are indentations in the mattress on either side of her hips, which leads me to conclude that the killer straddled the victim before going for her throat. Once she was dead, they laid her out and closed her eyes."

"Could a woman have done this?" Daniel asked.

Jason considered the question. "A strong woman could have done this, yes."

"Was the victim violated?"

"There are no signs of sexual assault, but the victim was not a virgin."

"Do you think that's relevant to the case?" Daniel asked.

Jason shrugged. "Depends on the motive for the killing."

"Could she have been with child?"

"If she were, she would have been in the early stages of pregnancy. I would need to open her up to know for certain."

"Time of death?"

"Before midnight. She's been dead for close to twelve hours."

Daniel nodded. "This was a very personal, frenzied attack. The killer didn't simply want to kill Miss Grant, he or she wanted to watch her die. Given that the killer had brought a knife, I think we can safely assume that the murder was premeditated."

"I agree," Jason said. "The murderer had the presence of mind to lay the victim out, remove the murder weapon, and escape from a locked room."

"Since there were no signs of forced entry, it must be someone who was already in the house," Daniel mused.

"Or someone who'd gained access without needing to break in."

"You're saying they had an accomplice?"

"Possibly. Or perhaps the person had managed to get in during the day when the doors were unlocked and remained hidden until everyone had retired."

Daniel removed his spectacles and cleaned them thoroughly with his handkerchief, something he did when he needed a moment to organize his thoughts. "I'd like to begin by speaking to everyone in the house. Do you need to return to the hospital?"

"I don't have anything scheduled for the rest of the day," Jason said as he unrolled his sleeves, donned his coat, and picked up his medical bag.

Mr. Grant, who was still in the library, had left instructions with the butler that they use the drawing room for the interviews. It was a pleasant room with large windows and comfortable furnishings upholstered in aquamarine blue and silver. Several occasional tables dotted the room, and there were arrangements of silk flowers, china figurines on the mantel, and stuffed birds taking flight beneath a glass cupola on a pedestal placed between two tall windows.

Daniel settled in an armchair and pulled out his notebook and pencil, while Jason took the opposite chair and crossed his legs, his gaze fixed on the door. They probably made for an intimidating pair, but sometimes fear made people babble and reveal details they might otherwise have kept to themselves, so Daniel and Jason made no effort to appear friendly or relaxed.

The first witness was Valerie Shaw, Miss Grant's maid. She was about thirty, with light brown hair and nut-brown eyes in a round, friendly face. She was of average height and weight, and her black dress was neatly starched and adorned with a modest white collar that matched her cap. The woman looked utterly bewildered as she entered the drawing room and sat on the edge of the settee at Daniel's request.

"How long have you worked for Miss Grant?" Daniel asked. It was always good to know how far back a relationship went when interviewing a witness.

"Just over two years, sir."

"Miss Shaw, can you tell us what happened this morning," Daniel said, giving Miss Shaw an encouraging smile.

She nodded stoically but looked like she was just barely holding back tears. "I went to wake my mistress at eight o'clock, as I did every morning. She liked to keep to a strict schedule. I set down her breakfast tray on the hallway table and tried the door, but it was locked. Miss Grant never locked her door, so I found this odd. I peered into the keyhole, but the key was still inside."

"What did you do then?" Daniel asked.

"I knocked and called out to her, but when she failed to answer, I summoned Mr. Hudson. He's the butler."

"What did Mr. Hudson do?"

Miss Shaw took a shuddering breath. "He called out and knocked, same as I did. It was at this point that we decided something was wrong. Miss Grant was not a heavy sleeper, nor would she ignore us if she were able to respond. Mr. Hudson was going to ask Mrs. Taft for a spare key, but I told him the key was still inside the door, so he called Steven—that's one of the footmen—and together they broke down the door."

"Were you the first person inside?" Daniel asked.

Miss Shaw nodded. "I was. I needed to make sure my mistress was decent before I let the men in. That's when I saw…" Her voice trailed off as a sob escaped her chest. "There was so much blood," she whispered, her eyes wide with the horror of what she'd found.

"Did you notice anything out of the ordinary besides the victim?" Daniel asked.

The woman shook her head. "No. Everything looked just as it should. Nothing had been taken."

"Was the window open or closed?"

"It was closed, sir. Locked."

"And the key?" Jason asked.

"The key fell out when the door was broken down, sir. It was lying on the floor, just inside the room. I picked it up. I still have it." She reached into her pocket and pulled out a brass key, which she handed to Daniel.

"Miss Shaw, who else has rooms on that floor?" Daniel asked.

"Only the master, sir. But his room is on the other side."

"And are there any places in the house where someone might remain undetected for a long period of time?"

"Why, yes, sir. There are several empty rooms where someone might bide, since no one goes inside after they've been cleaned. Do you think the intruder had been in the house all along?" Miss Shaw asked, her eyes widening in shock.

"There is that possibility," Daniel replied. "Miss Shaw, is there anyone you can think of who might have wished to harm your mistress? Did she say anything unexpected in the days leading up to her death? Was she frightened?"

"No, Inspector. She was in reasonably good spirits and looking forward to her trip."

"Where was she going?" Jason asked.

"She was going to the seaside and planned to stay for a fortnight."

"Was she traveling alone?"

"I was going with her. We were to stay at the cottage."

"What cottage is that?" Daniel asked.

"The family owns a cottage in Southend-on-Sea. There's a couple that looks after it. The Marches," Miss Shaw explained. "Miss Grant loved it there. It was her peaceful place, she called it."

"Had you accompanied Miss Grant to this cottage before?" Jason asked.

"Yes, I've been there twice before."

"Did she meet with anyone while in Southend-on-Sea?" Daniel asked. "Did anyone call on her at the cottage?"

"No, Inspector. She did attend church, of course, but she had no friends there. Not ones who'd come to call, at any rate."

"Did Miss Grant have any suitors?" Jason asked.

"No, sir. Why do you ask?"

"I'm only trying to get a clearer picture of her life," Jason replied. "It wouldn't be unusual for an unmarried young woman to have admirers."

"No, it wouldn't," Miss Shaw agreed.

"But there was no one?" Daniel asked, clearly unsatisfied with the answer.

"No."

"Miss Shaw, what did your mistress do?"

"Do, sir?"

"Where did she go? Whom did she meet with? Surely she must have done something to fill the hours," Daniel said.

"She was involved in charitable works and acted as hostess for her brother when he entertained. He's a judge, you know," Miss Shaw said reverently. "A very important man. She also liked to read. Miss Grant said that reading expands one's horizons and encouraged me to do it, but I'm not one for books."

"Thank you, Miss Shaw. Please send in Mr. Hudson," Daniel said.

Miss Shaw shot to her feet and was out the door in seconds, clearly relieved to be dismissed. It was understandable that she might need time to come to terms not only with what she'd seen but how it would alter her immediate future in a household where there was no other female who might require her services.

Only this morning, she'd had steady employment, but now her future was uncertain. Even if she received a glowing character reference, there'd be those who'd be wary of employing a woman whose last mistress had been brutally murdered in her own bed, as if Miss Shaw herself were tainted by association. Jason had seen many a servant left out in the cold in the wake of a murder inquiry. He wished he could help them, but he could hardly go hiring staff he didn't need.

Jason dragged his thoughts away from the unfortunate Miss Shaw, eager to hear what the butler had to say.

Chapter 2

Mr. Hudson was a man of late middle age with a full head of silver hair and pale blue eyes. He was stocky and tall, filling the room with his presence as soon as he entered. He declined to sit and stood before the two men, shoulders back, feet apart, as if facing a firing squad. Daniel couldn't help but wonder if the man felt responsible for what had happened. Miss Grant had been murdered on his watch, and he would face the wrath of his employer whether it was his fault or not.

"Mr. Hudson, I know we spoke when I first arrived, but can you take us through what happened one more time?" Daniel invited.

Mr. Hudson replied with a curt nod. "Miss Shaw rightly suspected that something was wrong and came down to the servants' hall to fetch me. We returned upstairs, where I called out to Miss Grant repeatedly. When the lady didn't respond, I decided to force the door, since I wouldn't be able to use the spare key to enter Miss Grant's bedroom on account of her key being already in the lock."

"Did you notice anything out of the ordinary while still in the corridor?" Daniel asked.

The butler winced. "Miss Shaw thought she smelled blood, and once she pointed it out, I could smell it as well."

"What did you see when you entered?" Jason asked.

"Miss Shaw went in first, to make sure her mistress wasn't in a state of undress. It was only when she screamed that I entered the room. I bade the footman to remain outside." Mr. Hudson took a deep breath, as if recalling that awful moment. "Miss Grant was on the bed. Her eyes were closed, and her throat looked like it had been savaged by a wild beast. There was blood on her face, hands, nightdress, and bedclothes. The bed was in disarray, as if a struggle had taken place. It was clear she was dead."

"Did you notice anything else about the room?" Daniel asked.

"Other than the smell? No, sir."

"Did you personally check the window and search the room before calling for a constable?"

"I did, sir. The window was locked, and nothing appeared to have been taken."

"You did not find the murder weapon?" Jason asked.

"I did not, sir, although, in truth, I'm not sure what the murder weapon would be, given the nature of the injury."

"What time do you lock up for the night, Mr. Hudson?" Daniel asked.

"Ten o'clock. I check all the windows and doors before retiring."

"Was everything as you had left it last night?"

"Yes, it was, Inspector. Both the front and back doors were locked when I first came downstairs this morning, as were all the windows."

"Mr. Hudson, could someone have entered the house earlier in the day and hidden in one of the empty rooms?" Jason asked.

"No, my lord. We had two callers yesterday, but I saw them out myself. And the tradesmen left by the tradesman's entrance after making their deliveries."

"When was the last time you saw Miss Grant alive?"

"Just before ten, sir. She said goodnight to me as she headed upstairs."

"And Mr. Grant?" Jason asked.

Mr. Hudson's lips compressed in obvious disapproval. "*Judge* Grant," he said, placing undue stress on the title, "was still in the drawing room when I retired." For a moment, the mask of stolid professionalism slipped, and Mr. Hudson suddenly looked old and tired. "I'd like to add that I have questioned the staff, and no one saw or heard anything untoward last night, your lordship," he said, his attention fixed on Jason.

Daniel felt an irrational stab of annoyance. The butler should be addressing him. This was his investigation, he thought petulantly, and instantly felt ashamed of his churlishness. Any man in service was conditioned to show respect to the highest-ranking personage in the room. It was only natural that Hudson would single out a nobleman over a mere inspector.

"Mr. Hudson, is there anyone you can think of who might have wished to harm your mistress?" Daniel asked, forcing the man to redirect his attention to him.

The butler's eyebrows lifted in astonishment. "Of course not. Miss Grant was well liked and respected by everyone who knew her."

"And yet someone murdered her in her own bed," Jason pointed out.

"I wouldn't know anything about that, sir," the butler said, his gaze growing anxious, his fear of being blamed obviously returning.

"Thank you," Daniel said. "You've been most helpful."

Daniel was about to summon the next servant when Mr. Grant entered the room, making a gesture of dismissal to the butler. "Inspector Haze, I really need to get out of this house for a short while or I'll go mad. If you'd like to speak to me, please do so now."

"Of course, sir. Please, have a seat," Daniel said, gesturing toward the settee. He felt somewhat foolish for inviting the man to sit in his own drawing room, but Oliver Grant didn't seem to notice and sank onto the settee, facing the two men and looking from one to the other. His eyes were red-rimmed, and his shoulders stooped, as if sitting up straight required too much of an effort. Daniel introduced Jason and the man nodded, as if having a member of the nobility examine his sister's remains after she was brutally murdered were the most normal thing in the world.

Oliver Grant was about forty, with hazel eyes and wavy brown hair untamed by pomade. He wore a neat beard, and his gray suit was exquisitely tailored and of the finest broadcloth. A paisley waistcoat of silver on burgundy silk and a burgundy puff tie provided a splash of color. Following Daniel's gaze, Judge Grant seemed to realize that he wasn't dressed in mourning attire.

"I really must change," he muttered. "I dressed before I knew what had happened to poor Sybil."

"We're very sorry for your loss, Judge Grant," Jason said.

"Thank you, your lordship." Oliver Grant turned his attention to Daniel. "How could this have happened, Inspector?" he asked, his voice shrill.

Even in a state of shock and grief, Oliver Grant was the sort of man who expected answers and needed someone to blame. He had an air of authority that couldn't be tamped down by tragedy or personal loss, and his gaze was angry and accusing, as if Daniel were personally responsible for every crime committed in the city.

"Had Sybil been attacked elsewhere, it'd be shocking and tragic, but feasible. But to be murdered in her own home, a place of safety and comfort, is incomprehensible. I keep going over what happened, and I simply can't understand it. How did the killer get in? How did he get out? Why did he target poor Sybil? She was such a kind soul, so generous with her time and affection."

"We're going to do everything in our power to discover who murdered your sister, but first, we need to ask you some questions," Daniel said. He felt for the man. For lack of a father or a husband, it had been up to him to protect Miss Grant and look after her interests. The knowledge that he'd failed his sister clearly weighed heavily on him.

"How long have you lived in this house?" Daniel asked.

"These past twenty years."

"And how many people do you employ?"

"Well, there's the butler, obviously, a housekeeper, a cook, kitchen and scullery maids, two footmen, a parlormaid, Sybil's maid, my valet, and a groom, who also acts as coachman."

"Are there any recent hires?" Daniel asked.

"No. Everyone's been with us for years," Oliver Grant said. "Except for the new boot boy."

"Judge Grant, unless someone managed to enter the house undetected, this was done by someone on the inside. Do you suspect anyone in your household?" Jason asked.

Oliver Grant thought about that briefly. "No, I don't," he finally said. "Not for a moment. This terrible thing was done by an outsider."

"But how would an outsider get in?" Daniel asked. "Mr. Hudson claims to have locked up for the night and said he found nothing to suggest that anyone had broken in during the night."

"I really don't know. But why would anyone in this house murder Sybil? She was a kind and considerate mistress. Too kind, some might say."

"You room is on the same floor. Did you hear anything last night?" Jason asked.

Oliver Grant shook his head. "No. I retired around half past ten and went directly to bed."

"What time did you get up this morning?" Daniel asked.

"I'm normally up by seven. I walk in Green Park every morning from seven-thirty until eight-thirty. I had just returned from my walk and sat down to breakfast when Hudson…" Oliver Grant's voice trailed off as he recalled the moment he'd heard the news.

"Judge Grant, did Miss Grant have any suitors?" Daniel asked.

"Suitors?" Oliver Grant reacted as if he hadn't quite understood the question.

"Yes. Had she received any gentleman callers within the past few months?"

"Not that I know of," Oliver Grant said sadly. "Sybil had no interest in getting married."

"Why was that?" Jason asked.

Judge Grant sighed heavily. "Because she still fancied herself in love with David Ellis," he said bitterly.

"And what happened with Mr. Ellis?" Daniel asked.

"He was killed during your war," Oliver Grant said angrily, pinning Jason with a belligerent stare. "He was a journalist, you see. He went to America to cover the war and was murdered for his pains."

"I'm sorry to hear that," Jason said.

"Miss Grant may not have been interested, but were there any gentlemen who'd tried to court her?" Daniel persisted.

"Are you suggesting that one of them killed her under my roof?" Oliver Grant exclaimed.

"I'm suggesting that we need to question anyone who might have had a grudge against her," Daniel explained patiently.

21

"There was Captain McHenry. He pursued Sybil for months, but she rejected him in the end."

"Where's Captain McHenry now?" Daniel asked.

Oliver Grant shrugged. "I really don't know."

"Judge Grant, whom did your sister spend time with? Did she have any particular friends?"

"She was in close contact with her school friends. Annabel Finch, Dorothea Parker, and Eleanor Gladstone-Smith. They saw each other regularly."

"Do you have addresses for them, sir?" Daniel asked.

"Ask Phillips."

"Who's Phillips?"

"The coachman. He'll know the addresses."

"I will," Daniel said, surprised the man couldn't be bothered to provide the addresses of his sister's friends. "Judge Grant, do I have your permission to interview the rest of the staff? I need to know everyone's movements, starting with dinner last night."

"Yes, of course," Oliver Grant said absentmindedly. His shoulders sagged again after his bout of anger, and his head drooped, possibly because he was tired of answering questions, or maybe because the reality of his loss was finally beginning to set it. "May I go now?" he asked desperately. "I really need some air."

"Certainly."

"Keep me informed of your progress, Inspector. And give my regards to Commissioner Hawkins. He's a close friend," Oliver Grant said, reminding Daniel that failure to solve the case would cost him dearly.

Chapter 3

Once Oliver Grant left the room, Daniel turned to Jason. "Are you absolutely certain Miss Grant's death couldn't have been an elaborate suicide?"

Jason's eyebrows lifted comically. "Do you honestly believe she did that to herself?"

"No," Daniel conceded, recalling the degree of savagery with which the poor woman had been killed. "I just can't figure out how the killer got out. If we are to assume that it was someone who was in the house at the time, then they must have left the room after killing Miss Grant. How did they lock the door from within, and how on earth did no one notice a blood-drenched person walking past? Surely there would have been a lot of blood, given the blood spatter on the headboard and bedlinen."

"Yes, there would have been a great deal of blood, but perhaps the person wore something to protect their clothing and removed it as soon as the deed was done. Did you search the wardrobe and the trunk at the foot of the bed?"

"I did," Daniel replied.

"We should search the rest of the house as well as the surrounding area in case they discarded the bloodstained garments once they left."

"But how did they lock the room?" Daniel asked again. "Had the room been locked from the outside, it would have been easy enough to comprehend, but how did the killer lock the room from within? And how on earth did they get out of the house if all the windows and doors had still been locked this morning?"

"Might there be a connecting door to an adjoining room?" Jason asked. "Or perhaps a back door no one had bothered to check?"

Daniel sighed. "I highly doubt there's a back door no one is aware of. And do you think this house is riddled with secret passages? It's not that old."

"What does its age have to do with it?" Jason asked, reminding Daniel that he wasn't well versed in British history.

"Some older homes are equipped with priest holes and secret passages, which were used after the Reformation to hide Catholic priests and to escape capture should the family's Catholicism come to the notice of the authorities. However, this house looks to have been built quite recently, so I doubt anyone had thought to add secret hideaways to the original plans."

"I see," Jason said. "Well, that's a shame because a secret passage would explain much in this case."

"Let's ask the housekeeper. She's bound to know if this house holds any secrets," Daniel suggested.

Mrs. Taft was in her mid-forties. She had dark hair liberally threaded with silver, shrewd dark eyes, and a thin nose that was pink at the tip. She was tall for a woman, and very thin, her black bombazine gown making her appear even more gaunt and forbidding. A prim lace cap covered her neat bun, and her white collar was stiffly starched. She looked at Daniel eagerly as soon as she took the proffered seat, as if expecting a reasonable explanation of the morning's events. Too bad he couldn't offer her one.

"Mrs. Taft, do you have any theories as to what occurred last night?" Daniel asked, rather than going through the usual list of questions. He had no doubt Mrs. Taft would mention anything unusual or unexpected.

The housekeeper shook her head. "I don't, Inspector. Everything was just the same. The master and Miss Grant had dinner at seven, then adjourned to the drawing room, where they remained until they retired. Mr. Hudson locked up for the night, and we all went to bed. We had no idea anything had occurred until Miss Shaw came to fetch Mr. Hudson this morning."

"Were there any strangers in the house?" Daniel asked.

"Not in the evening, sir."

"Who was in the house earlier?"

"Judge Grant had visitors around four. I sent up refreshments. Mr. Hudson saw them out just after five. And there had been deliveries from the butcher and the greengrocer, both before noon. Mr. Hackett and Mr. Grady are well known to us and make a weekly delivery. I saw them leave."

"Mrs. Taft, is there a door to an adjoining room in Miss Grant's bedroom?" Daniel asked.

"No, there isn't."

"What about a secret passage?"

"There are no secret passages that I know of, and I have been housekeeper here these nine years."

"Can you offer an opinion on how the murderer managed to get out of a locked room?" Daniel asked.

Mrs. Taft shook her head, her gaze reflecting her bewilderment. "I cannot."

"Were you close with your mistress?" Jason asked.

"Close, sir?" The woman looked even more baffled, if such a thing were possible.

"Did she ever confide in you?" Jason often confided in his own housekeeper, Mrs. Dodson, and thought other masters did as well, but that wasn't likely in a traditional household. Cool politeness and courtesy were the best a housekeeper could hope for from her masters.

"No, sir, Miss Grant never confided in me."

"Thank you, Mrs. Taft," Daniel said. "If you happen to think of anything, please send for me."

"Of course, sir."

"Who shall we speak to next?" Jason asked.

Daniel exhaled heavily. "I suppose the next logical choice is Judge Grant's valet. He is one of the few people who would have access to that floor in the evening. All the other servants would have retired after having their supper in the servants' hall."

Jason nodded in agreement. "Yes, there's a chance the valet might have seen or heard something."

Roy Nevins was a man of indistinct appearance. He was of middling height, middling weight, and middling attractiveness, the sort of person who could easily blend into the crowd and leave no impression on anyone who'd seen him. He did, however, exude an air of confidence and was smartly turned out.

"Mr. Nevins, can you describe your movements last night?" Daniel asked as he studied the man.

"Of course. I came upstairs just after ten to prepare Judge Grant's clothes. He likes to have everything ready when he gets up in the morning, so I laid out the clothes in his dressing room and left a clean nightshirt on his pillow. He came up shortly after. I helped him undress, hung up his jacket and trousers, deposited the day's linen in the laundry hamper, and wished him a good night before going to my own room."

"What time did you leave him?" Jason asked.

"Around ten-forty," Nevins replied.

"Did you see or hear anything unusual once you stepped out into the corridor?" Daniel asked.

Nevins shook his head. "I didn't go as far as Miss Grant's room, since it's at the other end of the corridor, but I didn't hear anything unusual. I did see a light under her door," he added. "I believe she liked to read before going to sleep."

"And Judge Grant? How did he seem?" Jason asked.

"He said he was tired, and I must say, he looked it. We chatted about the weather and his plans for the next day. He'd intended to dine at his club this evening. I assume he won't be going now that—" The valet didn't finish the sentence. His meaning was obvious. He sat silently, hands loosely clasped as he waited for Daniel to either ask him another question or dismiss him.

"Thank you, Mr. Nevins. You're free to go," Daniel said with a heavy sigh of disappointment.

Nearly three hours later, Daniel and Jason finally left the house in Half Moon Street, knowing no more than they had after examining the body, despite questioning every member of staff, down to the eight-year-old boot boy named Andy. They had searched the house from top to bottom, checking for secret panels in Miss Grant's bedroom and any sign of bloodstained clothes that may have been discarded or burned. The only person left to interview was Phillips, the coachman.

They found him in the carriage house, smoking a pipe while he cleaned the windows of the brougham with little enthusiasm. A tall, burly man, he had a full head of ginger hair with matching muttonchop whiskers and light brown eyes. His cheeks and nose were a mottled red, the spidery capillaries a testament to his love of strong drink.

"I'm Inspector Haze, and this is Lord Redmond," Daniel said as he showed the man his warrant card. "What is your full name?"

"Harold Phillips."

"Mr. Philips, first I will need addresses for Annabel Finch, Dorothea Parker, and Eleanor Gladstone-Smith. Judge Grant said you'd have them for us."

The coachman provided the addresses, which Daniel jotted down in his book. "Thank you," he said. "Now, when was the last time Miss Grant had gone out?"

"Yesterday," the coachman replied. "She went to call on Mrs. Finch."

"How long did she stay?"

"'Bout an hour."

"Did she come straight home afterward?"

"Yes."

"What time was that?" Daniel asked.

"'Round one."

"Did she seem in good spirits?"

Phillips stared at Daniel as if he were daft. "'Ow would I know?" he asked. "Not like we 'ad us a chat."

"Did she seem frightened or upset?"

"No."

"Did she ask you to take her anywhere unusual recently?" Daniel tried again.

"No."

"Did she ever meet any gentlemen on her own?"

"No."

"Mr. Phillips, is there anything at all you can think of that might have been out of character for Miss Grant?" Daniel asked, exasperated with the man's monosyllabic answers.

"No."

"Thank you for your help," Daniel said acidly. The man really was a dolt.

"Where to?" Jason asked once they had left Phillips to his task and his pipe.

"Mrs. Finch's. She was the last person who's not of the household to see Miss Grant alive. Perhaps she'll know something."

"I certainly hope so," Jason said. "No one else seems to know anything, which is odd in itself."

"Why do you say that?" Daniel asked as they walked down the street, keeping an eye out for a hansom.

"Someone entered the house, proceeded to Sybil Grant's bedroom, and hacked at her neck after first trying to strangle her. Something must have precipitated this savage act. I highly doubt it was a random killing, which suggests that someone knows more than they are saying, either about a visitor to the house or one of their own."

"Yes, I agree with you there," Daniel said, "but perhaps Sybil Grant had secrets they weren't privy to."

"In a house with a staff, there are no secrets," Jason pointed out. "The servants know and see all."

Daniel and Sarah kept only one maidservant at their rented house, but Daniel was sure she knew every minute detail of their lives. There were ten people looking after Judge Grant and his sister. Someone was sure to know something, especially if they had been with the family for years, as they all claimed.

"If anyone knows anything, it would be Miss Shaw. She was Miss Grant's lady's maid, so she'd not only see her comings and goings but also see to her soiled linen."

"Do you think Miss Grant was conducting an affair?" Jason asked.

"You said she wasn't a virgin. It's possible she had a secret lover."

"Yes, it is, but how did he get in the house?" Jason replied. "Unless her lover was one of the staff."

"A theory worth exploring," Daniel replied as a hansom pulled up to the curb. "Let's speak to her friends and see if we can learn something of Miss Grant's private affairs. Miss Shaw will be more likely to reveal her mistress's secrets if she thinks we're already privy to them."

"Agreed," Jason said.

Chapter 4

Annabel Finch lived in a lovely house in Marylebone, only a few streets away from Dorothea Parker, whom they'd visit next. A young maidservant opened the door.

"I'm Inspector Haze of Scotland Yard, and this is my associate, Mr. Redmond. We'd like to speak to your mistress." Daniel had automatically referred to Jason as Mr. Redmond, as he normally did in cases where Jason's title might intimidate the suspect, discouraging them from speaking freely.

The young woman stared at them in mute incomprehension before shutting the door in their faces and leaving them on the step, presumably to consult with her mistress. She was back mere moments later, the lady of the house hot on her heels. She was a beautiful woman with abundant chestnut curls styled in the latest fashion, wide blue eyes, and a heart-shaped face that was chalky white with obvious panic.

"What's happened?" she cried. "Is it the major?"

"Major?" Daniel asked, wondering what on earth the servant had said.

"Major Finch. My husband." The woman looked terrified and was wringing her pale hands in agitation.

"No, madam. I'm sure your husband is quite safe," Daniel assured her. "This is regarding Miss Sybil Grant. May we come in?"

Several curious faces had appeared in the window of the house across the street, the neighbors alarmed by the commotion.

"Of course. I'm sorry," Mrs. Finch muttered, her cheeks coloring with embarrassment. "Please come into the drawing room."

The maid went off after taking their coats and hats, and Daniel and Jason followed Mrs. Finch into the spacious drawing room, which was decorated in green and cream and boasted comfortable settees and a glass-fronted curio stuffed with exotic knickknacks. A portrait of an older man in uniform dominated the room, his dark gaze knowing and a little sly. If that was the major, he seemed far too old to be married to this young, beautiful woman.

Mrs. Finch sank into an armchair and looked from Daniel to Jason, her gaze anxious. "What happened to Sybil? Was she hurt?"

"Mrs. Finch, I'm sorry to inform you that Miss Grant was murdered," Daniel said.

"Murdered?" Mrs. Finch cried, her eyes widening with alarm. "By whom? Why? When did it happen?" She looked from Daniel to Jason and back again, her panic palpable. "I don't understand," she moaned.

Mrs. Finch was wringing her hands again, her chest heaving, and her breath coming in short gasps. Her pupils were worryingly dilated and her gaze unfocused. Daniel feared she might faint or become hysterical. The news of her friend's murder had clearly been too much for a woman with such a nervous disposition. Daniel looked to Jason for help.

"Mrs. Finch, may I get you a sherry, or a tot of brandy?" Jason asked solicitously. "For purely medicinal purposes," he added, when it looked like Mrs. Finch might refuse. Well-bred ladies didn't normally toss back brandies in the middle of the afternoon. "You're overwrought by the news," Jason added gently. "I'm sure the major would be very worried to see you this upset."

The mention of the major finally broke through the barrier of propriety, and Mrs. Finch nodded and bowed her head, breathing hard as she tried to compose herself. Jason returned with a glass of sherry, and she gulped it down, then set the empty glass

Mrs. Finch's hand flew to her bosom again. "Dear me, why would you ask such a thing?"

"Because it's important," Daniel replied.

"How can it be important, Inspector? David died three years ago. He wasn't the one that killed Sybil. And before you insist that I answer, I really don't know. We never spoke of such things."

Daniel nodded in acknowledgement. "What happened after Mr. Ellis died?"

"Sybil was devastated. So much so that she became ill. Oliver took her to their house by the sea and spent the summer with her, nursing her back to health. By the time she returned to London in the autumn, she was better, but not quite her old self."

"Were there any suitors after Mr. Ellis?" Daniel asked.

"There was Captain McHenry. It was the major who had introduced them, in fact. He thought Sybil and Crispin were well suited, but Sybil refused him, again and again."

"Why? Was she still grieving for Mr. Ellis?" Jason asked.

"I'm not really sure. She seemed to really like Crispin, more than any man she'd met since David died, but she wouldn't marry him."

"And where is Captain McHenry now?" Daniel asked, pencil poised over his notebook to write down the man's address.

"In Bombay. The major had a letter from him only last week."

"Is it possible that he has returned?" Jason asked.

"I don't believe so. Do you honestly believe Crispin McHenry could have killed Sybil?" Mrs. Finch looked appalled by the suggestion. "He's one of the most honorable men I've ever met. The major would gladly tell you so as well. The captain was heartbroken by Sybil's rejection, but he'd accepted her decision and left her in peace."

"How long ago did Miss Grant refuse him?" Jason asked.

"Well, it must be close to a year now," Mrs. Finch said. "Besides, he is to be married in September. Seems he's met someone in India. She's the daughter of some government official. Cora Leighton," she added, as if having just recalled the name. "I called on Mrs. McHenry after I had seen the announcement in *The Times*. She's very pleased that her son has finally moved on from Sybil. He deserves to be happy. She even showed me a photograph of the happy couple."

"Would you have an address for Mrs. McHenry?" Daniel asked.

"Are you really going to question her?" Annabel Finch demanded. "Mrs. McHenry is not in good health. Believing her son is under suspicion could kill her."

"Mrs. Finch, we have to follow every lead, wherever it takes us," Daniel explained. "And you have my word that we will be gentle. Captain McHenry is not under suspicion. We simply need to definitively rule him out of our inquiry."

Annabel Finch scoffed at that but provided Daniel with the address. She looked like she was more than ready to bid them a good day, but Daniel had a few more questions for her.

"What did Miss Grant do?" he asked.

"Do?" Annabel Finch asked, clearly confused by the question.

"What did she do all day?" Daniel clarified.

"She liked to read, and she was quite accomplished on the pianoforte. Oliver often asked her to play for him. He was very proud of her."

"Did Oliver Grant and his sister have a close relationship?" Jason asked.

"Oh, yes, which is not to say they didn't butt heads from time to time. All siblings do."

"What was the source of their disagreement?" Jason asked.

"Sybil's unmarried state, mostly," Annabel Finch replied. "Oliver had never approved of David Ellis. He thought the man feckless and believed him to be something of a radical. He did, however, like and respect Crispin McHenry. He thought Sybil should accept him and be grateful that such a good man was willing to take her on after the way she'd trifled with him."

"Was Sybil Grant a financial burden to Judge Grant, do you think?" Daniel asked.

"Oh, no. He only wanted her to be happy. To have a husband and children of her own, as every woman should. He'd even asked me to speak to her on the subject. I tried to describe to her what joy it was to have a child and a man who loved you above all others, but she said she didn't much care for children and had no desire to be dominated by some pompous old man."

Annabel Finch winced at that last part, no doubt still stung by her friend's unkind description of her husband. "Sybil said there were other paths to fulfillment," she added somewhat bitterly.

"Such as?" Daniel asked.

Perhaps David Ellis had planted some of his radical ideas in Sybil Grant's head. What sort of woman didn't wish for a home and family? To live with her brother for the rest of her days seemed like rather a barren existence, but he didn't know enough about Sybil Grant to pass judgment on her life choices, at least not yet.

"Where did Miss Grant go when she left the house?" Daniel asked.

He was growing more frustrated by the minute. They'd been speaking to Mrs. Finch for nearly a half hour now, but just as at the Grant household, they'd learned virtually nothing that might help with the investigation.

"She contributed to several charitable organizations for orphans, but the one place she went to regularly was St. Bridget's Home for Wayward Women. It's in Whitechapel, I believe."

"Wayward women?" Jason asked, his tone considerably more sarcastic than the situation called for.

Mrs. Finch seemed surprised by the question, but replied, nonetheless. "St. Bridget is the patron saint of fallen women, Mr. Redmond. Or so Sybil told me," she added, obviously thinking it didn't do for a respectable woman to know such things. "The rescued women are given a place to live until they can find respectable employment and lift themselves up out of the moral depravity they had succumbed to in their greed."

"Their greed?" Jason echoed.

"Of course," Mrs. Finch snapped. "The major says that a decent woman will take whatever employment is available to her. She'll sew till her eyes bleed or char all hours of the day rather than sell herself on the street. Women who find themselves turning to places like St. Bridget's were obviously seduced by the promise of easy money, too lazy to put in an honest day's work and prone to lustful ways. They're beyond help," Mrs. Finch announced. "Once they start down the path of wickedness, they never really recover. They always go back because they're sinful creatures at heart."

"You seem to have some very strong opinions on the subject," Jason remarked.

"Of course I don't. I'm guided by my husband in all matters of morality," she said primly. "He would never permit me to set foot in such a place, but Oliver Grant is more lenient. He thought Sybil should decide for herself, and look where her bleeding heart has led her."

"Are you suggesting she was murdered because she sought to help those less fortunate than herself?" Jason asked.

Daniel threw him a warning look. This wasn't the time or place to debate the plight of London's multitude of whores.

"Of course not. Sybil was kind and generous. But perhaps she'd been exposed to some criminal element at those places. I wager those women sneer at someone who's selflessly trying to help them and think a woman who's decent and chaste can't possibly comprehend their way of life."

"Quite so," Daniel said, eager to change the subject. "Mrs. Finch, was there anyone in the household Miss Grant didn't get on with?"

"Not that I know of."

"Was there anyone she was particularly fond of?" Jason asked.

"How do you mean, Mr. Redmond?" Annabel Finch asked.

"Was there anyone she felt close to?" Jason clarified.

"She was close with her brother. I think the reason she never married was because she couldn't find a man like Oliver. He always made her feel loved and respected without hemming her in. Sybil valued that about him." Mrs. Finch drew in a shaky breath. "Oh, I do hope Oliver doesn't blame himself for what happened," Annabel Finch exclaimed. "The major did say that Oliver should keep Sybil on a tighter rein. She might still be alive if he had."

"Thank you, Mrs. Finch. If you happen to think of anything that may be relevant, please send for me at Scotland Yard," Daniel said, rising to his feet.

"Yes, I will," Mrs. Finch said, but Daniel didn't think she'd recall anything relevant. She seemed like the sort of person who'd rather forget than remember.

Daniel hadn't met the major, but he was certain that once he heard about Sybil Grant's death, he'd tell his wife that her friend had done something to bring about the tragedy and they should speak of it no more, putting an end to this grisly chapter in their lives.

Once back out in the street, Daniel and Jason walked in silence for a moment, each lost in his own thoughts.

"I hope Mrs. Parker will have more to tell us," Daniel said. "It seems Miss Grant led a blameless life."

"And yet someone felt the need to end it," Jason pointed out.

Chapter 5

Dorothea Parker was a tiny, birdlike woman with pale green eyes and fiery auburn locks curled to frame a heart-shaped face. She wore a gown of green satin and an antique emerald necklace that must have been a family heirloom. The house was lavishly and tastefully decorated with furniture and carpets that looked brand new. Mr. Parker was clearly well off and spared no expense to keep his wife in style. Children's voices came from the back garden, where they were taking the air with their nursemaid.

"I'm afraid my husband it not at home," Mrs. Parker said once they were announced. She had been embroidering a sampler but set it aside out of courtesy.

"It's you we've come to see, Mrs. Parker," Daniel said. "It's regarding your friend, Sybil Grant."

"Oh?" she said, clearly surprised that the police would have anything to do with Miss Grant. "Do sit down, won't you?"

They settled in matching leather wingchairs and faced their hostess, who was looking at them expectantly.

"Mrs. Parker, we are deeply sorry to inform you that Miss Grant was found dead this morning. She was murdered," Daniel said.

Unlike Annabel Finch, Dorothea Parker did not give in to her emotion, although it was plain to see she was shattered by the news. She looked away, fixing her gaze on a lone bird perched on a branch just outside the window, her throat working as she swallowed back the tears that threatened to overwhelm her. It took her a few moments, but she got herself under control and turned to face them.

"Who would wish to harm Sybil?" she finally asked, choosing a euphemism to describe what had befallen her friend.

"We don't know yet," Daniel replied. "Miss Grant was killed in her bedroom, and nothing was taken. This was no random act."

"I see," Mrs. Parker said. "How can I help?"

"You can tell us about Sybil," Jason said gently. "What was she like?"

"Broken," Dorothea said, surprising Daniel with her assessment, all the more so since Annabel Finch, who'd just seen her, had said Sybil Grant had been in good spirits.

"How do you mean, Mrs. Parker?" Daniel asked.

"I mean she wasn't herself. She wasn't the spirited, idealistic girl I'd known at school, and for some years after. The death of her intended was a terrible blow. She had rallied and regained something of her buoyant nature, but something happened about a year ago that seemed to undo all the hard work she'd done to claw her way back to contentment."

"Might it have been something to do with Captain McHenry?" Daniel asked.

Mrs. Parker looked surprised. "Oh, you know about him?"

"Yes. Did something happen between them that might have frightened Miss Grant? Was that why she'd refused to marry him?" Jason asked.

Dorothea Parker shook her head. "No. Captain McHenry is a good man, and I thought Sybil had made a terrible mistake by refusing him. He would have made her happy had she given him half a chance. I thought that perhaps there still might be a chance for them, once he returned from his posting in India, but I hear he's to be married. Can't say I blame him," Mrs. Parker said. "Sybil didn't give him much hope."

"What do you think happened to cause a setback to Miss Grant's emotional wellbeing?" Daniel asked.

"I don't know. She wouldn't tell me, but I could see it was killing her. There was such angst in her eyes, such fear."

"Can you hazard a guess as to what may have been troubling her?" Jason asked.

Dorothea Parker looked away again, her indecision obvious. She didn't want to betray a confidence, but she was duty-bound to help catch her friend's murderer. Having come to a decision, she turned back.

"I think she was worried about Oliver."

"Why?" Daniel asked.

"Oliver's son, Marcus, is rather a dissolute young man. Oliver tried his best with the boy, but without the gentle influence of a mother, the child simply failed to thrive. He went to Eton, then Cambridge, but was forced to leave in disgrace, not only because of his dismal performance, but also because of his ungentlemanly behavior."

"What was he meant to have done?" Jason asked.

"I'm sorry, I can't repeat the things I've heard, but I can tell you that he has a fondness not only for strong drink and the gaming tables but for the pipe." She mouthed that last word as if not saying it out loud somehow meant that she hadn't shared the information with the police. "Oliver had threatened to withhold his allowance in the hope that the grip of addiction might lessen if Marcus couldn't afford to purchase the substance."

"Did it help?" Daniel asked.

"No. Marcus stole valuables from the house and sold them to support his habit. Father and son are currently estranged."

"Perhaps that's why Mr. Grant never mentioned him," Daniel observed.

"Why would he? Do you think Marcus is responsible for Sybil's death?" Dorothea asked, clearly horrified by the possibility.

"No," Daniel hurried to reassure her. "He wasn't in the house, as far as we know. Was Miss Grant close with her nephew?"

"She was when Marcus was younger. Marcus lost his mother at a tender age, and Sybil tried to step into the breach, but their bond became strained once Marcus went off to school. In fact, I think her opinion of him had changed drastically in recent years."

"Because of his opium habit?" Jason asked.

Mrs. Parker's face suffused with color. "Among other things. Sybil wasn't meant to know about his escapades, but she overheard Oliver berating his son after a particularly unsavory report had reached his ears."

"Did Miss Grant ever confront Marcus about his lifestyle?" Jason asked.

"I don't believe so. We never really discussed it. It was an embarrassing subject for us both."

"Mrs. Parker, can you think of anyone who might have wished Miss Grant harm?" Daniel asked.

The woman shook her head, making her curls bounce. "Sybil was lovely. She would never harm anyone, much less inspire a murderous rage. How did the killer get in and out?" she asked, her mind returning to Daniel's earlier comment.

"We've yet to figure that out."

"How odd that someone should violate the sanctity of that house. Oliver was always so particular about safety. He even interviewed all new members of staff himself to make sure they were up to scratch."

"What was it he feared?" Daniel asked.

"His son, presumably," Dorothea replied.

"Mrs. Parker, what about the charities Miss Grant patronized?" Jason asked. "Might there have been someone there who felt wronged by her?"

"I can't imagine why they would. Sybil genuinely tried to help people. In fact, she often donated her entire allowance just to make sure that the women at St. Bridget's got new clothes and had enough food. She said she felt an affinity with them. Lord knows why," Mrs. Parker added. "But she was like that. Generous of spirit. I think that's what drew her to David Ellis."

She checked to see that Daniel and Jason knew whom she was referring to and went on. "David was a crusader for justice, which made him less than popular in certain circles, and even less so with Oliver Grant. Oliver wanted someone solid and respectable for his only sister, not a reckless firebrand."

"Would he have refused David Ellis's proposal had he lived?" Jason asked.

Mrs. Parker shook her head. "Oliver loved Sybil and would never have done anything to hurt her. He would have accepted her marriage and been there for her should she ever need his help or support. But life had its own plan," Dorothea Parker said wistfully. "Poor Sybil, she certainly wasn't born under a lucky star."

"Thank you for your help, Mrs. Parker. Please send for me should you recall anything that might be material to the case," Daniel said as he stood to leave.

"Of course," Mrs. Parker promised with a watery smile. Daniel thought she might finally give in to tears once she was on her own.

45

Chapter 6

Having left the Parker residence, Daniel and Jason headed to a nearby chophouse. It was nearly two in the afternoon, and both men were hungry. Jason, in particular, needed to eat, since he often became shaky and felt faint if he didn't eat at regular intervals, a result of the hypoglycemia he had developed after a year of near starvation at Andersonville Prison in Georgia during the American Civil War. He hated to complain or whine like a hungry child, but his body wouldn't be denied. The two men settled at a corner table and placed their orders before turning their attention back to the case.

"We need to find out whether Marcus Grant was anywhere near the house last night," Daniel said after taking a long pull of ale.

"What reason would he have to murder his aunt?" Jason asked.

"Perhaps he'd asked her for money, and she refused him."

"Unmarried women rarely have access to money, so I doubt Sybil Grant would have been able to help him unless her allowance was very generous."

"Still, he might have felt enraged, or wished to retaliate against his father," Daniel argued.

"By killing an innocent woman?"

"She wouldn't be the first innocent woman to die at the hands of an angry man."

Jason nodded. "Yes, that's certainly true."

"And Oliver Grant, as well as the servants, might feel duty-bound to protect him. Losing one member of the family is bad enough. Having a second hang for murder would be disastrous, especially for someone of Judge Grant's standing."

46

"I was intrigued by Mrs. Parker's description of Miss Grant," Jason said. They waited until the waiter had placed the plates of roast beef and potatoes on the table and departed before continuing their conversation.

"How so?" Daniel asked.

"She described her as being broken."

"Why do you find that intriguing?"

"As far as we know, the biggest tragedy in Miss Grant's life was the death of the man she loved and hoped to marry. Not to downplay her pain, but a great number of people lose their partners, many of them after sharing a life with that person for years. Yet few would be described as broken, especially after several years had passed. Grieving, melancholy, lonely, bitter, but not broken."

"What are you suggesting?" Daniel asked, but he was nodding his head, having taken Jason's point.

"There's more to this story."

"There usually is," Daniel agreed. "Everyone has their secrets, and once we discover Miss Grant's, we'll be able to understand the motive for her murder."

"Whatever that motive was, it wasn't something mundane," Jason said. "The attack was frenzied and rage-driven. Whoever killed Sybil Grant didn't simply want her out of the way; they wanted to savage her."

Daniel nodded again, chewing slowly until he swallowed. "What in your opinion would drive someone to such fury?"

"Rejection. Fear. Possibly a desire to punish."

"Punish for what?" Daniel asked.

"That's what we need to find out. What did this seemingly ordinary woman do to drive someone to such an act of savagery, and how is it possible that no one saw or heard anything? Surely she would have cried out. It would have taken at least several minutes for the killer to first attempt strangulation, then reach for the knife and stab at her throat until they severed the arteries."

"I've never seen anything like it," Daniel said, shaking his head in disbelief. "It must have taken patience and planning to get to Miss Grant without being seen, but then the killer just gave in to madness."

"And having exhausted their rage, they were level-headed enough to get out unseen and cover their tracks," Jason agreed. "There was no blood on the floor or the doorknob, or even the key."

"The pitcher was clean, as was the basin, so the killer hadn't washed his or her hands before leaving the room."

"They must have worn gloves," Jason replied. "If the killer had the foresight to bring a weapon, why not a pair of gloves?"

"Are we dealing with someone extraordinarily clever or a raving lunatic?" Daniel asked.

"I think perhaps we're dealing with an extraordinarily clever lunatic," Jason replied. "Lunacy and intelligence are not mutually exclusive."

"I will check if anyone has been reported to have escaped from an asylum when I get back to the Yard," Daniel said.

"Unless that person was known to Miss Grant, I don't think they'd be our killer," Jason said.

"Perhaps it's someone she had helped as part of her charitable works," Daniel suggested. "You know what they say."

"No, what do they say?"

"No good deed goes unpunished."

"Yes, that's depressingly true," Jason said as he pushed away his empty plate. "Are you all settled in the new house?" he asked, since there seemed nothing more to say about the case.

"Yes, but Sarah misses her mother. Harriet promised to visit, but she has no wish to live in London year-round."

"And Charlotte?"

Daniel smiled happily. "She's in leading strings now that she's walking, and she's saying more words. She calls me Dada," he said proudly.

"Does Sarah take Charlotte outside?" Jason asked carefully.

"Only to the back garden," Daniel replied. "She doesn't trust herself after what happened with Felix."

"That's understandable, I suppose, but she won't be able to keep Charlotte on a leash forever."

"No. Perhaps one day we'll be able to afford a nursemaid. Since we no longer live with Sarah's mother, we only have my wages to rely on."

Daniel didn't normally allude to his financial situation, but Jason had made it clear that Daniel could always be direct when speaking to him. As an American, Jason didn't find talk of money vulgar or gauche. He was as matter-of-fact about a person's finances as he was about their physicality and was happy to discuss both.

"To tell you the truth, Sarah hasn't been feeling well these past few weeks," Daniel said.

"What's wrong?" Jason asked.

"I don't know, Jason. She seems fine in the morning, but then toward the afternoon she is tired and listless and can't seem to settle to anything. At times, she seems confused, other times she is suddenly happy and flits from room to room, but her good mood doesn't last long. Then, by suppertime she can barely keep her eyes open. She complains of headaches and seems to always be cold, even when the room is thoroughly heated."

"Would you like me to stop by and see her?" Jason asked.

"Would you?" Daniel replied. "I know you're very busy at the hospital, but I'm worried about her."

"I'm never too busy for you and Sarah, Daniel. Surely you know that."

"What do you think is wrong with her, Jason?"

"It could be something as minor as an iron deficiency. And the mood swings can be the result of being back in London and having to revisit the past. Has she been eating meat?"

Daniel shook his head. "She says she no longer cares for it. She prefers chicken and fish."

"Well, that could be it. An iron deficiency can cause fatigue, dizziness, headaches, and cold extremities. If that is the case, all Sarah would need to do is adjust her diet."

Daniel sighed with relief. "Thank you, Jason. I've asked her to see a doctor, but she refused. She says she's absolutely fine and I should stop fussing."

"Daniel, is there any possibility that Sarah might be with child?" Jason asked carefully.

Relations between Sarah and Daniel had been strained since last Christmas, when Sarah's involvement in a murder case had demonstrated just how unstable her mental state was. After months of avoiding the subject, and each other, Daniel and Sarah had finally reconciled and seemed to be getting along better and working on rebuilding the trust that had been lost, but Jason didn't think it appropriate to keep asking Daniel about the state of his marriage. When Daniel needed to talk, Jason was glad to listen, but he preferred to allow Daniel to take the lead when it came to Sarah.

Daniel suddenly smiled. "I hadn't thought of that. Yes, she might be with child. Oh, that would be wonderful. I think a baby would make her happy."

Jason chose not to remind Daniel that Sarah already had a baby and that Charlotte's birth had done nothing to dull the pain or guilt of losing her son. But if Sarah was indeed with child, her condition could explain a myriad of symptoms, from fatigue and mood swings to aversion to certain foods and occasional listlessness.

"I can't stop by today," Jason said. "Micah is coming home from school." He couldn't keep the smile off his face. "I've missed him."

When Jason brought orphaned Micah Donovan back to New York with him after their release from Andersonville Prison, Jason never imagined that he would grow so attached to the boy, but he loved Micah as if he were his own son and held Micah's sister Mary, who took a long while to locate, in high regard. After an extended stay, Mary had recently left them and returned stateside, a decision Jason would not question had Mary not left her small son Liam behind for the Redmonds to raise. Now Jason and Katherine were guardians to two Donovan children, and although Jason loved them both and could easily afford their upkeep, he felt Liam was too young to be parted from his mother.

"Will Micah remain with you for the entire summer?" Daniel asked.

"Yes, I think so. I might take the family to the seaside for a few weeks in August. I think Micah would enjoy that, and I know Katie would. She loves the sea."

"That sounds like a lovely holiday. Will you be taking the children?"

Jason's face clouded. "Child," he replied.

"What do you mean?"

"I had a letter from Mary. She recently married and has asked me to send Liam to Boston. It's only right that Liam should be with his mother, but I have yet to break the news to Micah. He's very fond of the boy and will miss him terribly. As will I."

Daniel gaped at Jason. "How does one send a two-year-old child to America?"

"I've placed an advertisement in *The Times*. I will hire a nursemaid to look after Liam on the voyage. There are plenty of women who are bound for America, in search of a better life. This is a way to earn some money for a few weeks' work."

"You will trust a stranger with Liam?" Daniel asked.

"I don't have much choice. Mary is not about to come for him. I think she's expecting, and Micah is too young to send to Boston on his own with a small child. Besides, he has no wish to go. I've asked him if he'd like to visit his sister this summer, but he didn't seem excited by the prospect."

"Is he still angry with her for leaving?" Daniel asked.

"More hurt than angry. He can't see why Mary couldn't have just remained here with us."

"He's too young to understand her motives," Daniel said, "but he'll come around. Knowing he's welcome in Boson should he wish to go is enough for now."

"It will have to be."

"Shall we go see Mrs. Gladstone-Smith?" Daniel asked as he took out a few coins to pay for the meal.

"Of course," Jason replied, and consulted his pocket watch. "I have an hour before I must head home."

Chapter 7

The Gladstone-Smith residence was in Clifton Hill, St. John's Wood, not too far from Daniel's own home on Springfield Road. It was a good-sized house but showed signs of neglect. The peeling window frames, a cracked step, and several tiles missing from the roof were just a few problems Jason noticed as they walked up the steps. The door was opened by a middle-aged housemaid, who invited them in after Daniel showed her his warrant card.

"The mistress is in the parlor," she said, and led them to a spacious parlor that faced the front of the house and was done in shades of mauve. Just like the façade, the room was a bit shabby, with faded velvet curtains, a worn settee, and two cracked leather armchairs before the marble-topped fireplace. A sad-looking potted palm sat in the corner, its leaves a yellowish brown that foretold its fast-approaching demise.

Mrs. Gladstone-Smith must have been a handsome woman once, but she was so wan, her complexion put Jason in mind of buttermilk. Her pale blue eyes almost exactly matched her gown, and her fair hair was cut short in the front and curled tightly, a fashionable hairstyle that suited few women, in Jason's opinion. Unlike her school friends, she wore no jewelry besides tiny pearl earbobs, and her simple gown wasn't adorned with yards of ribbon or lace.

She looked at the two visitors in obvious surprise, but good manners prevailed, and she invited them to sit down and make themselves comfortable, once Daniel introduced himself and Jason and explained the purpose of their visit. Mrs. Gladstone-Smith bowed her head and clasped her hands in her lap, needing a moment to absorb the terrible news and compose herself. When she looked up at last, she was even paler, if that were possible, and her eyes were misted with tears.

"I just can't believe it," she whispered. "How unfair life can be."

"Can you tell us something of Sybil Grant's life?" Daniel invited.

They'd decided that Sybil's schooldays were probably not relevant to the investigation, unless some clue pointed them in the direction of the Hawthorne Academy for Young Ladies, so decided to focus on the present instead.

"Sybil and I haven't seen each other much of late," Mrs. Gladstone-Smith said. She looked away for a moment, her pale throat contracting as she swallowed hard.

"Why was that? Were you not devoted friends?" Daniel asked.

"We were, or had been, but things had changed."

"Did you fall out?"

"Not fallen out as such, but grown distant," Mrs. Gladstone-Smith said.

"What was the reason for your estrangement?" Jason inquired.

Mrs. Gladstone-Smith bowed her head again and drew in a shaky breath. Whatever had happened between the two women had been upsetting for her. She finally looked up, and Jason noticed a spark of defiance in her eyes that hadn't been there before.

"Sybil and I met on our first day of school. That was also when I met her brother, Oliver. He was much older than Sybil, by ten years at least. I'm embarrassed to admit it, but I had something of a schoolgirl infatuation with him. Oliver was everything I imagined a husband should be. He cut a rather dashing figure to an impressionable, young girl." She went silent, staring off into space.

"Please, go on," Daniel invited.

"I'm sorry," Mrs. Gladstone-Smith said. "I was just recalling those happy days." She sighed deeply and returned to her narrative with obvious reluctance. "Oliver married before we left school, and I married my Robert when I was eighteen, but I saw Oliver from time to time when I called on Sybil and he was always most charming. Oliver was widowed early on, and my Robert passed three years ago. Cancer of the stomach," she said, a note of resignation creeping into her voice. "It wasn't a quick or painless death. Sybil was a great comfort to me during that time, often sitting with Robert while I went out for a walk or to the chemist for his medicines or spent some time with my son, who was only eight when his father became ill."

"So, what changed?" Jason asked kindly. Eleanor Gladstone-Smith was dancing around the reason for the estrangement, clearly embarrassed by whatever had taken place.

"Once I came out of mourning, I asked Sybil if she thought Oliver and I..." She allowed the sentence to trail off, but her meaning was obvious.

"You thought there might be a future for you with Oliver Grant?" Daniel asked.

"I didn't think as much as hope. He'd been on his own for many years, and I was lonely and uncertain about the future. Robert left us decently off, but the house needs repairs, and the school tuition must be paid. And I had always been very fond of Oliver," Mrs. Gladstone-Smith added, obviously realizing how mercenary she must have sounded.

"How did Sybil react?" Jason asked.

"She became visibly upset and said Oliver wasn't the man for me. She made it abundantly clear that I wasn't good enough for her brother and I should never bring the matter up again. After that, she called on me less frequently, and I was too embarrassed to call on her, for fear that she had told Oliver of my feelings."

"Might Sybil Grant have had other reasons for not wishing you and her brother to form an attachment?" Daniel asked.

"If she did, she could have told me what they were. I would have understood. But her reaction was so hurtful. It was as if she was repulsed by the very idea. Of course, if Oliver wished to marry again, he'd have his pick. He's an important man who has much to offer a wife."

"Perhaps Judge Grant has no wish to marry," Jason said.

Mrs. Gladstone-Smith shook her head. "I would understand if that were the case, but Sybil had mentioned that he was considering marriage. She seemed displeased with the idea. Perhaps because she had been fond of his late wife, but Helen has been gone for years, and it's not natural for a man to remain alone for so long."

"Might she have felt threatened by the possibility of her brother's new wife undermining her role within the household?" Jason asked.

Eleanor Gladstone-Smith shrugged delicately. "Perhaps. I hadn't considered that. I suppose Sybil enjoyed all the benefits of being a wife without having to marry."

"Had she wished to marry?" Daniel asked, even though he had already heard Sybil Grant's views on marriage. There was always the possibility of an opposing point of view, which could be helpful in assessing the victim's frame of mind.

"Yes," Mrs. Gladstone-Smith replied falteringly. "I believe she did."

"You hesitate," Daniel observed.

"Few women have the luxury of waiting for the perfect man to come along. We choose from whoever has chosen us. But Sybil wouldn't compromise. It was either all or nothing with her."

"And did she find it all with David Ellis?" Jason asked.

"She thought she had, but perhaps he hadn't been as certain."

"Why do you say that?"

"Because he chose to travel to a war zone rather than remain in London and marry the woman he loved. Far be it for me to question someone's dedication to their chosen profession, but surely there was news aplenty to cover right here in England. Perhaps he was looking for a way out," Eleanor Gladstone-Smith said. "He just didn't think he'd be making a permanent exit."

Daniel nodded at the obvious veracity of this statement. Jason had secretly thought the same thing when he'd heard how David Ellis had died. There had been plenty of field correspondents in the United States during the war, but if David Ellis had wished to report on the war, he hadn't needed to be in the thick of it. Associated Press, a news-sharing agency based in New York, would have been the most logical place for him to garner news of the war, and the South had established its own press association that sent out reports to Southern dailies. David Ellis could have dispatched daily or weekly bulletins by telegraph instead of traveling from engagement to engagement, as he must have done to get killed on the battlefield. David Ellis had either been a wholly new breed of journalist or a man desperate for an excuse to get away, possibly chasing danger instead of news.

"Can you think of anyone who might have wished Miss Grant harm?" Daniel asked.

"No. She was well liked by everyone."

"What about Captain McHenry? Could he have been so angered by her rejection that he'd decided to take revenge?"

Mrs. Gladstone-Smith looked genuinely shocked. "He's in India, Inspector. And no, I don't believe he'd be capable of such a thing."

"He's a soldier. He must have killed before," Daniel pointed out.

"Honorably, in the line of duty. I can't imagine that he would sneak into a woman's bedroom and murder her in her bed." Bright spots of color appeared on Eleanor Gladstone-Smith's cheeks, her anger obvious. "Really, Inspector. To suggest such a thing is just plain lazy, if you'll pardon me saying so. No one of Sybil's acquaintance could be capable of such a thing. If you think you'll find the killer among her friends or loyal staff, you're clearly looking in all the wrong places."

"Thank you, Mrs. Gladstone-Smith," Daniel said as he pushed to his feet. "I will certainly take your views on the matter under serious consideration. Good day."

Once outside, Daniel, still smarting from Mrs. Gladstone-Smith's criticism, and Jason parted ways. Jason had to get home, and Daniel needed to return to the Yard despite being within a stone's throw of home. He wished Jason a good evening and set off.

Chapter 8

Jason handed Dodson his hat and gloves, then shrugged off his coat. The house was unexpectedly quiet. Jason turned to Dodson, who looked as impassive as ever.

"Where is everyone, Dodson?" Jason asked.

"Her ladyship is upstairs with the children, and young Micah is in the drawing room, sir."

"Thank you, Dodson."

"Would you like some tea, sir?"

"Yes, I would."

"I'll have Fanny bring a fresh pot."

Jason walked into the drawing room, his face splitting into a grin when he saw Micah, whose mouth was full of jam tart. Micah swallowed, set down his teacup, and came forward to greet Jason. A year ago, Micah would have given Jason a hug, but now, after nearly a year away at school, he held out his hand instead, and Jason shook it solemnly.

"It's good to see you, Micah. How was the trip down?"

"Grand," Micah replied as he resumed his seat and eyed the last jam tart. "Do you want it?"

"You have it," Jason replied, glad to see Micah hadn't lost his appetite or passion for sweets.

"I sure did miss these," Micah said, helping himself. "There's still some tea in the pot."

"That's all right. Fanny is bringing more tea. And if I know Mrs. Dodson, more tarts."

"I like the new digs," Micah said, looking around the room. This was the first time he'd been to the London house, since he'd been at school during the move.

"I'm glad. Is your room all right?"

Micah nodded. "Are you very busy these days?"

"I volunteer at the hospital and teach. And I'm still assisting the police," Jason replied.

Micah instantly perked up. "Any new cases?"

"There is, as a matter of fact. A woman was murdered in her own bed," Jason replied, not too worried about Micah's reaction. As a drummer boy in the Union Army, Micah had seen enough violence to last him several lifetimes and was more interested in the logistics of a crime rather than its emotional impact. Jason thought Micah would make an excellent detective if his career interests ever turned in that direction.

"In her own bed?" Micah exclaimed, clearly scandalized. "Doxy, was she?"

"No, she was a lady."

"Cor," Micah exclaimed. "How was she killed?"

Jason was just about to reply when Katherine walked into the room. "Did I hear correctly and you have a new case?" she asked as she approached the tea tray and lifted the pot experimentally.

"Mrs. Dodson is sending up a fresh pot," Jason said.

"I hope she sends up some savories as well. I'm famished. I hardly had any lunch. Lily was fussing all afternoon."

"Is she ill?" Jason asked, ready to race upstairs to check on his infant daughter.

"She's fine. I think she was just hungry."

60

"Didn't you feed her?" Jason asked, hoping he didn't sound too autocratic.

"Of course I did. But—" Katherine's gaze slid toward Micah, who seemed bored with the conversation. "Can we discuss this later?" She gave Jason a meaningful look. "Tell us about the case," she said, clearly eager to change the subject.

"Are you sure you want to hear this, Katie?"

"You know I do. It'll be in the papers tomorrow anyhow," Katherine reminded him.

Well-bred ladies did not read the papers, but Jason took no issue with Katherine's desire to know what was going on in the world and arrive at her own conclusions. She was an independent, intelligent woman, and he valued her insights. He gladly shared the morning papers with her, to the great disapproval of Dodson, who'd offered many a time to take them away as soon as Jason was finished and throw them on the fire. Jason hoped that out of respect for the deceased, the editors would not stoop to printing photos of the crime scene, but he'd learned long ago that when it came to the press, respect was not a consideration when there was a profit to be made.

"Well, all right," he conceded, although the alternative had never really been an option. "Miss Sybil Grant was murdered last night."

"Sybil Grant?" Katherine exclaimed. "Sister of Judge Grant?"

"Yes. Did you know her?"

"I did. I met her last month at Mrs. Dixon's house. Remember she'd invited me to tea?"

"Yes," Jason replied, although he had forgotten. "What did you make of her?"

"She was pleasant and very passionate about the plight of the fallen woman," Katherine said, barely able to hide her disdain for those who thought they could help the women by advising them to pray for their souls. "I did notice an underlying sadness in her that seemed to have nothing to do with the topic we were discussing."

"Any idea to its cause?" Jason asked.

"She didn't say, and I could hardly ask," Katherine said. "It would seem intrusive."

"Did you ever meet her brother?"

"Yes. He came to collect her from Mrs. Dixon's, and she introduced him all around. Charming man. I hear he's been widowed for many years. I'm surprised he never remarried."

"Can we visit Drury Lane?" Micah cut in. "I hear the chorus girls are really something."

"Aren't you a bit too young for such entertainments?" Katherine asked, her brows lifting in disapproval.

"I'm nearly fourteen," Micah countered, even though he'd only just turned thirteen. "And if you're afraid that I'll see ladies of the evening, I've seen plenty already. Except they were 'ladies of all day long,'" Micah said, a grin tugging at the corner of his mouth. "There were plenty of camp followers, and they weren't discreet in what they were offering," he added, just in case Katherine hadn't taken his meaning. Katherine turned to Jason for support.

"Micah, some topics are not openly discussed in polite company," Jason said, hating himself for sounding like a pompous prig. Micah was only speaking the truth, which should be encouraged for its own sake.

"I'm sorry, your ladyship," Micah said, looking contrite, but Jason thought he detected a hint of sarcasm in Micah's use of Katherine's title.

"Micah, actually there's something else we need to talk about," Jason said, deciding this was as good a time as any.

"Yeah, I know," Micah said. "You're sending Liam away."

Jason had just opened his mouth to reply when Fanny bustled into the room, bearing a laden tray. She collected the cooling teapot and the empty tart plate before leaving them to continue with their conversation.

"We're not sending him away," Katherine said, clearly hurt by Micah's tone. "We're respecting Mary's wishes. She wants Liam with her. She's his mother, after all."

"She didn't think so when she abandoned him, and me, without a word," Micah grumbled.

"Micah," Katherine said gently, but Micah sprang to his feet.

"If you will excuse me," he said with forced formality, and left the room. Katherine turned to look at Jason, her gaze troubled.

"He'll come around," Jason said. "He's hurt, and he has every right to be. No child should ever suffer so much loss. He loves Liam, and he'll miss him."

Katherine nodded. "It's not easy to be a child, is it, when everyone else seems to be making the decisions for you and you have no choice but to adjust to what life has in store."

"No, it's not. But in some ways, it prepares you for what's to come. Life is rarely easy, even for those who are born to privilege."

Jason hadn't meant to sound self-pitying, and tried to cover up his momentary lapse by reaching for the teapot. He poured tea into a delicate porcelain cup, added a splash of milk, and passed the cup to Katherine before pouring tea for himself.

Katherine smiled and shook her head, her eyes soft with love. "You must wait for the lady to pour you tea," she admonished. "Will you never learn, Yank?" she asked affectionately, making Jason laugh.

"Nothing wrong with a husband making his wife a cup of tea," Jason replied. "Now pass me a tart, woman. I'm craving something sweet."

Chapter 9

After leaving Mrs. Gladstone-Smith, Daniel decided to call on Mrs. McHenry. The McHenry residence was on the way to the Yard, and before returning, he needed to confirm Captain McHenry's whereabouts. Mrs. McHenry was a plump, motherly woman of about fifty, who wore a satin gown of deep mauve accented with black lace and a black lace cap over her still-mostly-brown hair. Presumably, she was in half-mourning for her husband, or maybe one of her other children.

The drawing room was fussy and over-furnished, the heavy green velvet drapes keeping out most of the daylight and creating a dim and oppressive atmosphere. A stuffed owl glared at Daniel from beneath a glass cupola, its talons perched on a withered branch, its glass eyeballs covered with a layer of dust. Daniel would have hated to spend any time in this room, but Mrs. McHenry seemed extremely comfortable in her surroundings.

She received Daniel as if he were an honored guest rather than a detective of the police and offered him refreshments, which Daniel accepted despite having eaten not long ago. People were always more forthcoming over a cup of tea, and Mrs. McHenry seemed eager to talk. Daniel suspected she was lonely and glad of the unexpected company.

Once the tea had been made to their liking, teacakes dispensed, and small talk was out of the way, Daniel finally explained the reason for his visit.

"That poor, poor girl," Mrs. McHenry said, shaking her head in dismay. "I always knew she'd come to no good."

"Why do you say that?" Daniel asked.

"Some people just seem to court tragedy, don't they?" Mrs. McHenry said with an aura of a great oracle. "I told Crispin as soon as I met Miss Grant that she wasn't the one for him. She didn't love him, for one. You can always tell when a woman is in love. It's there in her eyes, and Miss Grant's eyes were sad. She reminded me of a child that gets lost in a crowd and looks around for its mother or nursemaid, desperate to be found and told they're safe."

"Not a very flattering description," Daniel said, wondering if Mrs. McHenry had heard about Sybil's feelings for David Ellis and thought she could never love her son as much.

"The truth rarely is, Inspector. I felt pity for her because I knew then and there that she'd never find contentment. I'm happy for my Crispin, though," she said, smiling happily. "That's him, right there on the mantelpiece, and his future bride, Miss Cora Leighton. They are to marry in September. Have a look," she invited.

Daniel set down his cup, walked over to the mantel, and picked up the silver-framed photograph. Dashing in his uniform, Captain McHenry looked down at the woman on his arm, his expression one of pride and admiration. Miss Leighton smiled up at him with such genuine happiness that it was hard not to envy the pair. There was no doubt in Daniel's mind that Captain McHenry had moved on and was ready to start a new life with his betrothed.

"Crispin wants me to come out for the wedding," Mrs. McHenry said once Daniel resumed his seat. "I'm a little apprehensive, I don't mind telling you. I've never been one for foreign parts, and Bombay is as foreign as it gets, isn't it? But I've made up my mind, Inspector. I will overcome my reservations and board that ship when the time comes. I will not miss my boy's wedding, not for the world. I can deal with the natives' heathen ways for a few weeks, I told myself, and I will, and without uttering a word of complaint. I only wish I didn't have to make the journey alone," she added, looking forlorn.

"I'm hoping to persuade my niece to join me. She could do with a change of scene. And might even meet some dashing officer while in Bombay. Ann is no longer in the first flush of youth, but maybe a respectable widower will be able to appreciate her finer qualities," Mrs. McHenry mused. "She deserves to be happy. She's such a kind soul and would make a loving mother to some poor motherless mite."

"I have no doubt she would," Daniel said, wondering how they'd got so off-topic.

Mrs. McHenry sighed heavily. "Do you have children, Inspector Haze?"

"A daughter. She just turned one."

"Well, allow me give you a piece of advice, if you will permit it. Have as many children as the good Lord blesses you with. Life becomes very lonely when you lose your beloved, and even lonelier without children and grandchildren to cherish. Crispin is my only child, and I've hardly seen him since he purchased his commission eight years ago. I pray he and Cora will return to England once his posting to India is at an end. I do so long to be a part of their family."

"I have no doubt you will be, Mrs. McHenry," Daniel said. He felt sympathy toward the woman and hoped her son would return and make a home nearby.

"I'm very sorry about Miss Grant," Mrs. McHenry said. "I do hope you will find whoever did this. No one deserves such a grisly end, no matter how broken they are."

There it was again, that description of Sybil Grant. What did it take for someone to seem irreparably damaged? Daniel wondered as he thanked Mrs. McHenry for the tea and stepped outside, relieved to be out in the fresh air. He could think of another young woman who could be described thus but forced his thoughts back to the case. His professional day wasn't yet finished.

Chapter 10

Daniel looked around for a hansom, then changed his mind and decided to walk instead. It was a fine day, and the late afternoon was fragrant with the scent of flowers and freshly cut grass. It would take him close to an hour to walk to the Yard, but he could use the exercise, and he needed time to think before meeting with Superintendent Ransome. Daniel still had mixed feelings about the superintendent, with whom he'd only worked these past few months since moving from Essex. John Ransome was a dedicated copper, there was no question about that, but although he personally oversaw every case to ensure justice was served and demanded a nightly progress report from each detective he supervised, he was also impatient, abrasive, and, at times, downright abusive.

He reminded Daniel of a tiger he'd seen at the London Zoo when he'd visited with Sarah and Felix shortly before Felix's death. The tiger had stood in the shadow of the enclosure, silent and watchful, tension coiled in its powerful body. It lived in captivity, but its wild spirit wasn't broken, only temporarily subdued. Daniel had no doubt that had an opportunity presented itself, the animal would have pounced instantly, taking down its prey in moments and ripping the hapless fool who got in its path to shreds. John Ransome would do the same to Daniel if he failed to conduct an investigation that lived up to his exacting standards. Daniel respected the man for his thoroughness and dedication, but he'd be lying if he said he didn't fear him just a little.

Hastening his steps, Daniel considered what he'd learned so far. The simple answer was nothing useful. Sybil Grant seemed to have led a blameless life, acting as hostess for her brother, playing the dutiful aunt to her nephew after he'd lost his mother, and donating her time to various charities. She'd suffered a romantic disappointment that seemed to have left a lasting mark, but aside from that, Daniel had learned nothing from either the staff or the people closest to Sybil that would explain what had incited someone to murder her in such a vicious, personal way. A jilted lover was always an obvious suspect, but unless there had been another man in her life, Captain McHenry was not only far away but happily engaged to another woman.

Daniel braced himself as he walked into the building and headed straight for Ransome's office. The door was open, so the superintendent saw him right away and beckoned for him to enter. John Ransome sat back in his chair and fixed Daniel with a belligerent stare. "Well?" he asked when Daniel failed to speak quickly enough to satisfy him. "Who killed Sybil Grant?"

"I don't know, sir."

"Then tell me what you do know," Ransome suggested with all the sympathy of an executioner who invites the condemned to lay his head on the block.

"All I know is that Miss Grant was murdered in a locked room by someone for whom the grudge was very personal."

"Bravo," John Ransome said sarcastically. "I could have told you that without leaving my office. Now tell me something I don't know."

"I have interviewed the staff, Judge Grant, and three of Miss Grant's closest friends, as well as the mother of the man whose proposal she had rejected," Daniel began.

"Would you like a round of applause?" John Ransome asked viciously.

"No, I would not. What I would like is to be granted the time I need to investigate this case properly. I have no doubt you would have solved it by now, sir, but sadly, I'm not as clairvoyant as you are," Daniel retorted, not caring if he were sacked on the spot. The man had crossed a line. It was his absolute right to request a report, but he had no right to taunt Daniel or belittle him for his lack of progress after less than a day on the case.

John Ransome actually laughed at that. "Very good, Haze. I see you've grown a pair of bollocks at last. Every inspector needs a fine set if he wants to succeed in this city of ours. Do what you need to do, but remember, Oliver Grant is a close friend of Commissioner Hawkins and will go straight to the top if we don't get a result. And just so you know what sort of man you're dealing with, allow me to enlighten you. Judge Grant is known as Hanging Grant. Know what that means? He's decisive and harsh, not a man to take failure lightly or to allow an offense to go unpunished. And if he doesn't have a criminal to hang, he'll turn his attention to the poor sod who'd failed to solve the case. And make no mistake, I will throw you to the lions to safeguard my own position. Good luck, Haze. Oh, and I have no objection to you consulting with Lord Redmond. I have great admiration for the man."

"So you have said," Daniel muttered. "Goodnight, sir."

"Whether this night will be good remains to be seen," Ransome replied, and bowed his head, returning to whatever report he'd been reading when Daniel had arrived. He'd been summarily dismissed.

Buoyed by John Ransome's backhanded compliment, Daniel left his office and was just about to leave the building when he was hailed by the desk sergeant.

"Inspector Haze, there's someone here to see you," Sergeant Meadows said.

Daniel looked around but didn't see anyone besides Sergeant Meadows himself. The man jerked his chin toward the corner, which was hidden from view by the tall counter. Daniel walked around the counter and peered into the corner, surprised to find a small boy hovering in the shadows.

"Andy, isn't it?" Daniel asked, approaching the child.

"Yes, sir."

"Do you have a message for me?" The boy nodded and handed over a folded piece of paper.

Daniel accepted it and looked at the child. "Will you be all right getting home on your own?"

"Yes, sir," Andy said, and disappeared through the door before Daniel had a chance to ask him any more questions.

Daniel unfolded the paper. The note was written in a neat, feminine hand. It read:

Inspector Haze,

Please meet me at Bambury's Coffeehouse on Piccadilly Road tomorrow at nine.

V.S.

Daniel folded the note and stuffed it into his pocket. The note could only be from Valerie Shaw, and she clearly had something to tell him that she didn't want the rest of the household to know about. That was promising.

Daniel said goodnight to Sergeant Meadows and exited the building. He was too tired to walk and wanted to get home in time for dinner, so he walked to the nearest underground railroad station and descended the stairs until he reached the gaslit platform. He still preferred to travel aboveground, but this was an efficient alternative to sitting in early evening traffic or walking. Once the train arrived, he'd get home in half the time.

Chapter 11

Tuesday, June 9

Daniel got out of bed, grabbed his clothes, and let himself out of the bedroom. Sarah had retired with a headache before he'd arrived home last night and was still asleep, her face pale in the morning light. This happened more and more often, and Daniel wondered if Sarah was truly unwell or simply wished to avoid spending time with him. He'd had a solitary dinner, stopped into the nursery to have a peek at Charlotte, and retired close to eleven. And he would leave for the day without so much as exchanging a word with his wife.

Having washed, shaved, and dressed in the spare room, Daniel instructed Grace to listen out for Charlotte, should she wake before Sarah, and left the house for his meeting with Miss Shaw. He'd arrive at Bambury's Coffeehouse early, but it was his plan to have breakfast before Miss Shaw arrived. He'd never been a lover of coffee, but Jason had taught him to appreciate his beverage of choice. With sugar and cream, it could be quite pleasing and surprisingly invigorating. Daniel looked forward to ordering a freshly brewed pot and maybe some fried eggs, sausages, and toast with butter and marmalade.

Daniel asked for a table in the corner, near the wall, certain that Miss Shaw would wish to keep their meeting private and wouldn't like to sit by the window, which he would have preferred. He liked watching the world go by, especially when eating on his own. It made him feel less lonely. Daniel was just finishing his meal when Valerie Shaw walked in. She spotted him and made her way over, taking the chair opposite.

"Would you care for some coffee, Miss Shaw?" Daniel asked.

She looked like she was about to refuse but changed her mind. "I'd love a cup."

Daniel signaled for a fresh pot and turned his attention to Miss Shaw. "What did you wish to tell me?"

Valerie Shaw looked distinctly nervous, her gaze sliding toward the door of the establishment, but no one had entered after her, and the few patrons who were already there hadn't spared her a glance.

"Miss Grant's letter opener is missing, Inspector," Miss Shaw said.

"And why do you think that's significant?"

Miss Grant would have kept the letter opener on her desk in the pretty sitting room designated for her personal use. He hadn't noticed a letter opener, but he'd seen the writing implements and creamy sheets of expensive paper she'd used for her correspondence.

Miss Shaw waited while the waiter placed a fresh pot of coffee on the table and set a cup and saucer before her. He poured Miss Shaw some coffee, refreshed Daniel's cup, and took himself off. Miss Shaw added cream and sugar and took a sip. She looked composed, but Daniel noticed that her hand trembled with nerves when she set the cup down.

"My mistress always kept the letter opener in the Rose Room. That's what she called her sitting room on account of the rose-patterned wallpaper," she explained. "Two days ago, she purchased a new book. *The Moonstone* by Wilkie Collins. She was looking forward to reading it," Miss Shaw said wistfully.

"Go on," Daniel prompted.

"Miss Grant liked to read before going to sleep. She said it helped settle her mind. She had asked me to fetch the letter opener from the Rose Room because the pages were uncut, and she needed a paper knife to separate them. When I helped Miss Grant

73

to prepare for bed, the letter opener was there, on top of the book. The next morning it wasn't."

Daniel nodded his appreciation. "That's a very important detail, Miss Shaw, and I thank you for bringing it to my attention."

"There's something else," Miss Shaw said. "I don't know why I did it, but I looked inside the book."

"What did you find?"

"A strip had been torn off the last page, and there was a smear of blood on the torn edge. I think perhaps my mistress tried to leave a message, sir."

"I can't imagine that Miss Grant would have been in any position to leave a message in the midst of her struggle," Daniel said gently. He didn't want to upset the woman any more than she already was. "Do you have the book?"

"I left it where I found it, on her nightstand. Do you think Miss Grant was killed with the letter opener, sir?" Valerie Shaw whispered, clearly horrified by the prospect.

"I think that's very possible. I will have to share this information with Lord Redmond and see what he thinks. Thank you, Miss Shaw. You were very brave to bring this to me."

Valerie Shaw nodded. She looked relieved to have delivered her message and concentrated on finishing her coffee. "This is good coffee," she said once she set the empty cup in its saucer. "Cook never makes coffee, since no one likes it."

"I'm glad you enjoyed it," Daniel said. "Please, let me know if you make any other discoveries."

"I'll send Andy if I do."

Miss Shaw wished Daniel a good morning and hastened out the door, presumably to return to her duties. Daniel briefly wondered what would happen to her now that her mistress was gone. Oliver Grant would have no use for a lady's maid, unless

Miss Shaw was given other tasks, although given the size of Grant's staff, Daniel couldn't imagine what there'd be for her to do.

Having settled his bill, Daniel headed toward St. George's Hospital. He needed to speak to Jason before interviewing any other suspects, since Miss Shaw's revelation certainly changed things. Jason usually scheduled surgeries for early in the morning, since he felt it was best to operate when both he and the patient were well rested. He also believed that the students who filed into the operating theater before every procedure were most alert at that time, unless they'd been out carousing the night before and would sleep till noon, in which case, he wasn't about to wait for them to get out of bed.

It took nearly an hour for Jason to finally emerge from the operating theater. He smiled when he saw Daniel. "Have you been waiting long?"

"Not too long. Can you spare me a half hour?" Daniel asked.

"Of course. But I'm afraid I can't leave just yet. I will need to periodically check on the patient I've just operated on. Stomach tumor," Jason explained as he pulled off his cap and stuffed it into his pocket. "Let's step outside. I could use a breath of fresh air."

There were several benches behind the building that were used primarily by patients and their visitors. They found an unoccupied bench and settled in the sun-dappled shade of a leafy tree. Daniel related his conversation with Miss Shaw and was surprised when Jason let out a low whistle.

"What was that for?" Daniel asked.

"Don't you see? This changes everything," Jason exclaimed.

"Does it? I agree that the letter opener is probably the murder weapon, but I don't see that it drastically alters the parameters of the case."

"But it does," Jason argued. "We were working under the assumption that the killer came to Miss Grant's room with the express purpose of killing her because he'd brought a weapon. But now we know that he didn't and grabbed whatever was to hand in the heat of the moment. It now also makes sense why the throat was torn rather than cut before the victim was stabbed. The letter opener wasn't sharp enough to slice through the skin, so after several attempts at slitting her throat, the killer resorted to stabbing Miss Grant. The letter opener severed the carotid artery, which was the ultimate cause of death. Had the killer brought a knife, it would have gone easier for Miss Grant, since death would have come quicker. As it was, she must have suffered a great deal in her final moments."

"I can't begin to imagine what that poor woman must have endured," Daniel said. "But one supposition remains unchanged. Whoever killed her was enraged at the time of the murder. This was a vicious, manic attack."

"Which makes it that much more unlikely that no one heard anything," Jason said. "It would have taken at least several minutes for the killer to administer the fatal stab. Miss Grant must have struggled and cried out at least once."

"Since the killer straddled the victim to keep her in place, it's possible that they used the left hand to stifle her screams during the attack."

"Yes, it is," Jason conceded. "Still, I can't imagine that Miss Grant was murdered by an outsider."

"Do you have a theory?" Daniel asked.

"The beginnings of one," Jason said.

"Then I hope you will share it with me because I'm drawing a blank at the moment."

"There are five men in the Grant household besides Oliver Grant. I think it's safe to rule out the coachman due to his age and personal appearance, but that still leaves four men with whom

Sybil Grant might have been conducting an affair. Let us suppose that her lover came to her room, expecting to join her in bed, only to be informed that she wished to end their relationship. He might have thrown her onto the bed and straddled her. Perhaps he wanted to frighten her or maybe he thought to arouse her, but Sybil Grant didn't respond in the way he'd hoped. She might have threatened him or insulted him in some way, which proved to be the turning point in the confrontation."

Daniel nodded. "Go on."

"Incensed, he wrapped his hands around her throat, intending to strangle her, when his gaze fell on the letter opener. So enraged that he wanted only to get the deed over with, he grabbed the opener and tried to slit her throat, tearing her skin and muscle and crushing the larynx and hyoid bone instead. Frustrated and terrified of being discovered, he turned the letter opener in his hand and used it to stab Sybil Grant in the throat." Jason illustrated the stabbing motion with his hand.

"Once Sybil Grant was dead, her lover came to his senses and realized that his only hope lay in hiding in plain sight. He did his best to minimize the damage. He laid her out, closed her eyes, took the murder weapon, and let himself out of her room. I have yet to figure out how he managed to lock the door from the inside, but he knew where he might hide until it was safe to come out, clean up, and return to his room as if nothing had happened."

Daniel nodded. "That theory certainly fits the facts, but we've searched the house from top to bottom and haven't found either the murder weapon or any bloodstained clothes. The killer would have been covered in blood. Even if he'd managed to get back to his room undetected, he would have had to dispose of the clothes. There were no men's clothes drying on the clotheslines, nor were there any remnants of burnt clothes in any of the grates. There were no stains on the floor or blood on the doorknob. Nor was there anything beneath Miss Grant's window. Had he washed his hands, he would have needed to dispose of the water, since the basin was clean when we arrived on the scene. And what of the bloodied page?"

Jason considered the question. "If either the killer or the victim had grabbed the book during the struggle, there'd be a lot more blood on it than a mere smudge. Did you examine the book when you first arrived on the scene?"

Daniel shook his head. "The book was on the bedside table, but I saw no reason to examine it thoroughly. I would have if I'd noticed traces of blood. The only explanation I can think of is that the killer cut himself in the process and stuck the paper to the wound for lack of a handkerchief."

"Perhaps," Jason said absentmindedly, his thoughts clearly not on the torn page.

"What are you thinking?" Daniel asked.

"The theory fits the facts, but there's a gaping hole in it."

"Which is?"

"How is it possible that Oliver Grant, whose bedroom is on the same floor as his sister's, didn't know of the affair? Whoever the man is, he took a great risk by coming to Miss Grant's room."

"Perhaps they didn't normally meet there. Maybe she told him earlier in the day that she wished to end the relationship, and he came to her room to try to talk her out of her decision," Daniel speculated.

"But where would they have met? They could hardly use the servants' quarters or the kitchen, or any of the downstairs rooms. Too risky."

"What about the nursery?" Daniel suggested. "The nursery's been empty since Marcus Grant was a child, so no one would go there at night, and there's a nursemaid's bed in there."

"Yes, that's certainly possible, since there'd be no one on the top floor at night," Jason agreed. "We need to reinterview the men, and I would like to be present, if you've no objection."

"When would be convenient?"

Jason pulled out his watch and checked the time. "Would you be able to meet me at the Grant house at three? I'm afraid I can't leave the hospital any earlier than that."

"Of course. In the meantime, I will go in search of Marcus Grant. He may not have been in the house when his aunt was murdered, but he might know something."

Chapter 12

It took Daniel several hours to track down Marcus Grant. He'd called at his lodgings and been directed to his club, then to a public house off the Strand, and eventually to a boxing gymnasium in Blackfriars. Marcus Grant, when Daniel found him at last, was nothing like Daniel had imagined based on the less-than-flattering description provided by Dorothea Parker, nor did he fit with Daniel's mental picture of a dissolute young man whose health had been undermined by excessive drinking and countless hours spent in opium dens.

In fact, Marcus Grant was the picture of health. His fair hair gleamed, his blue eyes twinkled, and his finely drawn eyebrows arched in obvious surprise to be the object of a Scotland Yard inspector's interest. His smile was easy and genuine, not a hint of anxiety in his gaze as he held out his hand in greeting.

"How can I help you, Inspector?" Marcus asked once the introductions had been made.

"Is there somewhere private we can talk?" Daniel asked, conscious of the dozen or so people at the gymnasium who had to be wondering what he might want with Marcus Grant, since they all seemed to have drifted closer in order to overhear the conversation.

Marcus didn't seem to care, but Daniel preferred to keep his interviews confidential, partly to protect the integrity of the investigation and the privacy of those he spoke to and partly to keep control of the information. He had been surprised to discover that no word of the murder had made it into the morning papers, possibly because Judge Grant had appealed to Commissioner Hawkins to keep the details of his sister's death from the press. Judge Grant had demanded that no crime scene photos be taken, saying that his sister deserved her privacy, even in death, but Daniel had refused the request, telling him that it was standard procedure to have a photograph for the file and that the images would not be made available to journalists. If Marcus Grant wasn't in contact with his father, he'd know nothing of what had happened, and neither would his friends.

Once Marcus had changed out of his gymnasium attire, he and Daniel adjourned to the Pig and Rooster, a public house a few streets away, where Daniel ordered a slice of game pie and a pint of bitter. Breakfast was a distant memory, and he was to meet Jason in less than two hours, so he'd have no other opportunity to eat. Marcus Grant ordered a plate of roast beef and a tankard of ale and asked for a loaf of bread and a dish of butter.

"Boxing makes me hungry," he explained as he buttered a thick slice of bread and took a huge bite. "Please, have some," he invited, pushing the plate toward Daniel.

"Thank you, but I'll wait for my pie," Daniel replied.

"Suit yourself," Marcus said through a mouthful of bread. "So, what's this about, Inspector?"

"Where were you on Sunday night?" Daniel asked.

"At a birthday supper with a dozen friends. We started out at Verey's, then eventually found our way to Madame Fleur's, where the celebration continued into the early hours with a dozen bottles of very fine claret and several charming ladies. I didn't get home until about six in the morning."

"Whose birthday was it?"

"Mine. I turned twenty-one."

"And your friends will vouch for you?" Daniel asked.

"Of course. As will Madame Fleur herself. I'm well known to her," Marcus Grant said with a smug smile. "Why do you ask?"

"I just need to be sure," Daniel replied. "Can I have the names of your friends?"

Marcus Grant rattled off a half dozen names, and Daniel took them down, as well as the address for the brothel. "What's happened, Inspector?" Marcus asked, his earlier playfulness replaced by obvious unease.

"Mr. Grant, have you heard from your father recently?" Daniel asked instead of answering the question.

"No. Why would I have?"

"Your Aunt Sybil has been murdered. Her body was discovered in her bed yesterday morning."

Marcus Grant dropped the half-eaten bread onto his plate, his eyes misting with tears. "No," he whispered. "No." He fixed Daniel with an accusing stare. "It wasn't in the papers."

"No, it wasn't. I believe your father had something to do with that."

"He would, wouldn't he?" Marcus said bitterly. "All he thinks about is protecting his reputation, even at a time like this. Did he tell you they call him Hanging Grant? That's right. I wouldn't want to be the poor sod who's dragged in front of him on his day of reckoning." Marcus Grant made a gesture that could only indicate a noose around his neck and pretended to yank it. "He has softened a bit these last few years, but not enough to lose the moniker."

"When was the last time you saw your aunt, Mr. Grant?" Daniel asked as the waiter placed their orders before them.

Marcus made no move to pick up his cutlery. "A few weeks ago. We used to meet in Hyde Park on every second Monday of the month."

"That's very precise," Daniel said, wondering if the young man was poking fun at him.

"My father and I are not on speaking terms, so Aunt Sybil and I thought it best to limit our communication for fear of it being read without permission or confiscated altogether. This way we knew exactly when we'd see each other."

"So, you saw each other regularly?" Daniel asked, wondering if Dorothea Parker had intentionally misled them about Sybil Grant's relationship with her nephew.

"We did, but no one knew. It was our secret," Marcus said, a sad smile tugging at his lips. He finally picked up his knife and fork and began to eat, the initial shock of Daniel's news having passed.

"Why did you feel the need to keep your meetings secret?"

"As I just mentioned, my father is something of an autocrat. I do not agree with his views, nor will I be ruled by his edicts and expectations. We fell out some time ago, and since Aunt Sybil lived under his roof, she preferred not to get in the middle. It made life easier for her, and I saw no reason to punish her for her desire to get along with her brother."

Marcus's mouth suddenly drooped, some belated realization coming to him. "She sent me a present for my birthday. It arrived on Sunday while I was out. That must have been one of the last things she did in this life." Marcus angrily wiped his eyes with the back of his hand. He seemed genuinely overcome.

"What did she get you?" Daniel asked.

"A silver snuff box with my initials engraved on the lid. It's a lovely gift. I will treasure it always." Marcus pulled out the box and showed it to Daniel, who agreed that it was a beautiful and thoughtful gift.

"And your father? Did he not wish you a happy birthday?" Daniel asked.

Marcus scoffed. "I doubt he even remembered. And even if he did, he'd never make the first move. If we are to reconcile, I would have to come crawling to him and agree to his terms. And the only reason I might ever consider doing that is to make sure I get my inheritance once he finally shuffles off his mortal coil."

Daniel considered that statement. Oliver Grant was considerably older than his sister but still young enough to sire a dozen children if he had a mind to do so. If he remarried, Marcus might never see a farthing of his father's money, but Daniel couldn't see how the threat of being disinherited might translate into the murder of his aunt.

"Was your aunt worried about the possibility of your father remarrying?" Daniel asked. "His wife would become the lady of the house, ousting your aunt from a position she'd held for years."

Marcus Grant shrugged. "She never said he was thinking of marrying, and no, I don't think she'd be worried. She'd be happy for him. That's the sort of person she was."

"Can you tell me more about your aunt?" Daniel asked, sensing that Marcus really needed to talk about Sybil Grant.

"She was a good person, regardless of anything you might hear about her."

"And what would I hear about her?"

Marcus looked away, clearly uncomfortable. "I don't know. Anything. All sorts of filth comes out about people who've been murdered, as if the mistakes they'd made justify what was done to them. That's all I'm saying," he added lamely.

"Mr. Grant, I'm going to ask you something, and please consider your answer. It might help us find your aunt's killer."

"Ask away," Marcus said, watching Daniel tensely.

"Might your aunt have been conducting a love affair?" Daniel asked, watching the young man's face for any change in expression or demeanor.

Marcus's eyebrows lifted comically. "Are you joking? Aunt Sybil? No. I don't have to think about it. She wasn't."

"How can you be so certain?"

"Aunt Sybil was in love with David Ellis. She would have followed him to the ends of the earth, and possibly to bed, but she hadn't felt strongly about anyone since he died. Captain McHenry tried to break through her fug of indifference but eventually gave up. I thought Aunt Sybil made a mistake by letting him get away and told her so. He was a good man and would have done his best to make her happy. Surely a marriage based on affection and respect is better than a life of barren spinsterhood," Marcus said with a shrug. "But what do I know? I've never been in love, so perhaps I have yet to understand what all the fuss is about. Anyway, why do you ask?" Marcus picked up his knife and fork and dug into his food, his appetite unaffected by the seriousness of the conversation.

"We believe Sybil Grant may have been killed by a jilted lover."

"How would he have gained access?" Marcus asked.

"It might have been a member of staff."

Marcus Grant nearly choked on his food. "A member of staff? Are you suggesting my aunt was at it with one of the footmen? Or Hudson?" The idea of Sybil Grant lying with the butler was apparently even more shocking.

"It's not impossible," Daniel protested.

"Oh, I think it is," Marcus Grant retorted. "Inspector Haze, if you ask around, you'll quickly learn that I'm not a person of unimpeachable character. I have too many flaws to list and have made many a miscalculation of judgment over the years, but I adored my aunt. She was the only person who genuinely loved me after my mother died and my father found that he had no time to devote to me. More than anything, I would like to see her killer brought to justice. But if you think that my aunt was having an affair with a footman and he killed her in a jealous rage, then the only job you're qualified for is to be a mutton shunter."

Daniel nodded, impressed by Marcus's impassioned speech and not at all aggrieved by the insult. He'd heard worse during his years as a peeler and would no doubt hear worse still. "Do you have any theories, Mr. Grant?" he asked, hoping Marcus Grant would offer him a lead worth pursuing.

Marcus set down his utensils and met Daniel's gaze. He seemed apprehensive and anxious, but he didn't look away. "I believe Aunt Sybil's death is a direct consequence of the past, Inspector."

"What are you referring to in particular?" Daniel asked.

Marcus finally looked away. "I don't know for certain. I only know that something changed drastically when David Ellis died."

Pushing his plate away, Marcus drained the rest of his ale and got to his feet. "I'm sorry, but I must go. I don't have anything more to tell you."

He threw some coins on the table, enough to cover Daniel's meal as well as his own, and walked away, his shoulders so rigid, he might have been going into battle.

Chapter 13

Jason arrived in Half Moon Street a few minutes early and watched Daniel approach on foot, his brows knitted together in either annoyance or consternation. Jason couldn't tell which.

"What is it, Daniel? Have you learned something?" Jason asked.

"I spoke to Marcus Grant, and he doesn't appear to be the scoundrel he's been portrayed as. He might be a skilled actor, but I think he genuinely loved his aunt and believes that the change that took place in her when David Ellis died was due to something more than mere grief."

"Did he give any indication as to what might have happened?"

"No, but he suggested we look at past events."

"Are you certain he's not simply trying to divert attention from himself?" Jason asked. "He might still have a key, which would explain how he got in and out undetected on Sunday night."

Daniel shook his head. "Marcus was celebrating his twenty-first birthday on Sunday. I verified his alibi with two of his friends before coming here. He was with them all night, so he's not our man. Besides, I see no clear reason he'd want to murder his aunt. They seem to have enjoyed a close relationship and met on a regular basis. He seemed genuinely devastated by news of her death."

"Is it possible that his friends are lying for him?" Jason asked.

"Anything is possible, but I didn't get that impression. They seemed sincere. What about you? Have you had any fresh thoughts on the case?" Daniel asked.

"I wonder if the body has been collected by the undertaker," Jason said. A theory was forming in his mind, and he hoped he wasn't too late to follow up on it, since Oliver Grant didn't seem disposed to let them handle his sister's remains any more than was strictly necessary.

"Why do you ask?"

"Because I'd like to have another look," Jason replied as Daniel knocked on the door, which had been decorated with an elaborate bow of black crape.

The door was opened by Hudson, who looked surprised to see them again so soon. He reluctantly stepped aside, allowing them to enter. Inside, the house had been decked out for mourning. The mirrors were covered with swathes of black crape, the clocks had been stopped, the hands pointing to the approximate hour of Sybil Grant's death, and there was a hush worthy of a mortuary.

"What can I do for you, Inspector?" Hudson asked. "Judge Grant is out at present."

"We're not here to see Judge Grant," Daniel said. "We would like to reinterview several individuals, since new questions have arisen."

"As you wish, Inspector," Hudson replied. "The judge has instructed me to assist you in your efforts, should you return."

"Mr. Hudson, has the body been collected by the undertakers?" Daniel asked. He thought the request to see the body would be better received from him, since he wielded official authority.

"Not yet, sir."

"Lord Redmond would like to have another look at Miss Grant's remains," Daniel said.

"But Miss Sybil has already been laid out, sir," Hudson protested.

"I will leave her exactly as I have found her," Jason promised.

"Yes, sir," Hudson replied, his expression closed. He couldn't very well object, but it was clear he thought his master wouldn't like it.

He led Daniel and Jason to the dining room, where Sybil Grant was laid out in a casket of polished mahogany. The brass handles gleamed dully in the light of the lamps, since the heavy velvet drapes were closed against the June sunlight. Sybil Grant looked at peace, the terrible bruises and wound on her neck covered by a lace fichu worn over a high-necked gown. She looked for all the world like she was sleeping and would wake as soon as Jason touched her, but her eyes remained closed, her face still in death.

"Please leave us, Mr. Hudson," Jason said, and waited until the butler departed, shutting the door softly behind him.

Jason pulled the curtains open, allowing the room to be flooded by natural light, then returned to the table. Sybil Grant was now garishly illuminated, her face no longer peaceful in repose but waxy and bloodless, her lips blue-tinged. She hadn't been dead that long, but the process of decomposition had already begun and would accelerate in the warm room.

"What are you looking for?" Daniel asked as Jason pushed up Sybil Grant's skirts to her waist. Jason pulled down the lace-trimmed drawers and lifted the bottom of the corset, which thankfully wasn't laced too tightly. He peered at Sybil Grant's milk-white stomach, then reached into his medical bag and extracted a magnifying glass.

"Jason?" Daniel prompted as Jason studied Sybil Grant's midriff.

"Just one moment," Jason replied as he set aside the magnifying glass and moved his hands over the lifeless flesh.

Having finished with his examination, Jason adjusted the clothing and pulled the curtains shut, plunging the room into near-gloom again before turning to Daniel.

"I conducted a thorough examination yesterday, but in view of what you've just told me, I thought it prudent to look again, in case I've missed something obvious."

"And have you?"

"I think I might have. Pregnancy leaves visible marks on the body. The more children a woman has carried and nursed, the more obvious those marks are. At first glance, it doesn't look like Miss Grant has had any children. Her stomach is flat, the skin and muscles in her abdomen still taut. Her breasts are firm and pert. However, upon closer examination, I was able to see faded stretch marks on her belly, and there's a barely perceptible flap of skin just above her pelvic area. I now believe Miss Grant had been pregnant, albeit several years ago."

Jason sighed and continued. "I can't tell you with any certainty if she carried the child to term, but I'm fairy sure she didn't nurse it. I think it's quite possible that she wore a tightly laced corset throughout the pregnancy, which would have prevented her abdominal muscles and skin from being allowed to stretch freely."

"Well that certainly changes things. Again," Daniel added. "However, I'm reluctant to reveal this information to the servants. Judge Grant would almost certainly take issue with me tarnishing his sister's reputation. Besides, he might not have been aware of the pregnancy, so we must tread lightly when asking our questions."

Jason nodded, acknowledging the validity of Daniel's observation. "I can't be sure that Sybil Grant wasn't pregnant at the time of death without dissecting her womb. Nor can I be one hundred percent certain that she had been pregnant in the past. I can only make an educated guess based on the evidence, which can be misleading. Stretch marks can be caused by weight gain. It's quite feasible that Sybil Grant was so devastated by David Ellis's death that she succumbed to a period of mindless eating brought on by extreme melancholy and grief. That can sometimes happen. Since she is not overweight now, we can assume that either she was able to shed the extra pounds or the marks on her body were caused by carrying a child. I think it's important that we find out the truth."

"I agree," Daniel said. "Miss Shaw might not know, but Mrs. Taft has been with the family for nigh on ten years. She would know if Sybil Grant had been overweight at any time during the past decade."

Daniel and Jason found Hudson hovering just outside the door. Jason couldn't be certain if Hudson had overheard their conversation, but it didn't matter. He wouldn't breathe a word. Not if he wished to retain his employment.

"Mr. Hudson, could you ask Mrs. Taft to join us in the drawing room?" Daniel asked.

"Of course, sir."

Mrs. Taft appeared a few minutes later, her gaze worried as she looked from Daniel to Jason, probably wondering what more they could ask her after yesterday's interview.

"Please, have a seat, Mrs. Taft," Daniel said, then glanced at Jason.

"Can you remind me how long you've worked for the Grants," Jason said, smiling at her kindly.

She seemed to relax a little. "It was ten years in February, your lordship."

"And who usually disposes of unwanted garments?" Jason asked, clearly deciding to start from afar so as not to alarm the woman.

"I do, sir. Miss Sybil's gowns were usually donated to St. Bridget's Home for Wayward Women, and Judge Grant's were either given to the two footmen or sold to a rag shop if they were too worn."

"Was there an occasion when Miss Sybil donated many of her gowns at once due to sudden weight loss?" Jason asked.

Mrs. Taft looked surprised by the question. "No, sir. Miss Sybil has been about the same size since the day I met her."

"And was there any time when Miss Grant had gone away for a prolonged period of time? A holiday abroad, perhaps?" Jason prompted.

"Judge Grant took her to Italy when she turned eighteen. That was nine years ago now. Master Marcus was away at school then, but he was upset to have been left behind all the same."

"How long were they away?" Daniel asked.

"They were gone for three months and came back so happy and full of stories about all the sights they'd seen. They brought gifts for everyone," Mrs. Taft said wistfully. "I still have the embroidered change purse Miss Sybil bought me in Florence. She was always very generous."

"Were there any other holidays?"

"Just the time the master took Miss Sybil to the seaside after Mr. Ellis died. Three years ago, that was. She was ill, and he thought the fresh air and peaceful surroundings would do her good."

"How long were they gone that time?" Jason asked.

"Judge Grant returned to London regularly, Southend not being so very far away. He could hardly ignore his professional commitments for months on end. But Miss Sybil stayed away a good long time. About four months, I'd say."

"And since then?" Jason pressed.

"Miss Sybil went to the seaside cottage a few times, but only for about a week or so."

"Did her brother accompany her?" Daniel asked.

"No, she took Miss Shaw."

"And who was her maid before Miss Shaw?"

"Her name was Anne Perkins. She was with Miss Sybil since she was seventeen or so, and she traveled with her to Italy, as did the master's valet."

"Would you have an address for Miss Perkins?" Daniel inquired.

Mrs. Taft shook her head sadly. "Miss Perkins died shortly before Miss Shaw came to us."

"What did she die of?" Jason asked.

"Pneumonia. Miss Sybil cared for Miss Perkins herself when she got ill, but there wasn't anything she could do other than keep her comfortable toward the end."

"Thank you, Mrs. Taft," Jason said. "You've been very helpful."

"Have I?" Mrs. Taft asked as she rose to her feet, ready to return to her duties.

"Without a doubt," Jason assured her. He turned to Daniel as soon as the door closed behind the housekeeper. "I don't think the trip to Italy is relevant. It was too long ago, but the time spent at the seaside could be significant. Four months would be long enough for Sybil Grant to hide a pregnancy from those close to her, and to have a few weeks to recover after the birth."

Daniel nodded. "If Sybil Grant had a child, she would most likely have had it there and then returned to London afterward. It's entirely possible that this has no bearing on her murder, but we won't know until we discover what really happened and who was involved."

"If the child was fathered by one of the men in this house, he might have only just found out about the pregnancy," Jason suggested, "which could have led to a confrontation."

"It makes no sense to interview the men until we know more, but I would like to speak to Valerie Shaw again. There's no hiding a pregnancy from a lady's maid."

"She's only been with Miss Grant for two years, so she wouldn't know anything about a previous pregnancy unless her mistress confided in her," Jason pointed out.

"I very much doubt she would have, but I shall ask. Jason, I'll be going to Southend-on-Sea tomorrow. Are you able to come with me?" Daniel asked.

"How far is it from London?" Jason asked.

"About forty miles. There's train service from Liverpool Street Station," Daniel replied.

"I will clear my schedule," Jason promised. "Now, let's speak to Miss Shaw."

Chapter 14

Valerie Shaw looked nervous when she entered the drawing room. Daniel had promised her that the rest of the household wouldn't know they had met earlier, and she was understandably worried that he'd betrayed her trust. The populace tended to mistrust the police and close ranks, especially when their livelihood might be at stake, or they could unwittingly reveal something their masters would prefer to keep secret. Then there was always the possibility that the killer was someone within the household, which would put Valerie Shaw's life at risk.

"Miss Shaw, Lord Redmond would like to ask you a few questions about your mistress's health," Daniel said, hoping to reassure the maid that these new questions had nothing to do with either the letter opener or the book.

"Of course, sir," Miss Shaw said as she accepted a seat.

Jason smiled at her in a friendly manner. "Miss Shaw, anything you say to me will be held in the strictest confidence," he said. "I know how important it is to have a spotless character reference, so nothing you tell me will ever leave this room."

Valerie Shaw nodded, now looking even more nervous. A lady's maid had to be the soul of discretion if she hoped to get a good character from her mistress.

"You said you've been employed as Miss Grant's maid for the past two years, is that correct?"

"Yes, sir."

"Did Miss Grant get her monthly flow regularly?" Jason asked.

"Yes, sir."

"When was the last time she had her courses?"

Miss Shaw looked ceilingward as she counted the days. "Her courses finished nine days ago, sir."

"Had the flow been regular, or perhaps lighter than usual?"

"It had been regular, sir. Lasted six days."

"Miss Shaw, did you look after your mistress's smallclothes?"

"Of course, sir."

"And did you ever notice–" Jason paused, clearly looking for the most delicate way of asking what he needed to know. "Did you ever notice evidence of sexual congress on her drawers?"

"You mean, were her unmentionables stained with a man's seed, sir?" Miss Shaw asked, trying in vain to hide her amusement.

"Yes, that is exactly what I mean," Jason replied, clearly relieved that his question had been correctly interpreted.

"No, sir. Not ever."

"What about the sheets?" Jason asked. "Were they ever stained?"

"If you're asking me if my lady ever had a man in her bed, the answer is an unequivocal no, sir."

"How can you be so certain?" Jason asked. "Rooms can be aired out, stains on sheets will dry overnight, and Miss Grant might have used cloths to protect her undergarments. Your room is not on the same floor, so you would not have seen or heard any comings and goings during the night."

Miss Shaw looked taken aback. "No, I suppose not, sir. I just never would have imagined…"

"I will ask you again, Miss Shaw, and please consider your answer carefully. Is it at all possible that your mistress was involved in a sexual relationship with someone in this house?"

Valerie Shaw opened her mouth to reply, then closed it, her cheeks suffusing with color as she considered the logistics of such a relationship. Jason waited patiently for her answer.

"Now that you put it that way, I suppose she may have, sir," Miss Shaw finally said. "Although I can't imagine who it would be."

"Was Miss Grant partial to any of the men who are employed in the household?" Daniel asked.

"She was always kind and polite to everyone, but I couldn't rightly say that she'd singled anyone out."

"The two footmen are rather handsome," Jason said, smiling at her encouragingly.

"I suppose they are, but I just can't see it, your lordship. Those two couldn't keep a secret if their life depended on it, which it would if one of them was making free with Miss Sybil. Judge Grant would have him up on charges of rape, and the poor fool would swing before he so much as had time to say he was innocent."

That was a valid point, Daniel decided. Due to his position, Judge Grant held the power of life and death in his hands. The man who dared to dishonor his sister would have to either be very cocky or unbelievably stupid.

"What about the judge's valet, Nevins?" Jason tried again. "Might he have found his way into your mistress's bed?"

Miss Shaw shook her head vehemently. "I'm sorry, sir, but I will not be party to speculating about a woman who can no longer defend herself against such base insinuations. I have never seen or heard anything myself, and that's all I can say for certain."

"Fair enough," Jason said, seeming satisfied with Miss Shaw's answers. "Please forgive me for making you uncomfortable. I'm only trying to get to the truth."

"I understand that, your lordship. I'm sorry I couldn't be more help."

"On the contrary, Miss Shaw. You've been most helpful," Jason replied, smiling at her kindly.

"You are free to go, Miss Shaw," Daniel said. "And thank you."

Miss Shaw nodded and left, shutting the door behind her.

"What do you reckon?" Daniel asked. "Think she's telling the truth?"

"I do," Jason said. "I don't think she knows anything, nor does she imagine her mistress capable of such brash behavior. I admire her loyalty."

"Loyalty is all well and good, but it doesn't help us solve the case. Do you have a theory?" Daniel asked, hoping Jason would put forth something they could expand on.

"I think that at some point over the past few years, Miss Grant had sexual relations with someone and found herself with child. Whether she was a willing participant or a victim of an assault is impossible to tell at this stage. Just as it's impossible to ascertain whether she was sexually active at the time of her death. I saw no signs of recent intercourse when I examined the body, which is not to say that she wasn't having an affair. Whether the murder was motivated by sexual jealousy or Miss Grant's rejection of her lover is impossible to determine without more evidence. I do, however, think that this is a crime of passion, and the motive is a very personal one."

"In other words, we know next to nothing," Daniel summarized bitterly.

"Precisely."

"I'd like to see the book Miss Grant was reading before she died," Daniel said, pushing to his feet.

"So would I."

They didn't bother to ask for permission to go up to Miss Grant's room. Hudson had no authority to refuse the request, and Judge Grant was not at home to ask. They found their way to Miss Grant's room and entered. The bed had been stripped and the linens changed, and the broken door had been taken away, albeit not replaced with a new one. There was nothing on or inside the bedside table or any other surface, and the ornate wardrobe had been emptied of Miss Grant's clothes. The room was utterly devoid of any personal objects.

"That was quick," Jason remarked as he looked around.

"Let's ask Mrs. Taft," Daniel suggested. "I'm sure Miss Grant's effects are still in the house."

They returned to the ground floor, then passed through the green baize door to descend to the basement level. Mrs. Taft was in her office and rose hesitantly when she saw them. She clearly hadn't expected to see them again so soon.

"Mrs. Taft, who cleaned out Miss Grant's room?" Daniel asked.

"I did, with the help of Miss Shaw."

"What did you do with Miss Grant's belongings?"

"Judge Grant ordered her things to be packed in a trunk."

"Where's the trunk?" Daniel asked.

Mrs. Taft pointed to a massive trunk in the corner. "The master said someone would come to collect it."

Daniel walked over and opened the trunk. It was full of dresses, shoes, undergarments, corsets, and stockings. Several hat boxes stood next to the trunk, and there was even a parasol.

"Mrs. Taft, Miss Grant had a book on her bedside table. *The Moonstone*. Where is it?"

Mrs. Tatt looked confused. "I didn't see any book, Inspector."

"Could someone have brought it to the library? How are the volumes organized?" Daniel asked.

"Alphabetically, sir. The master is very particular about that."

Jason and Daniel returned to the ground floor and found the library, where they checked under C for Collins, M for Moonstone, and T for The. They even checked under W for the author's Christian name but found nothing. Daniel and Jason then scanned every bookshelf for any book that looked new, but although they found several recently published volumes, there was no sign of *The Moonstone*.

"Someone's disposed of it," Daniel said unnecessarily.

"Perhaps they had used the strip of paper to write a message," Jason suggested. "Or maybe Miss Grant herself had written something damning before the murder, and the killer found it and tore it out."

"I suppose now we'll never know. That book has probably been given to a used book seller or thrown on the fire for all we know."

"Unless Judge Grant has it," Jason said.

"I do wish Miss Shaw would have brought it to me," Daniel said.

"Probably for the best that she didn't," Jason replied. "Especially if the killer is still in the house."

Daniel shook his head in dismay. "This case is becoming more convoluted by the minute. We've no motive, no obvious suspects, and no way of knowing how the killer got in or out."

"All we can do is try to piece together the events of Miss Grant's life and see if we find the motive that way."

"Shall we meet at the train station tomorrow at nine?" Daniel asked, ready to call it a day.

"I'll be there."

Chapter 15

"How is your case progressing?" Sarah asked when Daniel joined her in the drawing room before dinner.

Daniel was pleased to note that Sarah looked considerably better this evening, her cheeks rosy from the time she'd spent in the garden with Charlotte that afternoon. The child was already in bed, so this was their chance to talk and catch up on the day's happenings, but although Sarah had expressed an interest, there was a faraway look in her eyes, as if her mind were elsewhere and she was only asking to be polite.

"This case is most puzzling," Daniel replied, hoping to engage her attention. He poured himself a drink and sat across from Sarah, leaning forward in his eagerness to talk to his wife. "A woman—the sister of a well-known judge—was murdered in her bed."

Daniel felt it was important for Sarah to know that the woman had been respectable, someone who wouldn't normally meet with a brutal end. All too often he had to tell her of victims who were the sort of women no wife should have to hear about, but Sarah became upset when he refused to discuss his work, so he told her as much as he reasonably could without revealing the more disturbing details of their lives and deaths.

"And the killer?" Sarah asked.

"Escaped from a locked room, and no one in the house saw or heard anything. We've been investigating for two whole days and have yet to establish a motive or find a single clue."

Sarah considered this for a moment. "Are you certain this murder is not an intricate illusion?"

"How can it be?"

"A desperate woman's final act of revenge," Sarah said, a ghost of a smile tugging at her lips.

"Sarah, what on earth do you mean? Revenge against whom?"

"I mean that perhaps she had staged it all," Sarah replied. "As for whom it was meant to hurt, well, that's something you have to figure out."

"Why would a healthy woman in her twenties stage a murder and then kill herself in a way that would have caused her untold agony?"

Sarah cocked her head to the side and looked at him. Daniel thought he noticed a hint of derision in her gaze. "Perhaps it hurt more to live," she replied, her voice strangely flat. "And if everyone assumes she was murdered, she will not be treated as a suicide, not an end a well-known judge would appreciate," Sarah added matter-of-factly.

Daniel shook his head. "Impossible. The murder weapon is missing. Someone must have disposed of it."

"Have you searched behind the headboard?" Sarah asked. "Or underneath the mattress? She might have hidden the murder weapon intentionally, just to confound the police."

Daniel opened his mouth to reply but reconsidered his argument. Sarah had made a valid point. He'd searched the room thoroughly, but it wasn't outside the realm of possibility that the letter opener had become stuck between the headboard and the wall if Sybil Grant had tossed it behind the headboard in her final moments. They hadn't moved the heavy bed, only searched beneath it. Nor had Daniel checked beneath the mattress, although if there had been any blood on the side of the mattress, he would have certainly looked. The linens on the side of the bed had been clean, so it wasn't likely that a bloodied letter opener had been hidden underneath.

Closing his eyes, Daniel allowed himself to visualize the victim with dispassionate objectivity. The stab wounds to the neck were on the left. If Sybil Grant was right-handed, then she would have stabbed herself on the left side of the neck, just as she would

103

have applied greater pressure to that side when trying to slit her throat with the dull letter knife. The idea that a woman would do that to herself would be utterly preposterous if not for several undeniable facts that supported Sarah's theory.

There were no bloody footprints, no stains on the carpet or the wooden floorboards, and nothing on the doorknob. The door had still been locked from within when Valerie Shaw came to wake her mistress, and there was the complete absence of witnesses in a house full of people.

"Could a person do that to themselves, do you think?" Daniel asked, chilled by Sarah's immediate assumption that Sybil Grant had been so far gone in her mind as to go at herself like a madwoman.

"A person will do anything to stop the pain," Sarah said. "A few minutes of agony probably seemed a small price to pay for an eternity of nothing but peace."

"Jason doesn't think it was a suicide," Daniel said, but his voice sounded reedy, the statement lacking conviction.

Sarah nodded in acknowledgement, as if she had suddenly changed her mind. "Well, then you must continue with the investigation. I trust Jason's judgment implicitly."

But not mine, it seems, Daniel thought bitterly.

"Shall we move into the dining room?" Sarah asked after checking the time on the carriage clock on the mantel. "It's seven."

She smiled at Daniel, but the smile never reached her eyes, reminding Daniel of the china doll Harriet had purchased for her granddaughter, its chalk-white face forever frozen in a sinister grin.

Chapter 16

Wednesday, June 10

When Daniel arrived at Liverpool Street Station, he was surprised to see Micah waiting with Jason. Micah had a copy of the latest penny dreadful in his hand and looked excited at the prospect of an outing. The boy had shot up since Daniel had seen him last and was beginning to look like a well-turned-out young man rather than the coltish, undersized boy Daniel had first met two years ago.

"Hello, Micah," Daniel said, casting an inquiring glance at Jason, who looked mildly apologetic.

"Hello, Inspector," Micah said eagerly. "I'm coming with you."

"Micah thought he could help," Jason explained, as they walked into the station and purchased tickets for the next train to Southend. Daniel decided not to question Jason's logic. Micah had been helpful in the past, so maybe Jason had an idea he wasn't yet ready to share. And there was no harm in Micah tagging along. He could look after himself if the situation called for it.

"Have you ever been to Southend?" Jason asked Daniel once they were settled in a compartment, waiting for the train to depart.

"Once, with my parents when I was ten. That was several years before the railway came to the town. And before they built the pier. It has become quite the holiday destination in recent years, but back then, there wasn't much there save the beach and several modest guest houses."

"There is a beach? Can I go swimming?" Micah asked.

"There is a beach, and I believe they have bathing cabins, but you would need a swimming costume and a towel at the very least," Daniel said.

Micah looked crestfallen, then turned to Jason. "Why don't we go on holiday, now that I'm home from school? Maybe we can take Liam to the sea before you pack him off to Boston," he added unkindly.

"We'll talk about it later, Micah," Jason replied tersely.

"It's just that I've got nothing to do at home. And I miss Tom."

"Maybe you can help out at the hospital," Jason suggested.

"Really? Doing what?" Micah seemed intrigued. "Maybe I can be your surgical assistant. I can hand you the amputation saw and such."

"I'm not in need of a surgical assistant, but maybe you can visit some of the younger patients and read to them, or just talk to them to lift their spirits," Jason suggested.

"I'll think about it," Micah replied, and buried his nose in the penny dreadful, clearly not enticed by Jason's suggestion.

"I believe the Grant cottage is within walking distance of the railway station," Daniel said, relieved that Micah had stopped whining.

"Is it within walking distance of the pier?" Micah asked.

"It might be," Daniel replied.

"Captain, can I go explore while you visit the cottage?"

"I don't see why not. As long as you meet us on time."

"I will," Micah promised, and returned to his reading.

"Sarah had some thoughts on the case," Daniel said, lowering his voice. "She thinks Sybil Grant staged her own murder before committing suicide."

Jason's eyes widened in surprise. "What would give her that idea?"

Daniel sighed. "She thought that perhaps Sybil Grant wanted to punish someone, or maybe to ensure that she'd receive a proper burial. The church takes a dim view of suicide. Sarah suggested that she might have managed to hide the weapon in her final moments, which would account for the locked room and the lack of blood on the floor and the doorknob. It would also explain why no one had seen or heard anything. The stab wound was on the left, which is where it would be if Miss Grant had inflicted it herself."

Jason considered this theory, his gaze fixed on the verdant countryside rushing past the window as he weighed fact versus supposition. "I suppose that's possible," he said at last, "but not probable. If the killer is right-handed, then the wound would also be on the left side of the neck. I agree that a suicide would explain the locked room and why no one saw or heard anything, but I honestly can't imagine anyone inflicting such horror on themselves. Sybil Grant's throat was all but ripped out. Surely if she wished to resort to self-murder, she could have at least used a sharp knife."

"Perhaps she wished to ensure that her death was treated as a crime," Daniel suggested, playing the devil's advocate. He didn't really believe that Sybil Grant had committed suicide, but this line of reasoning could conceivably point them toward something they had hitherto missed.

"But why use a dull letter opener, if that truly was the murder weapon? We only have Valerie Shaw's word that it was even there. Surely if Sybil Grant had intended to end her life, she would have prepared and left nothing to chance."

"What if something had occurred to her just as she was getting ready for bed, and she grabbed the letter opener and tried to open her neck on the spur of the moment?" Daniel said.

"That seems unlikely," Jason said. "What would have to occur to someone to elicit such a swift and volatile reaction?"

"Beth McCardle hanged herself in the barn when she learned Ian Mackey was to wed Lara Simmons," Micah suddenly said.

"Are you suggesting that Sybil Grant had been jilted by her lover?" Daniel asked, studying Micah over the top of his spectacles, which kept sliding down his nose.

"Well, why not?" Micah asked. "Some women think they're nothing without a man."

Jason seemed to be considering Micah's suggestion but refrained from commenting.

"I suppose that's possible," Daniel speculated. "Sybil Grant had lost the man she loved when David Ellis died. If she had been rejected by a new love, then perhaps the prospect of spending the rest of her life alone proved too much for her. If something had happened earlier in the day, then perhaps the full extent of it hit her once she was alone in her room. If she was that distraught, she might have grabbed the letter opener off her nightstand and tried to slit her throat. Finding that it wasn't sharp enough to do the job, she turned it around and used it to stab herself instead."

"I'm still not convinced," Jason said. "This theory clears up some questions but raises many others. Who was her lover? Why did no one know about him? Sybil Grant was a grown woman, not a child barely out of the schoolroom. Why the need to keep him secret? Was he unsuitable? Married already and unable to offer her a future? Did she find herself with child and feel she had no recourse? And how could she have spent the entire evening with her brother, an experienced judge who's well versed in the caprices of human nature, without giving away anything of her feelings?"

Jason asked, his expression challenging Daniel to answer at least some of the questions he'd posed.

Daniel nodded, in full agreement with Jason's assessment. "And then there are the practical matters," he said. "If it was suicide, where's the weapon she used? We searched the room thoroughly but found no trace of anything that might have been used to account for the injury. The only place we didn't search is behind the headboard, but if Sybil Grant had tried to toss the bloodied weapon behind the bed, there would be blood not only on the woodwork but also on the wallpaper. There was nothing. And what of the book?"

"What book?" Micah asked, not even pretending to be reading at that point.

"There was a book on the bedside table, but someone has taken it away," Jason replied.

Micah's eyes lit up with excitement. "Maybe someone had used the book to convey a message," he said.

Jason nodded and smiled at his ward. "That's good thinking, Micah. We hadn't considered that."

"If someone had written a message on the last page, that would explain why Sybil Grant had torn it out. She didn't want anyone to see it," Daniel said.

"But what did she do with it?" Jason asked. "We didn't find any strips of paper in the room."

"She swallowed it," Micah exclaimed.

"I think you're getting a bit carried away," Daniel said, but Jason's expression grew thoughtful.

"I have heard of instances where couriers swallowed missives during the war to keep them from falling into enemy hands."

"Are you suggesting Sybil Grant was a spy?" Daniel asked, his lips twitching with amusement.

"No, but I think it's safe to assume the woman had secrets, and until we discover what they were, we have no hope of solving this case."

"Then let us hope that Southend holds some answers for us," Daniel said as the train slowed down, approaching the station.

Chapter 17

Once they disembarked in Southend, they made a plan to meet Micah by the pier in two hours before heading off to the Grant cottage on Pleasant Road. The cottage was built of gray stone and had a green-painted front door and shutters. The arbor that framed the tiny porch was smothered with crimson roses. Daniel could see why Sybil Grant might have wished to come here to get away from London. It was a peaceful spot, especially during the cooler months, when there were few visitors to the seaside town.

The door was opened by a middle-aged woman who wore a pinstriped pinafore, her hair pulled into a neat bun. She must have been pretty once, but now she looked severe and unyielding, her lips pursed in annoyance.

"Yes?" she asked, studying the two strangers on her doorstep.

Daniel showed his warrant card. "Are you Mrs. March?"

"I am."

"I'm Inspector Haze of Scotland Yard, and this is my associate, Mr. Redmond. We'd like to ask you a few questions."

"About what?" Mrs. March demanded, not budging from her spot by the door.

"About Miss Sybil Grant."

"I'm not at liberty to discuss my mistress, Inspector."

"I would rather not do this on the doorstep, Mrs. March," Daniel said, wishing the woman would invite them in, but she seemed determined to be obstructive.

"Do what?" she demanded.

"Your mistress was murdered two days ago."

111

Mrs. March's hand flew to her mouth, and her eyes filled with tears. "I didn't know," she choked out. "I don't read the papers."

"It wasn't in the papers. May we come in?" Daniel asked, taking a step forward and leaving Mrs. March no alternative but to step back.

Mrs. March led them to a pretty parlor decorated in pale blue and white and went off to make tea. Daniel suspected she'd offered them tea not to be hospitable but because she needed a few moments to compose herself. The woman was clearly in shock. She eventually returned with a laden tray and set it on the low table.

"Shall I pour out?" she asked, sounding more like a society matron than a housekeeper. Daniel had a feeling that Mrs. March had come down in the world, but her background was of no interest to him, at least not at the moment.

"Please," he said.

Once Mrs. March went through the ritual of pouring the tea and offering them slices of seed cake, Daniel got down to business.

"Mrs. March, the questions we must ask you are rather delicate, and you might feel disloyal to Miss Grant for telling us the truth, but I assure you, it's very important that we know what happened, since we believe her death is connected to past events."

Mrs. March nodded miserably. "I'll tell you whatever you wish to know."

"Can you tell us what happened when Judge Grant brought Miss Grant here to recuperate after the death of Mr. Ellis?"

Mrs. March set her teacup down and gazed out the window for a moment, as if trying to remember—or come up with a plausible response.

"It was in March of 1865. It was a cold spring, and there were few people in Southend, which suited Judge Grant just fine. Miss Sybil was very frail. She was devastated by the death of Mr. Ellis, and her melancholy had taken a toll on her health. She hardly left the house for four months. She read and slept and sat in the garden on fine days, but she was heartbroken and needed time to grieve."

"Did Judge Grant ever call for a doctor?" Jason asked.

"Yes, he did. Dr. Boswell attended on Miss Sybil several times, but he said there was nothing wrong with her that time wouldn't cure."

"And did Miss Grant bring a maid with her?" Daniel asked.

"No. It was just Miss Sybil and the judge. I looked after Miss Sybil's needs, which were very basic. She wore the same few gowns and kept her hair in a plait. And when the judge wasn't there, she only ate soup and poached salmon. Said she had no taste for anything else."

"Mrs. March, was Miss Grant with child?" Jason asked, his gaze fixed on the woman's face.

Mrs. March looked taken aback, her gaze sliding away from Jason's inquisitive stare. "No, sir," she muttered.

"Are you certain?"

Mrs. March didn't reply.

"Mrs. March, surely you would like to see justice done," Daniel said.

She nodded but remained silent.

"Is your husband here?" Daniel asked.

"Why do you want to speak to my husband?" Mrs. March asked, clearly alarmed.

"Because presumably he was here at the time, and we'd like to ask him a few questions."

"My husband is at home. We don't live here. I come by for a few hours every morning to dust and water the garden."

"I don't think that's quite true," Daniel said. "I think you live here all year around without the knowledge of Judge Grant."

Mrs. March looked stricken. "How would you know that?"

"Mrs. March, one doesn't have to be an inspector to notice that you had fresh milk and cake on hand when we called. Why would you bake a cake or bring one by if you only ever come to clean the place? There are men's slippers in the entryway, as well as a copy of yesterday's newspaper on the arm of that chair and a pipe on the mantelpiece. And there's coal soot in the grate," Daniel said. "I wager it gets cold here during the evening hours. Even in June," he added. "I expect you stayed somewhere whenever Judge Grant or Miss Sybil came to the cottage and then moved back in once they left."

Mrs. March nodded, her expression guilty. "We stayed with my widowed sister."

"You must have saved a pretty penny over the years, living here for free," Daniel said conversationally. "And it's such a pretty place. Much nicer than anything you might be able to afford on a housekeeper's wage. And is your husband employed?" he asked, watching the woman.

"He does odd jobs."

"Can't earn too much doing odd jobs in a town that only comes alive during the summer months," Daniel mused. "Shall I inform Judge Grant that you've been abusing his trust?"

Mrs. March went white to the roots of her hair. "Please, Inspector. We're not doing any harm. The house is empty nearly year-round."

"Still, you don't have express permission to live here, do you?" Daniel felt sorry for the woman, but she wasn't going to reveal anything unless she felt she had something to gain.

"Mrs. March, I will not say anything to Judge Grant. Your living situation has nothing to do with the inquiry. But you need to answer my questions truthfully. A woman is dead, and I need to know why."

Mrs. March nodded in resignation. "Thank you, Inspector. That's kind of you. My husband suffers from podagra. The pain prevents him from doing the sort of work that pays a decent wage, so we get by on what Judge Grant sends our way, which is not much. Not having to pay for lodgings makes all the difference to our situation and allows us to stay together. Otherwise, I would have to go into service," she explained, all previous defiance having been replaced by abject misery.

"Let's try this again, Mrs. March. Was Miss Grant with child when she came here in the spring of 1865?"

Mrs. March nodded. "About six months gone."

"And how did Judge Grant behave toward her while they were here?" Jason asked.

"He was solicitous, but he was also angry. It was obvious. He kept a close eye on her and didn't let her out of the house, not that she wished to leave. He bid us to report to him on Miss Sybil's activities whenever he returned from London."

"What happened to the child?" Jason asked.

"I don't know, and that's the honest truth."

"Was it born alive?"

She nodded. "A girl. Davina, Miss Sybil called her. After the baby's father. She was born on June second. I remember it as if it were yesterday."

"Who took the child?" Daniel asked.

"I don't know, Inspector. Judge Grant made all the arrangements. The child was delivered by a midwife, who took her away."

"Had Miss Sybil agreed to give up her child?" Jason asked.

"What choice did she have?" Mrs. March cried. "She could hardly have kept her, being an unmarried woman. Judge Grant would never allow it."

"Were relations strained between Miss Grant and her brother after the child was taken?" Daniel asked.

"She was heartbroken, the poor lamb, but she understood her brother's reasons. He was only trying to protect her from disgrace."

"And himself," Jason added. "A man of his standing would not welcome a scandal."

"No, I don't suppose he would," Mrs. March agreed.

"What was the name of the midwife?" Daniel asked.

"Jane something. We were never introduced."

"Did Judge Grant pay you to keep your silence?"

Mrs. March nodded. "He did, but he also threatened us. He said we'd be out without a character should we ever breathe a word. And now that I had to tell you, we'll lose our livelihood," she wailed.

"Not necessarily," Jason said.

Mrs. March's head snapped up, her gaze hopeful. "Sir?"

"I already knew Miss Grant had given birth to a child. I don't need to mention to Judge Grant that you have confirmed my suspicions."

"Oh, thank you, sir. That's most kind of you."

"However," Jason said, holding Mrs. March's gaze, "given that you were here, caring for Miss Grant during the final months of her pregnancy, I fail to believe that you didn't overhear any conversations pertaining to the child's future."

Mrs. March sniffled, her final barrier breached. "They argued all the time."

"About?" Daniel demanded.

"Miss Sybil begged her brother to place the child with a good family. She said she'd give it up without a fight as long as she knew it was well looked after and she could keep an eye on it from afar. And she wanted whoever took her baby to keep the name."

"And what did her brother want to do?"

"He said he'd do as she asked, but he wouldn't tell her the name of the couple. He didn't want her to have anything to do with the child ever again."

"And did Miss Grant agree to his terms?" Daniel asked.

"I believe they reached some sort of compromise, but I don't know what it was. All I know is that they made peace with each other."

"And how often did the Grants come to the cottage in subsequent years?"

"They came together every August and stayed for three weeks. Miss Sybil was due to come down at the end of this month, as it happens. She'd written to me, asking me to prepare the cottage for her arrival."

"Did she say why she wished to come on her own?" Jason asked.

"No, but she did come alone now and again and stayed a week or so. And before you ask, she didn't meet with anyone or have anyone visit her here. She brought her maid, Miss Shaw, probably because Judge Grant insisted on it, but she kept mostly to herself. She read a lot and went for long walks."

"Is there a possibility that Miss Grant was with child again?" Jason asked.

"I wouldn't know, sir, but she did say in her letter that she only wished to stay a week."

"Thank you, Mrs. March," Daniel said.

"Do I have your word you won't tell Judge Grant that we've been living here, Mr. March and I?" the woman asked anxiously.

"He won't hear it from me," Daniel promised, "but you are trespassing, Mrs. March, and I would strongly advise you to reconsider your living situation."

"Yes, Inspector. We will."

"Thank you for the tea," Jason said politely as they stood to leave.

Chapter 18

Jason and Daniel had some time before they were due to meet Micah, so they decided to walk down the Marine Parade toward the pavilion that led to the pier. The pier stuck out into the estuary like an accusing finger, but it was a fine place to promenade, and several well-dressed couples strolled along, the ladies shielding their faces from the sun with lace-trimmed parasols. The sunlight sparkled on the water, and the sky was a cloudless blue, the day too lovely to spend indoors. A few bathing cabins had been wheeled into the water for those brave souls who were willing to risk a dip in the still-frigid water, and they were clearly visible in their caps and bathing costumes as they splashed around.

"We now know that Sybil Grant gave birth to a daughter in June of 1865. The child was taken away and placed with a foster family chosen by Judge Grant. Davina has just turned three, but what could she have to do with Sybil Grant's murder?" Daniel mused as they strolled along. "If we are to assume that Judge Grant had exacted a promise from his sister never to see the child or have contact with the family, then this is just a bit of unfortunate family history."

"I'm afraid I don't see a connection either," Jason said. "We don't even know if the child is still alive. There are so many illnesses than can carry a child off before they are even out of babyhood."

"I'm glad we confirmed your suspicions that Sybil Grant had indeed given birth, but unless she was somehow in contact with her daughter, I fear this is a dead end. Whatever led to Sybil Grant's death was something that must have occurred recently."

Jason peered toward the pier. Two boys stood at the very end and appeared to be talking earnestly. "Is that Micah?" Jason asked.

Daniel squinted but couldn't be sure. He did think one of the boys had bright red hair peeking out from beneath his cap. "I can't tell from this distance. It could be."

"Looks like he made a friend," Jason observed. "I have no idea what I'm going to do to keep him occupied all summer. I don't want him roaming the streets of London on his own."

"He's too old for childish pursuits and too young to do anything that might be considered useful," Daniel said. "I don't suppose you'll have that problem for much longer. He's certainly matured this past year."

"Yes, he has," Jason replied with a sigh. "I only hope he doesn't run off to Boston before he has a chance to attend university. It would be a terrible shame if he were to forgo an education."

Daniel smiled. "Micah is a clever lad, but I don't need to tell you that. You already know. I doubt he'll throw his future away, not when he knows firsthand how the other half lives."

"People make irrational choices when their emotions are involved," Jason said. "If they didn't, you'd be out of a job."

"I can't argue with that," Daniel replied.

By this time, the two boys had turned around and were headed toward the pavilion, still talking animatedly between themselves, their steps unhurried. Jason and Daniel waited by the entrance and were surprised when Micah emerged alone.

"Oh, good, you're here," Micah said. "I'm starving. Can we get something to eat?"

"Of course," Jason replied. "Are you hungry, Daniel?"

"Surprisingly, yes. That cake didn't do much for me."

"What cake?" Micah demanded.

"Mrs. March gave us tea," Jason replied. "Who were you talking to?"

"His name is Walter. His father is the station master here in Southend. He's my age, and he is nice," Micah said. "He's going to work as a porter this summer to earn some pin money. We talked about all sorts of things."

"Really? Such as?" Jason asked.

Micah stopped walking and smiled up at Jason, his eyes dancing with mischief. "Such as Miss Sybil Grant," Micah announced, clearly pleased with himself.

"How in the world did Miss Grant come up?" Daniel asked.

Micah's grin broadened. "Well, being that Walter's father is the station master, I thought I'd mention that you are here investigating the lady's murder. You know, just in case he knew something. You'd be surprised what people happen to recall when prompted," Micah said, repeating something he must have overheard Daniel say. He even mimicked Daniel's stance and inflection. Daniel knew Micah meant no offense, so he ignored the impertinence. He was just excited about whatever it was the boy had learned.

"And did he know anything?" Jason asked, an admiring smile tugging at the corner of his mouth.

Micah nodded happily. "He said Miss Grant came to Southend once a month, even during the winter, and always on a Thursday," he announced as they entered a nearby coffeehouse and found a table by the window.

"Is he sure it was Miss Grant?" Daniel asked.

"He is. The Grants have been coming to Southend for years, and he's well acquainted with Judge Grant, who is a good tipper by all accounts. Walter's father worked as a porter when the railway station first opened," Micah added.

"It seems our Miss Grant had a fondness for routine," Jason said.

"Yes, she was very precise," Daniel agreed, recalling the meetings she had scheduled with her nephew.

"Did Walter say anything else? Did she come alone? Did she leave the same day? Where did she go once she arrived? I know you learned all you could," Jason said, his pride in Micah's abilities evident.

"Of course I did. She always arrived on the 11:27 from London and left on the 3:30. She came alone and took an omnibus that runs down the High Street. And," Micah added triumphantly, "I know the name of the omnibus driver. It's Matthew Garrett."

"Micah, you're a gem," Daniel said, grinning broadly.

"I'm glad you think so," Micah said, then turned his attention to the menu. "I'd like some cake and a pot of chocolate."

"You've earned it," Jason said. "Order whatever you like."

"Are you having anything?" Daniel asked Jason.

"Just coffee. I'm not really hungry after that seed cake."

"You really ought to eat something," Daniel said, worried that Jason might feel unwell if too much time elapsed between meals.

Jason smiled. "You sound like my wife."

"I'll take that as a compliment," Daniel replied, and glanced down at the menu, certain that Jason would take his advice.

Once finished, they walked to the omnibus terminal to ask after Matthew Garrett. He was out on his route but expected back shortly, since the omnibus only went to the end of the High Street and back. A quarter of an hour later, the omnibus pulled up, and the driver got out to stretch his legs before making the next trip. An

122

attendant brought out buckets of water for the horses, who must have made the trip several times already that day.

Matthew Garrett was a tall, lean man with iron-gray hair and kind brown eyes. His suit had seen better days, as had his shoes, but his clothes were neatly pressed, and the shoes were polished to a shine. This was a man who took pride in his appearance and his occupation. The omnibus looked clean, and the windows reflected the afternoon sunshine, not a speck of grime to be seen on the sparkling panes. He removed his hat and held it in his hands as he listened carefully to what Daniel had to say, his expression thoughtful.

"I don't rightly know if the lady's name were Miss Grant or not, since we'd never been introduced, but I reckon I know who ye're talking about. Not many ladies as fit her description ride the omnibus alone every last Thursday of the month. She were a sad little thing, all eyes and sighs, 'specially on the return trip. I don't know who she went to see, but it weren't an easy errand she undertook."

"Can you tell us where she got off?" Daniel asked.

"Got off at Bradley Street and walked quickly away, her head bowed. I reckon she didn't care to be noticed."

"Do you know anyone who lives in Bradley Street?"

"Can't say as I do, Inspector. I live in Prittlewell meself."

"Did Miss Grant ever speak to anyone while riding the omnibus or perhaps while waiting to board?" Daniel asked.

"Not that I noticed."

"Was she anxious as well as sad?" Jason asked.

"More so on the way back. I s'pose she were afraid to miss the train."

"Did she ever miss a month?" Daniel asked.

123

"Maybe once or twice, but usually she were there, like clockwork, ye might say."

"Did you ever think that someone might be following her?"

"I really couldn't say, Inspector. I keep me eyes on the road, if ye know what I mean. Can't really be watching pretty young women. There were other passengers who disembarked at Bradley Street from time to time, but I wouldn't think they was following anyone. Just going home."

"Does anyone else cover your route, Mr. Garrett?" Daniel asked.

"No, Inspector, it's just me."

"What about when you're ill?" Jason asked.

Matthew Garrett smiled, revealing even white teeth. "I'm never ill. Haven't missed a day of work since I took over the route eight years ago now."

"What did you do before that?"

"Used to drive a hansom in London, but me and me missus, we were ready for a quieter life."

"Thank you, Mr. Garrett," Daniel said.

"Was that helpful at all, Inspector?" the driver asked, his gaze hopeful.

"Yes, it was. Very." Daniel took out a sixpence and held it out, but Mr. Garrett refused.

"There's no need to tip me, Inspector Haze. Just doing what any decent man would do. She were a lovely lady, and I'm sorry she's come to a bad end."

"Are you heading out again, Mr. Garrett?" Daniel asked.

"In five minutes, I am," Mr. Garrett replied.

"Then I think we'll take a ride to Bradley Street."

"I'll be glad to take ye, good sirs. And the young gentleman," he said, grinning at Micah, who was petting one of the horses affectionately.

"What do you plan to do once there?" Micah asked Daniel once they'd boarded the omnibus. He was clearly fascinated with the direction the inquiry was taking.

"There's only one reason I can think of why Miss Grant would keep coming back to Southend on her own," Daniel replied. "This is where her daughter was born, so it's possible that the family the child was fostered with resides right here, in town."

"But how will you find them?" Micah asked as Mr. Garrett climbed onto the bench and took up the reins.

"Ask after a family that has a three-year-old girl. The foster family might have changed the child's name, but if that's who Sybil Grant was going to see, she shouldn't be too hard to find."

"And then what?"

"And then, hopefully, we'll find out more about the arrangement and whether it might have had a bearing on Miss Grant's death."

"Do you think it could have?" Micah asked as the omnibus pulled away.

"Mrs. March said that Judge Grant didn't want his sister to have any contact with the child. Unless he changed his mind, Miss Grant was going behind his back."

"I hardly think Judge Grant would kill his sister for trying to see her daughter," Jason said. "But perhaps the emotional strain had become too much for her. Especially if she happened to learn that the child had died."

"The birth of the child and her possible death would certainly explain the change in Miss Grant and the pervasive sadness so many had referred to when describing the deceased," Daniel said. "To lose a child conceived in love after the death of its father would be difficult for any woman to bear, especially one who had to pretend the child never existed."

"So, you think she topped herself?" Micah asked. "That's a mortal sin, and then she'd never be reunited with her girl in heaven."

"I think we need to discover the purpose of these monthly visits," Daniel replied. "Until then, all this is just baseless speculation."

Chapter 19

Bradley Street was not a holiday destination where beachfront promenades were dotted with elegant hotels that promised stunning views and fine dining. It was lined with red-brick houses that had identical front doors, black chimney pots, and windows that were too small to let in sufficient light. Daniel imagined the rooms behind them as gloomy and unwelcoming. Some windows were covered with lace curtains, while others were bare, facing the street like staring eyes. This was a street where respectable, hardworking people lived and died, since they weren't likely to afford anything better on their wages. If they moved anywhere, it was somewhere less desirable.

Two women stood on a doorstep further down the street, talking loudly, and several children played outside, their attention focused on the hoop and stick possessed by one of the older boys. A sixpence clearly visible in his hand, Daniel approached a boy of about nine, hoping he might be sufficiently swayed by the promise of a coin to answer his questions.

"Do you know of a family that lives in this street and has a three-year-old child?" he asked. He'd decided not to get too specific in case word of his search reached Davina's parents before he did.

The boy snorted with laughter. "It'd be easier if ye asked me which family don't, guv."

"It's a girl," Daniel admitted.

The boy shrugged. "There's lots o' girls. Got a name?"

"Davina," Daniel said, wishing he could have retained some control over the situation. The boy had a shifty gaze Daniel didn't like. Shifty boys grew up into shifty men.

The child laughed again. He was enjoying this. "Are ye the bailiffs?" the boy asked, sneaking a peek at Jason. He seemed confused by Micah's presence.

"Number twelve. The Kinnistons," his friend said. He looked a bit younger, but he had a direct gaze and a self-assured stance that Daniel found to his liking. "Their sprat's named Davina. Odd name, that."

"Thank you," Daniel said, and gave the child the sixpence, glad to note the look of outrage on the older boy's face. "You had your chance," Daniel said before walking away.

They found number twelve and knocked. A woman in her mid-thirties opened the door. She wasn't conventionally pretty, but there was a friendliness in her gaze that made Daniel feel more at ease. She wore a dress of cheerful yellow calico, and her dark hair was worn in a loose bun atop her head. She smiled in welcome.

"How can I 'elp ye, gentlemen?"

"Are you Mrs. Kinniston?" Daniel asked.

"Who's askin'?" She looked wary, the smile sliding off her face as Daniel held up his warrant card.

"Please, don't be alarmed, Mrs. Kinniston. We only want to ask you a few questions."

"Is it my Stan?" she cried. "'As 'e been 'urt?"

"No, it's not about your husband. Can we speak inside?"

Several people had appeared, the women standing in their open doorways to better see what was going on. They looked like hounds who'd caught the scent of a fox.

Mrs. Kinniston moved away from the door and let them in, closing the door behind them as soon as they stepped inside. She led them to a small parlor that wasn't nearly as dim or unwelcoming as Daniel had imagined. It was cozy and comfortable, with a pretty nautical landscape hanging over the mantel and a carriage clock that ticked loudly. The furniture and carpet looked newish, and an appetizing smell of roasting meat came from the kitchen.

"Why are ye 'ere?" Mrs. Kinniston asked once they were seated. She seemed particularly unnerved by Micah, whose flaming hair caught the light from the window and gleamed brightly.

"Mrs. Kinniston, we're investigating the death of Sybil Grant," Daniel began.

The woman looked blank. "I don't know anyone by that name," she finally said.

"Is your daughter's name Davina?" Daniel tried again.

"Yes," Mrs. Kinniston replied hesitantly.

"And is she three years old?"

"She turned three last week."

"Sybil Grant was Davina's natural mother. She was found dead two days ago in her home in London."

"Found dead?" Mrs. Kinniston echoed. "Ye wouldn't be 'ere if she died of natural causes."

"We believe she was murdered," Daniel clarified.

Mrs. Kinniston gasped. "I never knew 'er name," she said. "Not 'er real name, any 'ow. She called 'erself Miss Greene when she came. Oh, I am sorry for 'er," she said, but she didn't look sorry in the least. Hearing of the death of the woman who had the power to take her child away probably wasn't the worst news she could receive.

"Mrs. Kinniston, Davina is safe, and so are you. We simply need to clarify your arrangement with the Grants."

The woman nodded and sank into a chair that was as yellow as her dress. She no longer looked sunny. "Stanley and I weren't blessed with a child of our own," she began. "It broke me 'eart that I'd never be a mother, 'specially since me sister, Jane, has six strappin' lads. Jane knew 'ow desperate we were to 'ave a baby, and she were eager to 'elp."

"How did she help?" Daniel asked.

"Jane's a midwife. 'As been these past twenty years. She's well known in these parts."

"Did she deliver Davina?" Jason asked.

Mrs. Kinniston nodded. "When she told me a gentlewoman were to give away 'er baby, well, I jumped at the chance, but Stan weren't that keen. 'E were afraid there'd be conditions."

"And were there?" Daniel asked.

Mrs. Kinniston nodded again. "There was to be a monthly allowance for upkeep, and the gentleman as made the arrangement said there'd be no contact. Ever. Only thing 'e asked was that we keep the name, since 'twere to honor the child's father, so we agreed. T'weren't a name I would've chosen meself, mind, but it's pretty enough. Unique, Stan said. A name for a lady."

"But things didn't go to plan, did they?" Jason asked gently, noting Mrs. Kinniston's obvious distress.

"Davi was 'round six months old when Miss Greene first showed up at our door. She said she were the child's natural mother and asked only to see 'er. I tried to refuse, but she began to weep, and ye see 'ow nosy the neighbors can be. So I let 'er in. Well, she looked upon our Davi, asked to 'old 'er for a bit, then gave me five bob and left. I 'oped we'd seen the last of 'er, but Stan said that were just the tip o' the iceberg. And sure enough, 'e were right. She came back the next month, and the month after that. She swore she wanted nothing but to see the child and was 'appy to pay for the privilege."

"Did she try to tell Davina she was her mother?" Daniel asked.

"No. She never did. She only wanted to look at 'er and 'old 'er for a spell. She brought 'er presents. I didn't want 'er presents or 'er money, but Stan said we should save what she gave for Davi, to 'elp 'er out when she's old enough to 'ave need of it."

"And Miss Greene always came on the same day?"

"Last Thursday of the month. That were 'er day. She said it were so as I'd know to be at 'ome, but I think she 'ad 'er own reasons."

"Did you ever leave intentionally, so as not to be here when she came?" Jason asked.

"I wanted to, but she'd just come back another day. I felt sorry for 'er," Mrs. Kinniston said. "She were such a wretched little thing. She loved Davi with all 'er 'eart. I never doubted that. I reckon she loved 'er father something fierce."

"Mrs. Kinniston, what does your husband do?" Daniel asked.

"'E's a bricklayer, Inspector. Why d'ye ask?"

"And where was he on Sunday night?"

Mrs. Kinniston stared at him, comprehension slowly dawning. "Are ye saying it were me Stan as done for 'er?"

"I only need to know where he was, to rule him out," Daniel explained.

"Stan ain't no murderer, Inspector 'Aze. 'E's a good man who works 'ard to support 'is family."

"Where was he, Mrs. Kinniston?" Daniel asked again.

"Stan were 'ere, the whole night, with me and Davi." Mrs. Kinniston looked at Daniel fearfully. "What'll 'appen now?"

"I expect your arrangement with Mr. Grant will continue as before," Daniel said, although he wasn't at all certain Oliver Grant would continue to pay the Kinnistons their monthly allowance now that his sister was gone. Daniel hoped he'd honor the terms of the arrangement, but that wasn't really his business. "Thank you, Mrs. Kinniston."

"May I see her?" Micah suddenly piped up.

"Who? Davi?" Mrs. Kinniston asked. Micah nodded.

If Mrs. Kinniston was put out by the request, she didn't let it show. She led the three of them to a back bedroom, where a little girl slept in her cot. She didn't have her mother's coloring, but there was something about her that was unmistakably Sybil Grant's. The child looked the picture of good health, her chestnut curls lustrous and abundant as they fanned out on the pillow.

"She's beautiful," Micah whispered.

Mrs. Kinniston smiled proudly. "She is that."

"May the good Lord bless her and keep her," Micah said.

This seemed out of character, but Daniel thought that perhaps Micah was feeling emotional about Liam's imminent departure. He was about to lose a nephew he loved soon after his sister's unexpected exit, so maybe he felt a particular kinship with Sybil Grant, who'd lost the people she loved and had seemed unable to make peace with the way her life had turned out.

"Thank ye, young man," Mrs. Kinniston said, obviously bemused by Micah's interest.

"Thank you for your assistance, Mrs. Kinniston," Daniel said.

"Will I be 'earing from ye again?" Mrs. Kinniston asked, her forehead creased with worry. "Will ye let me know ye got the murderer? It's only that I worry for our Davi."

"I don't think what happened had anything to do with your daughter, Mrs. Kinniston, but I will write to you once we know more. You have my word," Daniel promised before they left.

Chapter 20

Micah fell asleep moments after the train pulled out of the station, leaving Daniel and Jason to discuss the case.

"Do you think Stanley Kinniston might have had something to do with the murder?" Jason asked.

Daniel shook his head. "No. Stanley Kinniston sounds like a practical man who was only too happy to take both Miss Grant's and her brother's money and use it to improve his family's prospects."

"Mrs. Kinniston feared these visits," Jason said. "Perhaps she thought Sybil Grant might devise a way to reclaim her child."

"The only way she could have done that was if she married and her husband agreed to take on her illegitimate daughter, but as far as we know, Miss Grant had no plans to marry."

"But the Kinnistons didn't know that," Jason pointed out.

"Let us say, for argument's sake, that Stanley Kinniston, bricklayer from Southend-on-Sea, decided to do away with his daughter's natural mother. How on earth would he have gained access to Sybil Grant's bedroom and escaped after killing her without a single person in the household noticing anything out of the ordinary? And why would he need to resort to such a scheme? Had he wished to kill her, surely there are easier ways of accomplishing that. He knew precisely when Sybil Grant would visit next. He could have lured her somewhere, bashed her over the head with a brick, and then disposed of the murder weapon by making it part of a wall. And he could have hidden her body somewhere no one would ever find it. This theory simply doesn't fit the facts."

"No, I don't suppose it does, but he did have a motive, or at least his wife did," Jason replied.

"Realistically, there was little chance that Sybil Grant would ever reclaim her daughter. She might have told Davina the truth and tried to establish a relationship with her, but she could never be a true mother to her."

"Judge Grant was the only person that stood between Sybil Grant and her daughter. Had Judge Grant suddenly died, Sybil could have taken her daughter and gone away somewhere she could either claim to be a widow or introduce Davina as her niece."

Daniel nodded. "Yes, she could have done that, but as far as we know, Judge Grant is in fine health, so this wasn't an immediate concern. Likewise, if the Kinnistons felt truly threatened, they could have left Southend and settled in a place where Miss Grant couldn't easily track them down. I'm sure the allowance is paid through a solicitor, so they could have simply informed the solicitor of their new address and explained the reason for their departure."

"Might they have contacted the solicitor and told him of Sybil Grant's visits?" Jason asked.

"I doubt it. Judge Grant would have put an end to the visits if he became aware of them."

"Perhaps he had," Jason suggested. "Losing her daughter a second time might have pushed Sybil Grant over the edge. If Judge Grant informed his sister that she would not be seeing her daughter again, the edict might have caused her to reach for that letter opener."

Daniel shook his head. "If she hadn't done away with herself after the baby was first taken from her, why would she do so now? She found a way to see her child. I think her reaction to her brother's orders would be defiance and a desire to outwit him rather than a decision to slit her throat."

"You have a point there," Jason conceded.

"Jason, do you believe Sybil Grant committed suicide?" Daniel asked decisively, needing to rule out the possibility once and for all. "I know it's physically possible, but the idea just doesn't sit right with me. This was a woman who'd maintained a relationship with her nephew despite her brother's decision to cut him off, and also managed to track down her child and worm her way into Davina's life despite the obvious reservations of her foster mother. I think the reason for her peculiar schedule was that Judge Grant believed she was someplace else on those days and didn't question her absence. She was involved with several charitable organizations. He most likely assumed she was going to meetings."

"That's very possible," Jason said.

"Sybil Grant was clever and resourceful, not to mention determined to retain some form of control over her life. She doesn't strike me as someone who'd just give up."

Jason cocked his head to the side as he considered Daniel's reasoning. "It is possible that she killed herself, but like you, I don't believe she did. I think Sybil Grant was murdered by someone who either couldn't deal with her rejection or who had felt threatened by her."

"To my mind, this is a murder investigation," Daniel agreed. There was a half-formed thought in his mind, and he found himself articulating it without considering what it really meant. "Jason, Oliver Grant lost his wife when Marcus was a child and never remarried. That is a long time to go without female companionship."

"What makes you think he has?" Jason asked.

"What I mean is that Sybil Grant was the lady of the house since Mrs. Grant died, and enjoyed all the privileges that went with that position. Mrs. Gladstone-Smith mentioned that Oliver Grant wished to marry again and that his sister wasn't pleased by the prospect. If he did indeed marry, Sybil Grant would be relegated to the position of burdensome unmarried sister, so perhaps she'd tried to dissuade her brother from marrying. She certainly didn't want to see him married to her friend. She made that clear. Perhaps she said as much to the lady her brother is courting."

"And you think the woman got into the house unseen and stabbed Sybil Grant in the throat after crushing her larynx with her bare hands?" Jason asked incredulously.

"No," Daniel said, realizing just how ridiculous such a suggestion was, "but what if Sybil Grant's death had nothing to do with her own secrets?"

"Go on," Jason invited.

"There's something Superintendent Ransome said that got me thinking. Oliver Grant is known as a hanging judge. What if killing his sister was revenge for a verdict he'd passed on someone's loved one? Perhaps someone's sister?" Daniel suggested.

"Daniel, I would readily agree with you that such a thing is possible if it weren't for the fact that the murder took place inside Miss Grant's bedroom." Jason's expression was thoughtful. "Did you personally examine the door when you first arrived on the scene?"

"No, I had Constable Napier do it. I turned my attention directly to the victim."

"And did you go back and look at the door afterward?" Jason asked.

"Yes, of course, but there was nothing to see. The door had splintered when it was forced, and the hinges had come loose from the frame. The key had fallen out and was on the floor, just inside the room."

"I think we should take another look at the door," Jason said, "before it's been disposed of."

"What do you hope to find?"

"I'll know it when I see it," Jason said cryptically. "In the meantime, we must focus our investigation on the victim. The sort of frenzy the attacker displayed was of a very personal nature. I can't see the Kinnistons or some wronged relative breaking into the house and going at Sybil Grant with a blunt knife. No, this murder was carried out by someone who was so enraged that they'd lost all reason, at least until the deed was done, and then steely calm prevailed. The killer is intelligent, practical, and cunning. And just cocky enough to think they can get away with it."

"And would you say that description fits any member of staff?" Daniel asked.

"I can't answer that based on one brief conversation, but it is quite possible that a member of staff had let someone in and then helped them to escape."

"So where do we begin?" Daniel asked, the insecurity he tried so hard to keep at bay creeping into his mind and whispering in his ear. It was as if Jason were in charge of the investigation and Daniel was an observer, a sidekick rather than the lead investigator. He quickly dismissed such thoughts as unworthy. Jason was only trying to help, and it was his intellect and unique way of looking at things that made him such a valuable asset.

"Miss Grant was very precise in scheduling her assignations," Jason said.

"Yes, she was, because she didn't want her brother to know what she was getting up to."

"But what if she had other standing appointments we know nothing about?" Jason suggested.

"Like with a lover?" Daniel asked.

"It's not beyond the realm of possibility."

"But how would we find out about other clandestine meetings if she walked or took an omnibus to get to her destination?" Daniel mused. "She certainly wouldn't mark these assignations in her diary."

"We need to ask Miss Shaw. Perhaps she didn't say anything sooner because she didn't think it was relevant, but if we were to ask her outright, she just might reveal something."

"She might. But if we work under the assumption that one of the staff let someone into the house, then it could have been anyone, even Andy the boot boy. I'd like to speak to Oliver Grant again, but perhaps I should wait until I have more to share with him. If I present him with indisputable evidence of his sister's comings and goings, he'll be more willing to tell us what he knows."

"You're assuming he knows something damning?" Jason asked.

"He knew about the child, obviously. Who's to say he wasn't privy to his sister's other secrets? He wants justice for Sybil, but he also wants to avoid salacious gossip about the deceased and wishes to protect his own reputation."

Jason nodded. "I suppose it depends on which he cares about more, justice or protecting his family name."

"Would you be able to meet me at the house at ten tomorrow?" Daniel asked. He could conduct the interviews by himself, of course, or take Constable Napier along to nose around belowstairs, but he found that Jason's clear-eyed approach helped him cut through the dissembling and extract the grains of truth hidden within the suspects' statements.

Many a copper he'd known formed a theory and then manipulated the investigation to make the facts fit, partly because they were under tremendous pressure to produce a result and partly because they were too vain to imagine they might be wrong. Jason didn't have to answer to anyone save himself, and Superintendent Ransome held no power over his future. He had the ability to approach an investigation in a careful and unbiased way, his opinions not colored by his desperate need to hold on to his livelihood or his good opinion of himself. Jason refused to commit to a theory until the facts formed an indisputable pattern, and only then was he ready to make an accusation.

"I'll be there," Jason replied. "I don't have to be at the hospital until noon."

"Excellent," Daniel said, embarrassingly relieved.

Jason pulled out his watch and consulted the time. "Would you still like me to call in today to see Sarah?"

"Sarah seemed better last night," Daniel said. "Perhaps give it a day or two?"

"Of course," Jason said. "I'm at your disposal."

Chapter 21

"Oh, the poor woman," Katherine said once Jason finished his account of the day's events.

They were in the garden, enjoying a quiet hour before changing for dinner. Jason held Lily in his arms, the sleeping baby's face gilded by the golden light of the summer evening. She was only three months old, but Jason could not remember a life in which she hadn't existed and had no desire to.

"Which one do you mean?" he asked, looking at Katherine's anxious face.

"Well, both of them, I suppose. To have to renounce the child of your heart is heartbreaking. I couldn't bear it if I had to give Lily up. I would do anything to keep her, anything at all. But to fear losing the child you've given your heart to is just as dreadful. Can you imagine how Mrs. Kinniston must have felt every time Sybil Grant arrived on her doorstep?"

"Would that give her a motive for murder, do you think?" Jason asked.

"I can see how Mrs. Kinniston would feel angry and frightened by the uncertainty of what was to come, but it's difficult to imagine this woman traveling to London, finding a way into the Grant house, and killing the mother of her daughter in such a brutal way," Katherine said.

"There's the husband."

Katherine shook her head stubbornly. "Had Sybil Grant been attacked in the street, then maybe you could lay suspicion at the Kinnistons' door, but the fact that she was murdered in her own bedroom rules out an outsider, in my opinion. I think Miss Grant trusted her killer, which would explain why she didn't call for help when she found the person in her room and why no one saw anyone enter or leave the house. The killer is within, Jason."

"I agree," Jason said.

"What does Daniel think?"

"As of last night, he wasn't completely convinced that Sybil Grant hadn't killed herself. Sarah seemed to think she might have committed suicide in a moment of utter despair."

Katherine's eyes widened in surprise. "You think that a woman would do that to herself intentionally? I can see someone wishing to end their life, but not like that, not unless they're mad. Was there any suggestion that Sybil Grant displayed symptoms of madness or hysteria?"

"No. But everyone did say she seemed broken and had been for years."

Katherine's face softened with sympathy. "A person who's been broken for a period of time will not suddenly reach for a dull knife and try to slash their throat. At least, I don't think they would. If this were an ongoing situation, one they couldn't hope to alter, I think they would plan their suicide carefully, not act on the spur of the moment. I think that would only happen if something had drastically changed for the worse. But I don't believe Sybil Grant succumbed to sadness. Not for a moment."

"On what grounds?"

"Davina. As long as both Sybil and Davina were alive, there was always a chance of them being reunited. Sybil Grant might not have been able to raise her daughter, but she knew Davina was well cared for and loved, which is the next best thing. And once Davina came of age, she would be able to approach her and perhaps develop a relationship with her. There was hope, Jason, and as long as there's hope, there's life."

Jason smiled. "I couldn't have phrased it better myself. Which brings me to my original assumption that Sybil Grant was murdered by one of the male servants."

"Do you think she was carrying on with one of the men?"

"It's more feasible than a stranger coming into the house unnoticed and killing her without anyone hearing a thing."

"Do you have someone in mind?"

"No, but we can't arbitrarily rule any of them out as there's no accounting for taste. Perhaps Miss Grant was attracted to older men, so she might have found herself drawn to the butler. Or maybe she liked them young and fit. The two footmen and the valet are in their twenties."

"How different her life would have turned out had her Mr. Ellis come back," Katherine said, reaching out to touch Lily's round cheek. "They would have married and become a family. And now they're both dead, and their daughter will never know anything about them."

"One decision can change the lives of so many," Jason said as he stood. "I had better take Lily up to the nursery. I could look at her all night, but she'll be more comfortable in her bed."

"All right," Katherine replied. "I'll be up in a minute."

"Take your time, Katie. It's a beautiful evening."

Katherine nodded and smiled, but Jason was sure she still had the case on her mind.

Chapter 22

Having reported the latest developments to Superintendent Ransome, Daniel waited for the inevitable dressing down, but it never came, at least not in the vein he'd expected.

"Well, well, well," Ransome said, twirling the end of his waxed moustache absentmindedly. "So, Judge Grant let the fox into the henhouse and then shut the door once it was too late for the hen."

"How do you mean, sir?" Daniel asked.

Ransome looked at him as if he were a dolt. "He carried on as if no man was good enough for his sister, when all the while she had not only been despoiled but had given birth to an illegitimate child. I've no doubt David Ellis would have married her, but a decent woman would have saved herself for the marriage bed instead of allowing herself to be taken like a common whore."

There was a bitterness in Ransome's tone that instantly raised Daniel's suspicions. "Did you know Miss Grant personally, sir?"

Ransome had the decency to avert his gaze after denigrating Miss Grant so thoroughly and forced a cough, possibly to cover up his embarrassment at being so easily read. "Eh, yes. Our paths crossed some years back, but she had no time for a common policeman. She didn't seem to have similar reservations when it came to journalists."

"I hope you can remain objective about the case, sir," Daniel said, regretting the words as soon as they left his mouth. What was wrong with him? Why was he baiting the man who wielded so much power over his future?

Superintendent Ransome fixed Daniel with a narrowed gaze, his lips pursed in anger. "Do you imagine me incapable of being objective, Inspector?" he asked, his voice dangerously low.

"Not for a moment, sir," Daniel replied.

"Well, you happen to be correct. Miss Grant is the victim of a crime, and regardless of my own feelings toward her, which are nothing but professional at this stage, she will be treated with the respect she deserves. Now, I commend you on discovering her secret. No doubt it played a role in her death, directly or indirectly. This tells us much of her character and therefore confirms my belief that she was carrying on an affair. Find her lover, and you'll have your murderer. Dismissed," he barked, clearly still rankled by Daniel's insinuation.

"Goodnight, sir," Daniel said.

"Hmm," was all that Ransome could muster.

When Daniel finally arrived at home, he was tired, hungry, and frustrated. They'd discovered much today, but he was no closer to figuring out what happened to Sybil Grant. Ransome's assumption that she had been done away with by her lover was reasonable, but Daniel had yet to identify a possible candidate. No one he'd met thus far seemed even remotely likely to have been the man, and then there were Ransome's personal feelings to be considered. If he'd been rejected by Sybil Grant, he'd probably find a grim justice in her being murdered by a jilted lover. It would somehow soothe his ruffled feathers. Not for the first time, Daniel wondered if John Ransome was married, and what sort of woman his wife might be. He'd have to ask a few discreet questions at the Yard and see what the men knew of Ransome's domestic situation.

Sarah was in the drawing room, a book in her lap, but had her gaze fixed on the window, watching the street outside. She gave Daniel a wan smile when he kissed her cheek.

"How are you feeling today?" Daniel asked.

"I feel well."

"Good. Would you care for a drink before dinner?"

"No. But you go ahead."

Daniel poured himself a whisky and settled in his favorite chair, hoping they could talk about the case as they had done last night, but Sarah's gaze drifted back toward the window, as if he weren't even in the room. Her lack of interest felt like a rejection.

At first, Daniel had been overjoyed when Sarah had finally agreed to move to London to be near him, but although their relationship had improved somewhat since the move, he still felt as if a part of her was forever lost to him. He had assured her again and again that she hadn't been to blame for the tragedy at Ardith Hall the previous December, but Sarah couldn't forgive herself, nor could she find it in herself to be a true wife to Daniel. They shared a bed, but it was as if Sarah's mind went elsewhere whenever Daniel touched her. During the day, she cared for Charlotte and oversaw the running of the household, but toward the evening, she was often quiet, withdrawn, and painfully uninterested in anything that had to do with him. Most days, he hardly recognized the woman he'd married.

"I went to Southend-on-Sea today," Daniel said. "It's a lovely place. The water must be cold, but there were people bathing. Do you think you might enjoy a few days at the seaside?"

Sarah tore her gaze away from the window and turned to face him. "That would be nice, but Charlotte is too young to appreciate it, so perhaps we should wait until she's older. It's such an expense."

"Charlotte is too young, but we are not," Daniel protested.

"Felix would have loved to see the sea," Sarah said dreamily. "Remember that little boat he had that he sailed in the pond?"

"Yes, I remember."

Daniel didn't want to talk about Felix, but he could hardly say so. Felix had been gone for more than four years, but Sarah still brought him into the conversation daily. Daniel supposed it helped her to cope with her loss, but he found it wrenchingly painful and wished Sarah would finally accept that Felix was gone. His remains rested in the graveyard at St. Catherine's in Birch Hill. He would never see the sea or sail his boat or grow into a man. Felix was gone, but Charlotte was here, and she deserved better than a mother who floated through her day in a haze of grief.

"Sarah," Daniel began, but Sarah lifted her hand to silence him.

"Yes, I know, Danny, Felix is dead. You don't need to remind me. I remember all too well. Now, tell me about your day. Why did you go to the seaside?" she asked, startling him with the sudden turnabout.

"Jason thought Sybil Grant might have had a secret child."

"And had she?"

"Yes. The child was given to a family in Southend. She is loved," Daniel added, knowing that would be important to Sarah.

"A child should always be loved," Sarah said. "I'm glad you love Charlotte. So, do you now know who the killer is?"

"No, but we know Sybil Grant had secrets," Daniel replied.

"Everyone has secrets, Daniel."

"I would hope we have no secrets from each other," Daniel said, a sinking feeling settling in the pit of his stomach. He wanted Sarah to tell him that there were no more barriers between them and that in time they would reclaim the closeness they'd once shared, but Sarah smiled in that absentminded way that told Daniel louder than any words that their moment of frankness was at an end.

Daniel glanced at the carriage clock on the mantel. "It's seven. Shall we go in to dinner?"

"Of course," Sarah said.

She stood, and Daniel suddenly realized that she'd lost a considerable amount of weight since coming to London several months ago. He opened his mouth to suggest she see a doctor but promptly shut it. He'd hoped it might not be necessary, but Jason would need to look in on her after all.

Chapter 23

Thursday, June 11

Oliver Grant was out when Jason and Daniel arrived at the house. Despite his sister's death, he still kept to his usual schedule and had gone to his chambers after his morning walk, which had been followed by a hearty breakfast. Miss Shaw had gone out to run an errand, so Daniel decided to start with the two footmen: Steven and Michael Bakewell, who were cousins and the epitome of a matching pair. They were strapping young men with sandy hair, blue eyes, and enviable bone structure.

Steven came in first. Having already been interviewed once, he didn't appear too nervous. Since there was no clever trick to entrap either man into admitting to an affair with their mistress, the only way forward was to ask them straight out and watch for a reaction, since they likely weren't expecting the question, especially straight out of the gate.

"Mr. Bakewell, were you having sexual relations with Miss Grant?" Daniel asked, unblinking as he waited for a response.

Steven stared at Daniel, his mouth opening in astonishment. Once the question finally penetrated the fug of confusion, he blushed furiously at the suggestion, his eyes widening with the sort of shock one couldn't easily fabricate.

"No. I never... Do you think...? Good Lord!" he sputtered, staring at Daniel as if Daniel had just asked him if he drank the blood of infants for breakfast. "Why would you...? Oh, God, you think I killed her!" he exclaimed, all color draining from his face.

"Not anymore," Daniel said, witnessing the man's obvious distress. There was no way he was that good an actor. "Mr. Bakewell, did you ever see anyone entering Miss Grant's bedroom who didn't belong there?"

148

"No." Steven Bakewell was so upset, he could barely focus on the question. "I was never anywhere near Miss Grant's room at any time during the day or night. There was no reason for me to be there."

"Thank you," Daniel said. "Please ask Michael to join us."

Steven Bakewell practically sprinted from the room, sending in his cousin, who'd been waiting outside.

Michael Bakewell was the cockier of the two and took a seat before he'd been invited to. He looked from Daniel to Jason, obviously curious why he'd been summoned again.

"Mr. Bakewell, were you having sexual relations with Miss Grant?" Daniel demanded.

Unlike his cousin, Michael Bakewell burst out laughing at the suggestion. "Are you joking, Inspector? What would Miss Sybil want with the likes of me?"

"The same thing women generally want with a good-looking young man."

"If you happen to know any of those women, please send them my way, 'cause I sure as hell don't have the coin to pay for their services."

"Miss Grant was an attractive woman," Daniel tried again.

"Inspector, I might be just a lowly footman, but I value my life. If Judge Grant ever caught me with his sister, he'd have skinned me alive first and then seen me hang. And I assure you, it wouldn't be a quick death. A few minutes of pleasure are hardly worth that sort of risk."

"I take your point, Mr. Bakewell," Daniel said, and he did. "Did you ever see anyone entering Miss Grant's room who had no business being there?"

Michael shrugged. "*I* had no business there, so I wasn't anywhere near it."

Daniel nodded and turned to Jason to see if he had any questions, but Jason just shook his head. They were done with Michael Bakewell.

"What do you think?" Daniel asked once the door closed behind the footman.

"I think their reactions were too genuine to be scripted."

"As do I," Daniel said with a sigh of frustration. "Let's speak to Roy Nevins."

Their previous interview with Roy Nevins had yielded little. He had seen nothing, heard nothing, and knew nothing. Daniel hoped that when asked more specific questions, Mr. Nevins would let something slip, but given the interviews with the Bakewells, he wasn't feeling overly optimistic.

Roy Nevins looked worried when he entered the drawing room and accepted a seat across from Daniel and Jason. "I already told you, Inspector, I didn't see anything," he said.

"I remember, Mr. Nevins," Daniel said. "But I have several more questions to put to you, and I hope you will think carefully before answering."

"I will," Nevins replied.

"What time did Judge Grant retire on Sunday?"

"Ten. He always went to bed at ten when he wasn't entertaining."

"Did you attend on him?" Jason asked.

"I did."

"So, you would have been the last person upstairs besides the judge and Miss Grant," Daniel stated.

"Yes, I suppose I would be, but that doesn't mean I know anything," he said defensively.

"I'm only trying to work out a timeline of events," Daniel said, wondering why the valet seemed so unnerved. "Miss Grant was a handsome woman," he observed, watching Roy Nevins intently.

"Yes, I suppose she was," Nevins replied.

"Did you ever see her privately?"

Roy Nevins opened his mouth to reply, shut it, then stared at Daniel in disbelief. "Are you suggesting I was carrying on with Miss Sybil?"

"Were you?"

Nevins snorted with derision. "You are not very good at this, are you, Inspector?" he said nastily. "You're just groping in the dark."

"I may be better at this than you imagine. Your word is hardly enough to prove that nothing was going on between you two," Daniel replied, more to frighten the man than because he really believed Sybil Grant had been having an affair with Roy Nevins. To date, the only person she seemed to have feelings for was David Ellis. She'd made no secret of her love. It would be entirely out of character for her to sneak around with this weasel.

"No, I don't suppose it would be, but if you can find anyone to suggest that there was anything between us, I'd be interested to hear what they have to say."

"You had cause to be upstairs when Miss Grant retired for the night," Daniel said.

"Yes, I did. I had a legitimate reason, as Judge Grant will confirm. I wasn't loitering," he added.

"Still, you had access to Miss Grant's room," Daniel tried again.

"What of it? Just because you see a door doesn't mean you have to walk through it, does it?"

"But what if you had?" Jason asked conversationally.

Nevins shrugged in response. "I would have walked right back out again. Miss Sybil was a good woman. Respectable. She would never have debased herself with a member of staff."

"So, why was she killed, in your opinion?" Daniel asked.

"That's for you to figure out, Inspector. If I had your considerable skills," Nevins said without bothering to disguise the sarcasm in his tone, "I wouldn't be spending my time getting spots out of Judge Grant's shirts and folding his drawers."

"Mr. Nevins, does Mr. Grant keep a mistress?" Daniel asked, clearly taking the man by surprise.

"Not that I know of," Nevins replied, his lip curling with scorn. "You're determined to prove someone was having it off, aren't you?"

"Did he keep a mistress in the past?" Jason asked.

"He did have a lady friend until about two years ago. He saw her regularly."

"And then what happened?" Daniel asked.

"He doesn't confide in me."

"Do you know if the judge was courting someone with a view to getting married?" Jason asked.

"I believe he was fond of Mrs. Applegarth," Nevins said.

"Did he tell you that?"

"No, but I overheard him talking to Miss Sybil about the lady. He said she would make an excellent wife should he decide to marry again."

"And how did Miss Sybil respond?" Daniel asked.

The valet's gaze slid away from Daniel, fixing on the door. "Miss Sybil said he had no business marrying anyone," he said at last.

"Did she give a reason?"

"She said he was bankrupt in all the ways that mattered."

"Do you know if your master was having financial difficulties?" Daniel asked.

"I have no idea."

"Would you have an address for Mrs. Applegarth?"

"I can get it for you."

"Please do."

"Can I go now?"

"Yes. See if Miss Shaw is back. We'd like to speak to her," Daniel said to the valet's retreating back. "I wish I could arrest him, if only on a charge of insolence," Daniel muttered angrily.

"If you were to start arresting people for insolence, you'd have no time left to solve real crimes," Jason pointed out.

"No, probably not, but it would be awfully satisfying."

"He certainly seems confident of his place in the household," Jason remarked. "Henley would never dare speak to anyone like that, much less a police inspector."

"I suppose he's secure in the knowledge that we found no evidence to tie him to the crime."

"Yet," Jason replied just as Valerie Shaw knocked and entered the room.

153

Chapter 24

Miss Shaw didn't seem overly pleased to see them either. She looked tired and harassed and clearly would have preferred to be elsewhere.

"I told you everything I know, Inspector," she said as she took a seat.

"Are you all right, Miss Shaw?" Jason asked.

She shook her head. "I've been dismissed. I can't say I'm surprised, but I had hoped that Judge Grant might find a use for me."

"Did you receive a good reference?"

"I did, yes, but I don't relish having to look for work. If I don't find new employment in a fortnight, I'll have to find a place to live. My savings won't last long if I have to pay for lodgings."

"I wish you luck, then," Jason said.

"Your lady doesn't require a maid, does she?" Valerie Shaw asked, searching Jason's face.

"I'm sorry, but we're fully staffed."

Miss Shaw nodded. "I understand. Thank you for your concern, your lordship."

"If we might return to the subject at hand," Daniel said. He felt sorry for the woman but was in no doubt she'd find a suitable position. She looked capable and trustworthy.

"Of course, Inspector. I'm sorry to burden you with my troubles."

"Not at all," Daniel replied automatically. "I only have a few more questions to ask you, Miss Shaw. Did your mistress have any standing appointments?"

Miss Shaw looked taken aback by the question. "Standing appointments?"

"Yes. We now know that she met with her nephew on the second Monday of every month. And we also know that she went to Southend on the last Thursday of every month to visit a friend," Daniel said, not wishing to divulge that he knew of Davina's existence. There was no reason for the servants to know that about their deceased mistress.

Miss Shaw considered the question. "I knew about the meetings with her nephew. Miss Grant spoke of him and said he needed guidance and understanding more than he needed judgment and sanctions."

"Did you know she went to Southend?" Jason asked.

"I knew she went somewhere, but I didn't know it was to Southend. She left early in the morning and returned in the late afternoon. She said it was for her charity work."

"Did Judge Grant ever inquire after his sister on those days?" Daniel asked.

"He never asked me, so I simply assumed that she had told him whatever it was she wanted him to believe. It wasn't my place to tell tales, especially where the judge's son was concerned."

Miss Shaw was just about to say something else when Mrs. Taft exploded into the room. "I'm sorry to disturb, but we need a doctor downstairs," she cried.

Jason was instantly on his feet. "Who's hurt?" he asked as he hurried after Mrs. Taft.

Daniel dismissed Miss Shaw and headed downstairs. He found Jason in a small room near the butler's pantry. Andy lay on a cot, his eyes closed, his face white as a sheet. For a brief moment, Daniel thought the child was dead.

Jason sat on the side of the cot and laid his hand on the child's forehead, then pressed two fingers to his neck to take his pulse. Mrs. Taft hovered behind him, peering at Andy anxiously.

"Mrs. Taft, would you get Andy a cup of water, please?" Jason said. Mrs. Taft bustled out, leaving the three of them alone.

"What happened?" Daniel asked.

"It seems Andy let out a cry and fainted dead away. When he didn't come to right away, Mrs. Taft came to get me."

"Will he be all right?"

"I don't see anything obviously wrong with him," Jason said. He was looking at the child intently, his expression puzzled.

Andy's eyelids fluttered, and he slowly opened his eyes. He looked terrified until he recognized Jason and Daniel. Andy reached out and grabbed Jason's hand, his gaze anxious. "She went to the Angel," he muttered. "That's where she got 'em."

"Got who?" Jason asked, but Mrs. Taft had returned with a cup of water, effectively silencing the boy.

"Is he all right, my lord?" Mrs. Taft asked.

"Yes. I think something frightened him," Jason replied. "Andy, what did you see?"

Andy shook his head. "Nothin', m'lord. I seen nothin'."

Jason turned to Mrs. Taft. "What happened just before Andy lost consciousness?"

"Why, nothing, your lordship. Someone came to collect the trunk for the charitable organization Miss Grant patronized."

"Had Andy eaten today?"

"Andy, I saw you eating breakfast this morning," Mrs. Taft said reproachfully. "Are you telling tales?"

156

"No, ma'am," Andy murmured.

"I think Andy had better rest for a little while, then have something to eat," Jason said.

"Lazy sod," Mrs. Taft said affectionately. "Don't you worry. I'll feed you."

She wasn't about to leave, so Jason and Daniel left the boy to her care. Jason pulled out his watch and checked the time. "I must leave you, Daniel. I have a lecture in an hour."

"I'm going to interview Mrs. Applegarth. Jason, do you think you could come by later this evening?"

"To discuss the case?" Jason asked as they stepped outside into the gray, misty morning.

"To see Sarah. I'm worried about her."

"I thought you said she was feeling better. What's changed?" Jason asked, no longer a friend but a doctor ready to catalog his patient's symptoms.

"I thought she was, or maybe *hoped* is a more accurate word. I noticed last night that she's lost quite a bit of weight. She's just not herself. I fear she's ill."

"Will Sarah allow me to examine her?" Jason asked.

"I doubt it, but maybe you could just talk to her. Take her measure, so to speak."

"Of course. I can stop by around four. Will you be back by then?"

"Five would be better. I must report to Ransome before I can leave for the day."

"All right. Five it is. I'll see you then."

Chapter 25

Jason arrived at the Haze residence just before five and was shown into the drawing room. Sarah sat in the corner of the settee, her gaze fixed on Charlotte, who was playing at her feet. The little girl was stacking wooden blocks and pushing them over, laughing joyously when her tower collapsed. Charlotte was Jason's goddaughter, but he hadn't seen much of her, mostly because Sarah had not been very sociable of late. Jason and Katherine had seen Sarah only once since her arrival in London, and then it had been because they had invited the Hazes to dine. Sarah had been gracious and polite, but aloof, and had not invited them back.

Sarah looked up when Jason entered the room. She smiled, but the smile didn't quite reach her eyes. She looked distracted and seemed to need a moment to rouse herself from her reverie.

"Jason, what a pleasure to see you. I'm afraid Daniel is not back yet."

"I'll wait, if that's all right," Jason replied, his gaze on Charlotte. "She's beautiful, Sarah. I hear she started walking."

"She can get around by holding on to furniture, but she hasn't taken any unassisted steps yet. She does say a few words, though," Sarah said proudly.

As if realizing that they were talking about her, Charlotte looked up and said, "Kitty."

"She likes cats," Sarah explained. "Grace keeps a tabby in the kitchen to deal with the mice."

"Well done," Jason said to Charlotte, who smiled happily and returned to her blocks.

"And how have you been?" Jason asked.

Sarah's skin looked waxy, and she had lost weight. He would have noticed the change even if Daniel hadn't pointed it out.

Sarah had been slender before, but now she was bordering on gaunt.

"I'm well," Sarah replied cautiously.

"You've lost weight," Jason said, deciding to forgo any subterfuge.

"Did Daniel put you up to this?" Sarah asked, angry spots of color blooming in her cheeks.

"He's worried about you."

"Well, there's nothing to worry about. I'm absolutely fine," Sarah replied sharply.

"Are you eating?" Jason asked, ignoring the outburst.

"I'm not terribly hungry these days," Sarah admitted, her anger having burned out as quickly as it had flared.

"Are you sleeping?"

"Yes."

"Getting fresh air and exercise?"

"I try to," Sarah replied vaguely.

"Sarah, is there anything troubling you?" Jason asked softly, hoping she would see him not only as a doctor but as a friend.

"I am tired," Sarah said.

"Would you permit me to examine you?"

"Thank you, but I saw a physician not long ago. There's nothing wrong with me."

Jason would have liked to ask if Sarah's courses came regularly but thought she might take offense at such familiarity. He wasn't here in his professional capacity, after all.

"Is the fatigue physical?" Jason asked instead.

The question seemed to surprise Sarah. Clearly the physician had not asked her that during his examination.

"Yes, but it's also mental," Sarah replied. She sounded utterly defeated. "I know Daniel is right and I need to put certain events behind me, but as much as I would like to, I just can't seem to do that. My mind keeps returning to the most painful moments of my life. It's exhausting, Jason, having to relive it all again and again. And being back in London..." Her voice trailed off.

"Yes, I can imagine how it must have brought it all back. Do you think you'd feel better if you returned to Essex?"

Sarah shook her head. "It doesn't matter where I am."

She stood and bent down to pick up Charlotte, who didn't take kindly to her game being interrupted. She squirmed and whined, but Sarah ignored the child.

"It's time for Charlotte's dinner," Sarah said. "Do excuse us. I think I hear Daniel at the door."

Daniel walked in a few moments later and settled across from Jason, a look of wariness on his face. "What do you think?" he asked without preamble.

"How long has Sarah been suffering from a lack of appetite?" Jason asked.

"At a guess, the last few months."

So it may have been longer, Jason thought, since Daniel and Sarah had been living apart for months before she finally joined him in London. "Daniel, is Sarah taking anything?"

"Such as?"

"Such as a restorative tonic of some sort or a sleeping draught. I see plenty of cures advertised in the papers, but they're useless at best, dangerous at worst if taken for a prolonged period."

"No, she's not," Daniel replied.

"Are you sure?"

"Quite. The only thing Sarah takes is cod liver oil. Her mother swears by it and has been giving it to Sarah since she was a little girl."

"Well, that can't do any harm, at least," Jason said.

"Why do you ask if Sarah is taking a tonic?" Daniel asked, clearly concerned.

"Most tonics serve one of two purposes. They either sedate or invigorate, and they're often laced with either cocaine or opium to achieve the desired effect. Sarah seems torpid. There isn't a trace of her previous vitality."

Daniel winced. "Jason, do you think she's ill?"

Jason sighed heavily. He owed Daniel the truth but knew it wouldn't be appreciated. Not in this instance.

"I think Sarah might be anemic. She must eat meat several times a week and add more fruits and vegetables to her diet. But the problem is not only physical. Little is known about the workings of the mind. There are those who attribute a woman's moodiness to hysteria and believe it can be treated surgically, but we both know that Sarah's affliction stems from past events. I have a theory, but I'm reluctant to share it with you for fear of causing offense."

"Jason, please, speak your mind. I would rather hear it from you than from some quack who thinks the only way to help Sarah is to remove her womb."

"All right," Jason said, hoping he wasn't making a terrible mistake. "Daniel, I believe that some people are prone to melancholy. Whereas most people experience melancholy from time to time, they're able to overcome it on their own and find a way forward."

"But Sarah is unable to do that?" Daniel asked.

"Sarah's mind keeps returning to the day of Felix's accident; she's admitted as much. She is unable to let go of her grief and find joy in the life she has. No even Charlotte can break through the wall of self-recrimination Sarah has erected around herself. I think Sarah believed that revenging herself on the person who was responsible for Felix's death would set her free, but if anything, her guilt and grief have spiraled out of control since Roger Stillman's death. She now feels responsible for two deaths rather than one."

"So, what do I do?" Daniel asked, his desperation obvious.

"I don't know, Daniel. I'm out of my depth. I do, however, think that Sarah must want to move on, if not for herself, then for you and Charlotte. Until she makes a concentrated effort to put the past behind and forgive herself, she will remain forever trapped between life and death."

Daniel bowed his head to hide his tears, and Jason wished he'd kept his mouth shut. What did he know of the mind and its capacity for rebirth? What if he was wrong and Sarah was suffering from a physical ailment he couldn't diagnose simply by speaking to her? He wished he could walk back his uninformed opinion, but deep down he believed in what he'd said. It'd been four years since Felix's death. Tragic as it was, it was human nature to overcome. Sarah had a loving husband and a beautiful daughter. She could have more children if she wanted to, but she couldn't find the strength to let go. Or perhaps she simply had no wish to.

Would he be able to move on if they lost Lily? Jason couldn't begin to imagine the pain of losing his child, but deep down he knew that eventually he would find it in himself to get on with his life and try to find happiness. Katherine would too. She was strong and resilient, qualities he had admired in her from the very start. Life was hard, and often cruel. A person had to learn to protect themselves from its unexpected blows. Jason's mother had told him that. *Remain strong without losing your humanity*, she had said, and he'd carried that advice with him through the war. But now that he had a family of his own, he was more vulnerable than ever, so he couldn't take it upon himself to judge Sarah. All he could do was try to help.

Having collected himself, Daniel looked up, meeting Jason's gaze head on. "Thank you, Jason."

"I'm sorry…" Jason began, but Daniel held up his hand.

"You have nothing to apologize for. I asked for your opinion, and you gave it to me. I would be upset if you felt the need to lie to me or resort to euphemisms. You are right, Sarah was always prone to melancholy, even before Felix was born. Perhaps it was her fragility that attracted me to her. I wanted to protect her and offer her security and comfort. I dreamed of being her knight in shining armor, but instead I feel more like her jailer. She's not happy here, Jason."

"Was she happier in Essex?" Jason asked.

"No."

"What would make her happy, do you think?"

"I can't begin to imagine," Daniel replied.

"Well, I think you need to start small. Manageable steps."

"I don't understand."

"The first step is to alter Sarah's diet. Feeling stronger physically might help to improve her overall well-being. The second step is to find activities that will, if not make her happy, at least distract her from her sad thoughts for a while."

"Like what?" Daniel asked, looking a bit more hopeful.

"What did Sarah enjoy doing in the past?"

"She liked to walk in the park on fine days. And she enjoyed visits to the portrait gallery and the British Museum. Then we would go to a tearoom and have tea and cake," Daniel said, smiling wistfully at the memory.

"So why not try that? Plan an outing for just the two of you. Do something that will remind you how life used to be before tragedy struck. I don't know if it will work," Jason added. "I don't pretend to have experience in these matters. I can only offer what I think is a feasible solution."

"Thank you, Jason. I think that's very logical. I don't know why I hadn't thought of that myself. Sarah spends too much time in the house and has no one to talk to except Grace. She needs a diversion. I will suggest an outing as soon as we're finished with this case and I have a day to myself."

"I hope Sarah will like the idea," Jason said, glad that Daniel wasn't angry with him. "Shall we discuss the case, or would you rather I left you to spend time with your family?"

"The sooner we figure out what happened to Sybil Grant, the sooner I can focus on Sarah's well-being," Daniel said, clearly relieved to move on to a different subject. "I spoke to Mrs. Applegarth this afternoon. She didn't even know Sybil was dead. It seems Oliver Grant had not called on her in over a week."

"How did they meet?" Jason asked.

"She met Oliver Grant through her late husband, who was a barrister. She said Grant has been the perfect gentleman throughout their acquaintance and Sybil was very gracious. Mrs. Applegarth had hoped for an offer of marriage but understands that one won't be forthcoming until Oliver Grant has had time to grieve."

"He certainly didn't waste any time in having her things cleared out," Jason observed. "It seems almost indecently quick."

"Some people can't bear to have any reminders of those they loved," Daniel said, "while others are unable to let go."

Jason didn't need to ask about Felix's belongings. He was sure Sarah hadn't parted with a single item and his things were lovingly packed in some trunk, where they would reside for eternity.

"Were you able to make any sense of what Andy said?" Jason asked.

"I've been wondering about that as well. If we are to assume that he was referring to Sybil Grant, I can think of only two possible explanations. Either she went to visit a grave with an angel statue, or she had an assignation at the Angel, which is a crossroads in Islington."

"She might have visited David Ellis's grave," Jason replied.

"Yes, but in my experience, headstones with angels are more common to women and children. It is possible, of course. Or perhaps it was someone else's grave," Daniel speculated.

"Why would she go to a crossroads?" Jason asked.

"Perhaps she was meeting someone. There are several coaching inns in that area, since it was originally on the Great North Road. The road has been renamed, but the inns are still there. There's one called the Angel Inn, as it happens."

"How would Andy know that's where Sybil Grant had gone?"

"I don't know, but I think we need to get Andy on his own. He won't talk in front of Mrs. Taft or Mr. Hudson. You saw his face when the housekeeper walked in. The boy knows something, but he's scared to admit it."

"How do you wish to proceed?" Jason asked.

"Tomorrow morning, I will visit the offices of *The Times*, where David Ellis worked until leaving for America. At the very least, maybe I can discover where he's buried, if he's buried in England at all. I would also like to visit the Angel Inn. I took the liberty of helping myself to one of these."

Daniel reached into his pocket, took out a folded card, and passed it to Jason. Jason unfolded the card, which was a black-edged invitation to Sybil Grant's funeral, scheduled for Friday morning. Oliver Grant had spared no expense, and an oval picture of his sister graced the card, her lovely face caught at a moment of reflection, a faraway look in her eyes.

Jason nodded. "It certainly helps to have a photograph, since we know Miss Grant wasn't averse to using false names."

"That's exactly what I thought. I had expected her picture to appear in the paper, but the story is yet to break. I believe Judge Grant called in a favor with Commissioner Hawkins and had a gag order issued to keep the sordid details of the murder from coming out."

"I can see why he would prefer to keep it quiet," Jason said.

"The public has a right to know what happens in their city," Daniel replied.

"Surely reporting every gruesome murder that takes place only causes alarm, and perhaps strokes the ego of the person responsible."

"Not if they're caught." Daniel sighed as though the weight of the world were resting squarely on his shoulders. "What sort of day do you have tomorrow?"

"I have to be in theater at eight. I can be with you by eleven," Jason replied.

"Splendid. I'll meet you at the hospital. Give my regards to Katherine," Daniel said as Jason stood to leave.

Jason wanted to say something encouraging about the situation with Sarah, but words failed him, so he wished Daniel a good night instead.

Chapter 26

Friday, June 12

Daniel was relieved when morning finally came. He'd spent the night suspended between wakefulness and sleep, disturbing dreams and an even more worrying reality fighting for dominance in his mind. Sarah had locked him out of the bedroom last night, angry that he'd confided in Jason and fearful that he meant to take medical measures that would see her either surgically interfered with or confined to an asylum. Daniel had tried to explain, to make her understand that he only wished to help and had no intentions of taking any drastic measures, but his words had fallen on deaf ears. What had become clear to him last night was that Sarah didn't trust him anymore and didn't believe he was on her side.

Daniel had slept in the spare room, almost relieved to be on his own, Jason's words twisting and turning in his mind and forcing him to acknowledge the unbridgeable chasm that had opened up in his marriage. For a short while, he'd been full of hope for the future, but his hopes had been dashed, and he no longer believed he could reach Sarah in the way Jason had suggested. He feared she would not only rebuff his attempts but drag him down into the purgatory her life had become. What was he to do? How could he reach her? Doctors went so far as to pay graverobbers to bring them fresh corpses so they could study the human body and the effects of various illnesses. Why did no one study the mind or the lasting effects of loss and grief?

Daniel dragged himself out of bed, shaved, dressed, and went to check on Charlotte before leaving. Charlotte wasn't in her bed, and he felt a momentary wave of panic before realizing that she was probably downstairs with Grace. Daniel made his way to the kitchen and smiled guiltily when he saw Charlotte sitting in her highchair, a piece of buttered bread in her chubby hand.

"I hope it's all right that I took her down, sir," Grace said, noting Daniel's expression. "She woke early, and I thought I'd let Mrs. Haze sleep."

"It's perfectly all right, Grace. Thank you. That was very considerate of you."

Grace looked relieved and smiled at Daniel. "Can I get you some breakfast?"

Daniel was about to refuse, since his stomach was still in knots from his restless night, but he knew he should eat something before heading out. "Just some tea and toast, please. I'll have it right here with Charlotte," he said as he settled at the pine table.

"Of course, sir."

Grace cut a thick slice of bread and speared it with a toasting fork before putting the kettle she'd already boiled back on the hob. A few minutes later, Daniel was presented with strong tea, toast, butter, and marmalade. Despite his grim mood, he liked having breakfast with Charlotte, who held out her hand for bits of toast, enjoying the tart sweetness of the marmalade.

'She's got a sweet tooth, that one," Grace said affectionately.

"Yes, she does. We'll have to hide the jams and jellies from her once she gets older."

"Come on now, Miss Charlotte," Grace said. "We'd best wash your hands and face before you soil your smock." She lifted Charlotte out of the chair and took her over to the sink, where she wet a towel in a basin and cleaned the child.

"Have a good day, Inspector," Grace said once Daniel had finished his breakfast. "Wave bye-bye to your papa," Grace said to Charlotte, who obediently waved.

Feeling marginally more cheerful, Daniel set off, intending to visit the offices of *The Times*. He had no expectations of seeing

John Thadeus Delane, who was the general editor of the newspaper and only saw visitors by appointment, but Daniel hoped to speak to someone who might have known David Ellis on a personal level.

He was directed to the office of Clive Bannon, who'd been writing for the paper for the past twenty years, first as a freelance journalist and then as a full-time contributor. Clive Bannon was a short, wiry man with wavy dark hair that was parted on the side and fell into his face, obscuring his right eye and forcing him to keep sweeping the hair back in irritation. He wore round spectacles in a heavy tortoiseshell frame and sported a pencil moustache that looked like a third eyebrow above his thin upper lip. He reminded Daniel of a penny dreadful villain, depicted in a top hat and velvet-lined cape as he stalked his victims down gaslit alleyways swirling with nearly impenetrable fog.

"Inspector, how can I help?" Clive Bannon asked affably once Daniel was seated in the guest chair. Bannon was probably hoping for a story, and perhaps he'd get one if his information proved helpful.

"I'm investigating the murder of Miss Sybil Grant."

Clive Bannon's shock was obvious. "I know—knew—Sybil. I had no idea. There was nothing in the papers."

"No, there wasn't," Daniel agreed.

The man nodded in understanding. "There are still gatekeepers, even when there's free press," he said. "How was she killed?"

Daniel quickly filled him in on the details but left out all the supposition, in case Clive Bannon decided to print Daniel's words without his authority.

"How do you think I can help?" the reporter asked, flipping his hair back yet again.

"I was told you were quite close with David Ellis when he worked here," Daniel said, hoping the reporter would be eager to talk.

He was. "David was a cherished friend," Clive Bannon said, his mouth drooping. "I still mourn him."

"What sort of man was he?"

"Kind, loyal, and incredibly decent."

"Mr. Bannon, why did Mr. Ellis go to America?"

"He wished to report on the American Civil War," Clive Bannon replied. "Or at least that was the reason he gave at the time. I think there were other, more personal motivations."

"Did he ever share them with you?"

Clive Bannon glanced toward the open door of his office, then sprang to his feet, shut the door, and returned to his seat. "The walls have ears in this place," he said. "David confided in me, and I've never told this to anyone, but in view of what happened to Miss Grant, I think it might be relevant."

Daniel took out his notebook, ready to get down the facts, but Clive Bannon waved at the notebook dismissively.

"Put that away. What I'm going to tell you is off the record, and I will deny saying it should you quote me."

"All right. Off the record," Daniel said, putting the notebook back in his pocket.

"David asked Sybil to marry him about a month before he left, and she said yes. He was ecstatic. He said he'd never met a woman who understood him the way Sybil Grant did. Those two were truly soulmates, if you ask me." Clive Bannon lowered his voice conspiratorially, even though the door was firmly shut. "David was planning to ask Judge Grant for his blessing, even though Sybil would have married him whether her brother gave his permission or not, but it was just around that time that David stumbled onto something pertaining to the judge. David never told me what it was he'd discovered, but he said it would destroy the man's reputation and put an end to his career. He asked me for advice."

"What did you tell him?"

"I told him to forget whatever it was he'd learned if he hoped to marry the man's sister. He had to choose. He couldn't have both."

Clive Bannon absentmindedly twisted the signet ring on his finger, his gaze fixed on something beyond Daniel's shoulder as he recalled his meeting with David Ellis. "David never broke the story, but I believe he shared what he'd learned with Sybil. He wasn't the sort of man to enter into a marriage without being completely honest with his intended. Whatever he told Sybil proved to be the end of them. She ended the relationship, and he left for New York. He died three short months later."

"What could he have discovered that would have such dire consequences for his personal life?" Daniel asked.

Clive Bannon shrugged. "I can only assume he found proof that Judge Grant was corrupt. To be fair, I've never heard a bad word said about Oliver Grant. He has a reputation for being harsh in his pronouncements, but no one has ever accused him of being unfair or biased. When someone finds themselves in his courtroom, they are treated the same, be they a vagrant or a nobleman. I also happen to know that he's been offered bribes but has never accepted a single one, as far as anyone knows."

"Where is Mr. Ellis buried?" Daniel asked.

"Since David had no family to speak of, it made no sense to ship his remains home. He is buried somewhere in Virginia, I believe."

"Mr. Bannon, do you have any theories as to why Miss Grant might have been murdered?"

Clive Bannon looked thoughtful. "I honestly don't know, Inspector. She was an admirable woman. I can't imagine anyone hating her enough to kill her in such a savage way."

"Thank you," Daniel said, and pushed to his feet.

"David would want me to help you find whoever did this. I hope what I shared with you might shed some light on the motive for this murder."

"If only it would, Mr. Bannon," Daniel said, and took his leave.

Once outside, Daniel found a public house, where he ordered a pot of tea. He had an hour until he was due to meet Jason, and he needed time to think. Marcus Grant had said that the motive for the murder lay in the past. Well, now he knew that David Ellis might have unearthed something the Grants wished to keep quiet. Whether Sybil Grant had confronted her brother with David Ellis's findings or not, if the allegation of corruption was true, then Oliver Grant would certainly have something to hide. And his sister had been steadfast enough to sacrifice the love of her life to protect her brother.

Or had she? What if Oliver Grant had given her an ultimatum or had threatened her in some way? Perhaps she'd had no choice. Had she known she was with child at the time, or had she found out after David Ellis left? Had she hoped for a reconciliation? It was certainly convenient that David Ellis died, leaving Oliver Grant free to get on with his life, the threat having been eliminated. Had Judge Grant known of the allegations against him? Were they even true? A man of Oliver Grant's standing was sure to have enemies. Were those enemies known to him, and would they resort to killing his sister to silence him?

Daniel drank the last of the tea before paying the bill and heading to the hospital. He looked forward to sharing his findings with Jason.

Chapter 27

Daniel looked around as the hansom approached the Angel crossing. He hadn't been this way in years and noted all the changes that had taken place. The New Road had been renamed the Pentonville Road, and new buildings with shops on the ground floor had sprung up like mushrooms to accommodate increased traffic and residential development. The owners of the Angel Inn had sold off some of the land, but the inn was still in business, although not the thriving concern it had been when it had stood at one of the entry points to London on the Great North Road and had been surrounded by nothing but fields. The Angel had been around since the sixteenth century, but the current building was not the original structure and was built of brick rather than the post and wattle of the original Tudor inn.

"Why would Sybil Grant come here?" Jason asked as they alighted from the hansom and stood before the entrance.

"This is still a coach stop and a post house," Daniel replied.

"But why would she need either?"

"Perhaps she was meeting someone," Daniel said, although he couldn't imagine whom Sybil Grant might wish to meet here of all places and wondered if Andy had meant something entirely different or hadn't been referring to Sybil Grant at all.

They entered the inn and approached the barkeep who stood behind the polished counter, wiping pewter mugs in preparation for the midday crowd. The man was bald as an egg, but the wooly mutton chop whiskers that were connected by a rather luxurious moustache more than made up for the lack of hair on his head. He appeared to be in his mid to late forties and was stocky and broad of shoulder, a man who could acquit himself in a fight. He reminded Daniel of Davy Brody of the Red Stag in Birch Hill, and he wondered if the man was involved in any criminal activity.

"'Ow can I 'elp ye, gents?" he asked, smiling in a friendly manner and revealing crooked, tobacco-stained teeth. "Drink?"

Daniel was about to decline, but Jason smiled back. "Please. A pint of your finest ale. And one for my friend."

The barkeep set their pints on the counter and went back to wiping.

Jason took a sip and nodded appreciatively. "We don't have ale like this where I come from."

"No? And where might that be?" the barkeep asked. "Ye do 'ave a funny way of talking."

"Born and bred in New York," Jason replied proudly.

"So, what'ya doing 'ere, then?" the man asked. "Fancied a bit of a change?"

"Yes," Jason said. "I like it here."

"Never been anywhere else meself," the man said. "I were born upstairs."

"Are you the owner, then?" Daniel asked, glad Jason had warmed him up a bit. He didn't bother to introduce himself or show his warrant card. This man would probably respond better to a casual chat.

"I am that, as was me father afore me. Alf Perkins at yer service," he said, giving a mock bow. "I don't need to be 'ere, mind, but I like to keep an eye on things, know the patrons personal-like."

A plump woman with frothy fair curls stepped out from what must be the kitchen, the opening of the door releasing appetizing smells into the taproom.

"Me wife," the publican said proudly. "Cooks all the food 'erself. She's a fine cook, Jinny is. The finest in all of London."

"Oh, go on with ye," Jinny said, but she looked pleased all the same.

"There's someone we're looking for," Daniel said as he took another sip of the ale he really didn't want. "Name of Miss Grant."

The barman shook his head. "Sorry, never 'eard of 'er. So many people passing through."

"She might not have given her real name."

"What's she look like, then?" Jinny asked, her curiosity piqued. "Can ye describe 'er?"

"I can do better. I can show you a photograph." Daniel had folded the funeral announcement, leaving only the photograph of Sybil Grant and not the print, but the black border on the top and sides was still clearly visible.

"She dead, then, this Miss Grant?" Jinny asked.

"Yes."

"The poor lamb," Jinny said as she peered at the photo. Despite being reproduced for the funeral cards, the image was remarkably clear. "I seen 'er. Called 'erself Mrs. Pallister. Bit unlucky, she were."

"In what way?" Jason asked.

"Well, couldn't keep a maid, could she?"

"How do you mean?" Daniel asked, wondering what keeping a maid had to do with anything. Valerie Shaw had been with Sybil Grant for two years, and most of the staff at the Half Moon Street house had been with the family for ages.

"Lots of young girls come this way," Jinny explained patiently. "Come in on the London-bound coaches 'oping to go into service."

"And Miss Grant came here in search of maids?"

Jinny nodded. "She ain't the only one. Good place to pick one up on the cheap. They 'ave their plans and their fancy notions, but once they arrive, they all look the same—like frightened sheep. Never seen nothin' bigger than their village, I reckon. They 'ave the desire to work but don't know 'ow to go 'bout getting a place."

"Do many come here to find cheap help?" Daniel asked.

"Some do. Those as don't care for a character. Don't really need one for a skivvy, do ye. Don't take great skill to scrub pots or peel potatoes. 'Tis the lady's maids as need a good character, or even parlormaids, on account of working upstairs and being seen."

"And how many times have you seen Miss Grant here?"

"Oh, a few. Come every few months, she did. Always in a 'ansom. I reckon it cost 'er a pretty penny to keep paying the cabbies."

"And did she always leave with a girl?" Jason asked, his expression grim.

"Oh, aye. Always took the pretty young ones. I told Alf 'ere, what d'ye care if a skivvy's fair? Get a homely one, and she'll not give 'erself airs. Better yet, find a woman of middle years if ye want 'er to stay put," Jinny said. "Young girls want better for theirselves, but the older ones just want a steady wage."

"And then she came back again? For more?" Daniel clarified.

"Ain't that what I just said?" Jinny replied, looking at him as if he were daft.

"You did," Daniel agreed. "Do you recall the first time you'd seen her?"

"When would that a' been, Alf?" Jinny asked her husband.

"Don't rightly know," Alf said, scratching his bald head. "Three years, mebbe."

"Three years or thereabouts," Jinny said. "I even told 'er, 'Ye sure go through them fast,' and she said, 'Good 'elp ain't easy to find, Mrs. Perkins.'"

"Did she ever take any boys?" Jason asked.

Jinny looked to her husband. "Did she, Alf?"

He shrugged. "Once, mebbe. Took a little lad. 'E come down with 'is sister."

"Thank you both," Daniel said, and set down his tankard.

"Why'd ye want to know?" Alf demanded. "She is dead, ain't she, so what do it matter?"

"She was murdered," Daniel said.

"Ye private inquiry agents?"

"I'm a detective with Scotland Yard," Daniel replied, finally producing his warrant card.

Alf looked wary. "And ye think we 'ad something to do with it, *Inspector*?" He enunciated the word as if it were a slur.

"No, you're all right," Daniel reassured him. "Thank you for the information, though."

Jason deposited several coins on the bar, and they left the premises, walking along in silence until they found a hansom.

"Where to?" the cabbie asked.

"Twenty-three Half Moon Street," Daniel replied.

Chapter 28

"Are you thinking what I'm thinking?" Jason asked once the hansom pulled away from the curb.

"If you're thinking that Miss Grant was procuring young girls, then yes," Daniel replied, his voice thick with disbelief. "From interviewing the staff, we know that only Miss Shaw and Andy were hired less than three years ago. All the other servants have been with the Grants for years, even the scullery maid. And she came to the Angel in a hansom and gave a false name to preserve her anonymity. Judge Grant's carriage and driver might be remembered, but no one pays attention to cabbies."

"What do you think her intention was?" Jason asked.

"I can think of only one reason anyone would target young, innocent country girls."

"I'm with you there, but why would Sybil Grant participate in such a scheme?" Jason asked again. "She was a gentlewoman who devoted her time to charitable works and had a daughter of her own, albeit one that didn't reside with her."

"I think someone was leaning on her. Perhaps blackmailing her with the knowledge of her illegitimate child or even threatening to cause Davina harm."

"Who would know, apart from the Marches, the midwife, and the Kinnistons?" Jason asked. "Do you think they might be involved somehow?"

"I honestly think it was someone closer to home. Someone right here in London. Consider the chain of events," Daniel said. He needed to arrange his thoughts and lay them out for Jason to see if there were any flaws in his argument. "David Ellis discovers something that could destroy Judge Grant's reputation. He doesn't submit the story to his paper, but he does tell Sybil, unable to keep the truth from the woman he loves. Instead of Sybil's undying gratitude, he gets the boot and leaves for America, needing to put

178

as much distance between himself and the Grants as the ocean will allow. David Ellis is killed shortly after his arrival, while back in London, Sybil Grant discovers she's with child.

"Turning to her brother for support, she allows him to take charge. He whisks her to their seaside cottage and stays there with her until the child is born and placed safely out of Sybil's reach. At which point they return to London. Only Sybil somehow discovers the whereabouts of her daughter and starts paying unwelcome calls on the family, compensating them for their silence."

Jason nodded. "Everyone said something changed for Sybil Grant about three years ago. We assumed it was the child's birth, but perhaps there was something else as well."

"Exactly," Daniel exclaimed. "Just around that time, she starts coming to the Angel Inn to meet the coaches and offers employment to newly arrived girls, taking them away with her in anonymous cabs. We know she didn't take them back to Half Moon Street, so where did she deliver them, and how much does Andy know?"

"But did Oliver Grant know what his sister was doing?" Jason asked.

"We know she was good at keeping secrets, so perhaps he had no inkling what she was up to."

"Or perhaps he was being blackmailed as well," Jason speculated. "In which case, he might know what happened to his sister and is keeping quiet to protect himself. That might also explain why he's been so eager to keep the story out of the papers. He wants it to die down as quickly as possible for fear of being implicated."

"If that is the case, then it's entirely possible that it was Oliver Grant who let the killer in. Perhaps it was never the intention to murder Miss Grant, but something happened that night, something that changed everything."

"How do you intend to proceed?" Jason asked.

"I am going to confront Oliver Grant," Daniel said.

"Daniel, wait," Jason said as the hansom neared Half Moon Street. "All you have at this juncture is speculation and circumstantial evidence. Oliver Grant is a judge. He'll tear your argument apart in moments, especially if he already knows who killed his sister and is protecting the killer to safeguard his own future. What you need is an iron-clad version of events to present to him, one he can't poke holes in. Only then will he break."

"How do you suggest we go about getting this iron-clad version?" Daniel asked, feeling deflated. He'd been raring to confront the man with the evidence he'd gathered, but Jason was absolutely correct. Oliver Grant would not go down without a fight.

"I suggest we question Andy. He clearly knows something, but we need to get him alone. He will never talk in front of the other servants. He's too scared, and probably with good reason. If he's the boy Miss Grant took from the inn, then he must know what became of his sister."

"For lack of a hall boy, Andy performs other menial tasks within the household," Daniel said. "He takes out the upper servants' chamber pots to the privy behind the house. If we wait long enough, he's bound to make an appearance."

Jason nodded. "Never thought I'd be lurking behind privies when I came to England, but if the situation calls for it, I'm your man," he said with a smile. "However, Andy's absence will be noticed when he doesn't return."

"Which is why I will call at the house the moment you have him. That should serve as a distraction for Mrs. Taft and Mr. Hudson, and I would like to examine the door. You believe I missed something?" Daniel asked. "Tell me what I should be looking for."

Jason shared his theory with Daniel, who nodded. "All right. Where will you be?"

"I'll ask the cabbie to wait around the corner. Once I speak to Andy, I'll return to the hansom."

"That sounds like a good plan. I'll meet you at the corner once I see that Andy has returned."

"I'll be waiting," Jason replied.

Chapter 29

It wasn't long before Andy emerged from the house, carefully carrying a full chamber pot toward the privy. Jason waited until Andy emptied it and came back out, then came around the side of the brick outhouse, which blocked him from view should one of the other servants look out the window and see him with Andy.

"Andy, do you remember me?" Jason asked. Andy nodded.

"May I speak to you for a few minutes? It's important. And it might help us catch Miss Grant's killer."

Andy looked fearfully toward the house, clearly torn between taking flight and telling Jason what he knew, but the need to unburden himself won out.

"Andy, how did you know Miss Grant went to the Angel?" Jason asked.

"Because that's where we met 'er," Andy replied.

"Who's we?"

"Me and Alice."

"Is Alice your sister?" Andy nodded.

"I need you to tell me what happened when you met Miss Grant at the Angel Inn," Jason said.

Andy stared back at him, his clear blue gaze unflinching. "And what will 'appen to me once ye 'ave what ye need, yer lordship?" he demanded. "Ye think I'll be permitted to keep my position? I've nowhere to go if I get sacked."

"Andy, you have my protection," Jason said.

"Oh, yeah? And what does that mean, m'lord?"

"It means I will see you safe."

"Do I 'ave yer word?" Andy asked, still fearful.

"You have my word of honor that I will see you safe and cared for," Jason replied, his heart going out to the poor child. He couldn't begin to imagine what it must be like to find yourself alone on the streets, with no one to care for you or offer you sustenance or shelter.

Andy's gaze clouded, his words tripping over each other as he told Jason his story. Jason hoped no one would come out to use the privy and overhear their conversation, but he had a good view of the back door and would warn Andy if he saw anyone coming. Jason's heart contracted with pity and anger as he listened to the boy, and he wished he could take Andy away right then but doing so would jeopardize the investigation.

Meanwhile, Daniel had presented himself at the front door, which was opened by the butler.

"How can we help you today, Inspector?" Hudson asked, his tone bordering on jeering.

The public held the misguided view that the police should be able to solve a murder case in days, if not in mere hours. The fact that Daniel kept coming back but hadn't made an arrest made him a laughingstock in the servants' hall, no doubt, but Daniel wasn't bothered. Each case was unique, and those that were a conundrum, like this one, took time to untangle. Sometimes all it took was one loose thread, and then the whole thing would unravel, one clue leading to the next until the culprit had nowhere to hide and no one to offer him or her shelter.

"I wish to see the door to Miss Sybil's room," Daniel said.

"It's in the cellar," Hudson said. "Stephen can show you."

"Actually, I'd like both you and Mrs. Taft to accompany me."

The butler looked taken aback by the request but didn't argue. "If you wish," he replied, and led Daniel through the baize door and down the corridor toward the housekeeper's office, where she was drawing up some sort of list.

"Inspector Haze wishes to see the door from Miss Sybil's room and would like both of us to accompany him," Hudson announced, his tone even more mocking than before.

"As you wish, Inspector," Mrs. Taft said. Her tone wasn't as obviously derisive, but she was clearly annoyed by the request.

Mrs. Taft lit an oil lamp, and they made their way to the cellar, where the household liquor was kept under lock and key and there were stores of coal, root vegetables, and other foodstuffs that needed to be kept cold. The door was propped up against the back wall, and Daniel was exceedingly grateful that it hadn't been thrown away or used for firewood. Had he been the culprit, he would have seen the door disposed of.

"What do you hope to find, Inspector Haze?" Hudson asked as he stood at Daniel's shoulder, staring at the door as if he expected something to happen.

"Evidence," Daniel replied obliquely.

"Well, you have here a broken door that's been torn off its hinges. If that's the evidence you were hoping for, then you're in luck," Hudson said acidly.

"Mr. Hudson, would you kindly hold the door away from the wall, just so," Daniel said, making sure there was at least a foot of space between the wall and the door. He then carefully examined the floor. It was clean, with not so much as a layer of dust or a cobweb. "Mrs. Taft, may I have the lantern?"

The housekeeper handed him the lantern, and Daniel held it up to the keyhole, allowing himself a grim smile of satisfaction when the light failed to shine onto the wall behind the door. He removed his spectacles and inserted the metal arm into the hole, which stared back at him darkly. Almost immediately, he encountered resistance. Daniel pushed harder, mindful of breaking his glasses, then replaced his spectacles on his nose and checked behind the door. Even before he saw what lay on the floor, he could see the surprise on Hudson's face.

"How did you know it'd be there?" Hudson asked.

Daniel didn't bother to reply. He lifted the tight little ball that had fallen out and unfurled it carefully. It was a strip of paper, the edge bloodstained and the bottom showing tiny print, which upon closer inspection proved to be the name of a publishing house.

"Thank you both," Daniel said, hoping that Jason had got what they needed from Andy and it was safe for the butler and housekeeper to return upstairs.

On their way to the servants' hall, they encountered Andy sitting on a bench, a pair of boots before him as he applied polish to a thick brush. Andy didn't meet Daniel's gaze, but Daniel could tell the child was relieved not to have been caught loitering outside by the upper servants, who were both silent as they followed Daniel down the corridor.

"I'll see myself out," Daniel said, leaving the servants to gape after him.

Chapter 30

"Did you find it?" Jason asked as soon as Daniel climbed into the hansom.

"I did. I could almost kick myself," Daniel said ruefully. "It really should have been obvious. And you? Were you able to get Andy to talk?"

Jason nodded sadly. "Let's go somewhere where we can speak privately."

They retreated to a coffeeshop a few streets from Scotland Yard, where they ordered a pot of coffee and a plate of ham sandwiches.

"Let's have it, then," Daniel said.

"Andy came to London with his sister Alice after their father died at Christmas. He was a tenant farmer, so the children were left with nothing once he was gone, and they were told to clear off by the New Year. They sold what they could and decided to try their luck in London. Alice believed she could find a situation for them both."

"Didn't they have any family that could take them in?" Daniel asked, not that it mattered at this stage. They weren't the first or the last children to find themselves on the street after their parents died.

"No, and Alice refused to go into a workhouse. When Alice and Andy arrived in London, the coach stopped at the Angel Inn, where they were told by the driver that those who weren't too picky about character references sometimes came to find domestic help. Alice was approached by a well-dressed woman who said she was in need of servants and would take them both on. The children couldn't believe their good fortune and instantly agreed. They left with Sybil Grant, who took them to a well-appointed house and passed them over to what she referred to as the housekeeper. The woman was kind and welcoming. She fed them and led them to their quarters. It was only when she locked them in that Alice began to worry."

Daniel shook his head, all too aware of what was coming. "Sybil Grant took them to a brothel?"

"The Orchid, near Covent Garden. Miss Cherry, as the madam is known, kept the children under lock and key until they were ready to listen to what she had to say."

"And what might that be?" Daniel asked, disgusted.

"She said that she'd let them go free if they weren't amenable to her offer, but first, they had to pay back the house for the food, lodging, and clothes that had been provided for them. Of course, she named an astronomical sum that the children couldn't hope to repay, so Alice had no choice but to agree to Miss Cherry's terms."

"And what was Andy's role to be?" Daniel asked, his stomach clenching with apprehension. Andy couldn't be more than eight, but Daniel knew there were those depraved enough to use a young boy to gratify their sexual needs.

"They never got to find out because Sybil Grant returned to the brothel a few days later and demanded to see Andy. She told him there was nothing she could do for Alice, but she could offer him honest employment. Alice was terrified to let Andy go, but Sybil gave the girl her word—whatever that was worth to Alice after she'd been so cruelly deceived—that he would be safe. That's how Andy came to be part of the Grant household."

"Why did she do that?" Daniel asked. "It doesn't make sense."

"I think she may have felt guilty," Jason said. "Andy said most of the girls at the brothel were in their upper teens, and he hadn't seen any other boys. Or perhaps Miss Cherry had decided to chuck Andy out, realizing she had no use for him, and Sybil Grant felt sorry for him."

"I suppose Andy should be grateful to her, but given the role she had played in his life, I'm not sure gratitude is warranted," Daniel said. "How did he know she went back to the Angel?"

"Andy said Miss Grant often asked him to run to the corner and find her a hansom. Once she came out, she told the driver to take her to the Angel Inn within Andy's hearing. She also told him that if he kept quiet, she'd take him to see Alice."

"And did she?"

"Once. He said Alice was like a different person, but she was glad Andy was safe. She told him to bide his time and save his wages."

"Do you think she meant to escape?" Daniel asked.

"Possibly. Or maybe she wanted to make sure Andy would have something to fall back on if Miss Grant's guilt ran out."

"I can't imagine he's paid much, the poor lad," Daniel said. "He wouldn't last long on his own."

"No, I don't suppose he would." Jason poured himself a second cup of coffee but made no move to take another sandwich.

"You were right about the door," Daniel said. "The strip of paper torn from the book was inside the keyhole. The killer must have rolled it into a ball and forced it inside after he'd locked the door from the outside, then slipped the key beneath the door. Unlike some of the older keys, this key if fairly sleek and flat, so it wouldn't have been too difficult to push it through the gap between the door and the floor, even though it's too narrow to be obvious," Daniel said, then continued with the explanation.

"When Miss Shaw peered into the keyhole, she saw that it was blocked and thought it was the key. Once the door was broken down, the key was found inside, next to the door, which led everyone to assume that it had fallen out of the keyhole when the door was forced. Once the killer realized the book might be used as evidence, he removed it. Too bad he forgot to extract the paper from the keyhole."

"So, we now know that the killer let himself out, locked the door from the outside, and made his escape. Despite the frenetic nature of the attack, he was calm enough to think things through afterward. He made sure not to leave a trail of bloodstains and was able to fool us into thinking that the murder had been committed inside a locked room. He also returned the next day to remove the book, which once again points toward someone within the household.

"Given that Oliver Grant was the only person in the vicinity at the time of the killing, I think the evidence leads directly to him. All he would have had to do was return to his room, clean up, and go to bed. He went out for a walk early the following morning, before anyone suspected anything had happened. He could have very easily disposed of the bloodied garments somewhere along his route, and he could have spilled the water out his bedroom window to keep anyone from suspecting anything," Jason said.

"The theory certainly fits the facts, but I find it hard to believe that he'd kill his sister so brutally," Daniel replied. "Unless he felt he had no choice. Perhaps Sybil threatened him, or he'd discovered what she'd been doing and lost control. If anyone got wind of her connection to the Orchid, Oliver Grant would be implicated as well. His tenure as judge would be over."

"The threat of exposure would certainly be a motive, and he had the opportunity and the means. He may have grabbed her by the throat initially, but in his rage looked around for a weapon, perhaps needing to be sure she was truly dead," Jason mused. "Having killed her, he came to his senses and went about covering his tracks."

"But why was Sybil Grant procuring girls for the Orchid?" Daniel asked. "How did that arrangement come about? Did Andy happen to mention anyone else he might have seen there?"

"He said he only saw the other girls and Miss Cherry. She seemed to be in charge. Oh, and he saw the ruffian who manned the door. He was the one who came to collect Sybil Grant's trunk from the house."

"Was that why Andy fainted?"

Jason nodded. "Perhaps he thought he'd come for him."

"If Sybil Grant's things were going directly to the Orchid, then Oliver Grant had to have been the one to arrange it," Daniel said.

"The Grants are obviously connected to the place. It's up to us to discover in what capacity."

"And how do we do that?" Daniel asked sourly. "I highly doubt Miss Cherry will simply admit to any wrongdoing. Like all brothel owners, she'll say the girls are there of their own free will and can leave at any time. Most girls will back her up out of fear of being punished or thrown out. And I doubt she'll implicate Grant. If anything, his involvement will give her something to blackmail him with, if she's not blackmailing him already."

"Perhaps if we could speak to Alice," Jason suggested.

"What would she know of the secrets the owners are trying to hide?"

"Probably not much, but having been at the brothel since January, she would have seen and heard a lot," Jason replied. "It would help if we had a photograph of Oliver Grant."

"I can obtain a photograph easily enough," Daniel said. "His likeness appeared in the *Illustrated London News* a few months back when he presided over a sensational trial. There must be a copy of the paper at the newspaper's offices. The more difficult task is to get to Alice. I doubt she's allowed out on her own."

"Then we must get in," Jason said.

Daniel studied Jason's determined expression. "Somehow I don't think you mean we should simply present ourselves at the door."

"There's only one way to get inside. As a client."

"Are you volunteering?" Daniel asked. "No one would ever mistake me for a client. I don't look the part, but you're one posh cove."

"A lonely American visiting London and looking for a bit of female company," Jason added.

"And how might the wife of this lonely American feel when she finds out her husband is planning a visit to a brothel that very likely specializes in young girls?"

"I have no secrets from Katherine," Jason said, his expression darkening. "She won't be pleased, but she'll understand."

"I don't think Sarah would understand," Daniel replied.

"Good thing it won't be you going, then," Jason said, smiling for the first time that afternoon.

Chapter 31

Katherine sat on the bed, watching Jason tie his cravat. Her lips were pursed, and her arms crossed, her hair tumbling about her hunched shoulders. Her bare legs crossed at the ankles, she resembled an intricate knot in her posture of fuming outrage.

"I still can't believe it," she exclaimed. "How could any woman do such a thing? To deceive those poor, innocent girls into thinking she was offering them respectable employment. Why, that's downright Machiavellian, Jason. And that poor boy. What is he to think, knowing his sister had been tricked into sexual slavery? Why, if Sybil Grant wasn't already dead, I think I might like a go at her."

"Katie, let's not jump to conclusions," Jason said, knowing full well that Katherine was nowhere near finished.

"I don't, as a rule, but in this case, I'll make an exception. I don't care about her reasons. If she was being blackmailed, then she should have dealt with the consequences head on rather than sacrifice countless children to protect her own reputation. Perhaps Sarah was right, and she committed suicide because she could no longer live with herself after what she had done."

"We've ruled out the possibility of suicide," Jason replied. "There's no doubt in my mind that she was murdered."

"I won't say she deserved it, because no one deserves to die so horribly, but I will say that it was probably divine retribution."

"Your father would be proud of that assessment," Jason replied, smiling sheepishly.

That broke through Katherine's fury. "You're right. I have no business passing such judgments. I'm just so angry. And helpless. There should be a place for orphaned children to turn to for help. It shouldn't be a choice between the streets or the workhouse. Few find respectable employment, but I suppose they have no choice but to try. What are the chances that Alice and Andy would have found someone to take them in?"

"Katie, I agree with you wholeheartedly, but we're not going to solve the problem of orphaned children tonight. I am sorry, but I must get going," Jason said apologetically. He hated leaving her in such a dark mood, but it was nearly ten and the optimal time to head to a brothel, in his estimation.

"Jason, I want you to take Joe along," Katherine said. "For protection. I need to know that you'll be safe."

"Katie, I'll be fine, but yes, Joe is coming with me. He'll wait in the carriage."

"I certainly hope he has a cudgel stowed under his seat," Katherine said, her glare daring Jason to argue with her.

"He does."

"Maybe you should take your pistol."

Jason walked over to the bed and bent down to kiss Katherine. "I know you're worried, and I love you for it. But I will be all right. I always am."

"Even cats run out of lives," Katherine grumbled.

"I think I still have a few more left. Please go to sleep, and I'll tell you all about it over breakfast. How does that sound?"

"Sounds like you're trying to pacify me," Katherine said, but a small smile was playing about her lips. "I love you, Yank."

"And I love you, my fiery vicar's daughter," Jason replied with a grin. "Now, off to bed with you."

"I'm not a child," Katherine muttered.

"No, you're not, but I'll be able to better focus on what I must do tonight if I don't have to imagine you sitting here, looking like a thundercloud."

"Fine. I will go to bed. But I won't sleep," Katherine said, now fully smiling. "I will wait up for you."

"Deal," Jason said, and kissed her again. "I'm off."

"Be careful," Katherine called out as he left the bedroom.

Chapter 32

As the brougham approached Covent Garden, Jason was overcome with nerves. He'd been to a whorehouse once, years ago, when he was a newly certified doctor and a young woman had tried to self-abort an unwanted child. In the light of day, the brothel had looked seedy and sad, the garish furnishings overly bright and more than a little threadbare. Jason hadn't been able to save the girl; despite his best efforts, she'd hemorrhaged to death, but what stood out in his memory were the frightened faces that had looked on from the doorway, the girls young and vulnerable. He could understand the reasons some turned to prostitution, but surely there were other options, he'd thought at the time. Surely one always had a choice.

Now that he knew how the Orchid got its workforce, he had to reconsider his initial assumption. Sybil Grant had taken several newly arrived girls from the Angel Inn, so at least some of the girls that been duped and were now held prisoner, forced to service countless men without any hope of escape. Their earnings would never be enough to buy back their freedom, their tab growing by the day as they were given new gowns, food, and possibly medical attention, if Miss Cherry cared about her girls enough to keep them in decent health.

What would happen if they tried to escape? Would the thug Andy had seen be sent after them? Would he hurt them to teach them a lesson or go as far as killing them, tossing their bodies into some dark alley or the river to show the other girls the price of rebellion? Katherine was right, the government should take responsibility for the countless orphans that showed up on the streets every year. They were England's citizens, its future generation. Surely it would be a good investment to teach them skills and send them out into the world with a view to earning a living. But as he'd told his passionate wife, these were questions for another day. The carriage had pulled up before the address Jason had given Joe, and it was time to play his part.

Jason alighted from the carriage, approached the orchid-painted door, and waited until a burly youth opened it and stared at him balefully.

"What ye want?" he asked ungraciously. "I ain't seen ye before."

"What everyone wants when they come here," Jason replied. He hoped there wasn't some secret password or gesture he had to know to get in.

Having decided that Jason probably had the means to pay for his pleasure, the man finally stepped aside to reveal a lavishly furnished drawing room at the end of the short hallway. A wall must have been knocked down to create a room that size, but he supposed the madam wanted to be able to keep everyone in one place, both the girls and the clients, where they could remain under her watchful eye until they retired upstairs for a bit of privacy.

She came forward to greet Jason. The woman had to be in her mid-forties. Her dark hair was artfully piled on her head, and her face was pale with powder, her cheekbones and lips skillfully accented with rouge. She was attractive at first glance, but without the enhancements and the gentle light of the gas lamps to soften her countenance, Jason thought she might look older and more careworn.

"Good evening, sir," the woman said. "My name is Miss Cherry."

Jason bowed over her hand. "Robert Corrigan."

That had been his maternal grandfather's name, and he hoped his grandfather would forgive him for uttering it in a place like this. But it was for a good cause, and to give his own name would have been foolish in the extreme. London was a vast metropolis, but when it came to its upper classes, it may as well have been a tiny settlement. Everyone knew everyone, or at least of everyone, and Jason's name as well as his involvement with the police and work at St. George's Hospital were well documented.

"Welcome, Mr. Corrigan. You are far from home, are you not?"

"I am. I'm in London on business, and a hotel room can be a lonely place."

"And who recommended us to you?" Miss Cherry asked, her painted mouth curving coyly.

"A business contact."

"Does this contact have a name?"

"Surely you don't want me to bandy about the names of your clients," Jason said, smiling at her sardonically.

It was a stalling tactic, but he hoped that if he gave enough evasive answers, Miss Cherry would stop questioning him. What did it matter, as long as he was able and willing to pay her price?

"And did your acquaintance recommend any particular girl?" Miss Cherry asked.

"He did. He recommended Robin, but I would like to take a look for myself before I make my choice."

Jason breathed an inward sigh of relief. Andy had mentioned a girl named Robin who'd tried to console Alice when the children found themselves at the brothel. She was one of the older girls and had tried to convince Alice that there were harder and far less profitable ways to earn a living. Robin had taken to her new life and had possibly even been coached by Miss Cherry to comfort the new arrivals and reassure them in order to defuse some of their defiance.

"Very wise of you," Miss Cherry said. "Some of our clients prefer Robin, but I wouldn't trust someone else to know your desires. Shall I introduce you to the girls who are currently available?"

"Please," Jason said.

She invited him to sit down and offered him a drink before clapping her hands to summon the girls. Jason was surprised that despite the size of the room, he was the only man present. That could mean one of three things. He was either unfashionably early, the business was struggling, or the usual clients preferred to keep their identities secret and were taken directly upstairs, where their chosen girl was brought to them.

Seven girls lined up before Jason, and he had to work hard not to show his dismay. They were children, the youngest probably no older than eleven or twelve. He expected them to look frightened, but they had the dead-eyed look of people who no longer cared what happened to them and were merely trying to get from day to day. Jason nodded as if in appreciation and allowed his gaze to wander from one girl to the next. His gaze settled on a girl of about fifteen, who had flaxen hair and wide blue eyes. She resembled Andy enough to be the one he was seeking.

"What's your name, darlin'?" he asked, smiling at her.

"Alice, sir," the girl muttered.

"And this is Robin," Miss Cherry said, pointing toward a buxom girl of about sixteen who had riotous dark curls and soft brown eyes. In the soft light of the gas lamp, she could have been Katherine's younger sister.

Jason allowed his gaze to return to Alice and forced a smile to his lips. He hoped it was seductive, but given how he was feeling, it was probably more a grimace of distaste. "I'll take her."

Miss Cherry gave him a look that could only mean, *You're not taking her anywhere until you pay.*

"How much?" Jason asked.

"Didn't your friend tell you?"

"The price of whores is generally not discussed between gentlemen," Jason said with disdain.

Miss Cherry inclined her head in acknowledgement. "I do apologize, sir. That was clumsy of me."

She named her price, and Jason handed over the money, his gaze never leaving Alice's face. He saw no apprehension or fear, only indifference. She smiled at him, but the smile never reached the eyes as she held out her hand and led him to the staircase, their progress observed by Miss Cherry.

Alice took Jason to a room at the end of a long corridor. Like downstairs, the floor plan had been altered, creating many small rooms with their doors alarmingly close to each other. Jason heard the unmistakable sounds of men taking their pleasure and the occasional moan or whimper from the girls. He was glad he hadn't eaten anything in hours, since the very situation made him feel ill.

Alice shut the door behind them and advanced into the room, which was tastefully furnished in shades of pink and cream, like the bedroom of a little girl, not the boudoir of a woman. She turned to face him.

"Shall I undress, sir, or did ye 'ave something particular in mind?" she asked.

Jason came as close to her as he could without alarming her. She didn't flinch or step back. He couldn't bear to think of how many men this fifteen-year-old girl had serviced over the past five months.

"Andy sent me," he said softly, and watched a spark of hope light her eyes.

"Andy?" Her voice quavered with anxiety, probably in fear that Andy was some man named Andrew or Adrian and not her little brother.

"Your brother. He's well," Jason replied.

Alice's eyes filled with tears. "Who are ye?" she whispered. "Why are ye 'ere? Surely not just to tell me that Andy is fine. Or is 'e?" Alice exclaimed, and instantly looked terrified of alerting whoever was on the other side of the wall or outside the door with her outburst.

"Alice, I'm with the police, and I'm going to get you out of here, but first, I need you to answer a few questions for me." She nodded.

Jason pointed toward the bed. "I think we'd better talk there, in case we're being watched."

Jason removed his coat and tossed it over a chair, ignoring Alice's terrified gaze when she spotted the Colt in its holster. Jason sat down on the bed and patted the space next to him. If someone looked through the keyhole or a specially made opening, they would see two people on the bed, their exact activities distorted by the gauzy bed hangings that made the bed look like a ship in full sail.

Alice sat next to him, then slid downward, the move clear to Jason. If someone were watching, they might think she was pleasuring him. "Ask your questions," she whispered.

"Who brought you here?" he asked.

"A woman I met when Andy and I got off the coach. She said she were looking for a kitchen maid and that Andy could come too. She gave 'er name as Mrs. Pallister. She turned us over to Miss Cherry as soon as we arrived. It were the middle of the day, so she weren't wearing any rouge and 'er dress were modest. Mrs. Pallister said she were the 'ousekeeper and introduced 'er as Mrs. Newton. She welcomed us and fed us and said we could share a room. She were kind, and we felt relieved to 'ave found a position so quickly. I were terrified that we'd run out of money and find ourselves on the street."

"What happened then?" Jason asked.

He heard someone outside and shifted his weight on the bed, making the springs creak. He was surprised when Alice moaned, the sound coming from deep in her throat, but her expression never changed and then she did it again, just in case.

"She's always checking up on the punters, to make sure they're enjoying themselves," she whispered, and gave Jason a meaningful look. He was mortified but made the appropriate noises so as not to put Alice in any danger.

"Alice, have you ever seen this man?" Jason took out the drawing of Judge Grant from the *Illustrated London News* and showed it to Alice.

She shook her head. "Never seen 'im before."

That took Jason by surprise. If Oliver Grant had no ties to the brothel, then why had his sister been procuring girls for Miss Cherry? Something didn't add up.

"Have you seen any men here who are not clients? Punters," Jason amended.

"There's Seth. 'E mans the door, and there's Miss Cherry's son. 'E comes round once a week. They take tea in 'er parlor. Sometimes 'e comes in the evening. He likes Lucy."

"And how old is Lucy?"

"She's sixteen. 'E don't like the younger ones. Lucy has the biggest bosoms of all the girls," Alice explained. "'E likes that."

"What happens to the girls once they get older?" Jason asked.

"They get sold off to other brothels. Robin's the oldest. It won't be long till she goes."

"Is she afraid?"

"Nah. She can't wait. She 'as plans, Robin does."

"Are you allowed to go out?"

Alice shook her head. "I 'aven't left this place since the day I got 'ere. I 'ad no idea if Andy were all right. I were so worried. I 'aven't seen 'im in months."

"Alice, can you describe Miss Cherry's son? Do you know his name?"

Alice shook her head again. "They never use their real names. Miss Cherry jokingly calls 'im Lord Cherry."

Jason winced at the grotesqueness of that. What sort of people took children and sold them to grown men? Prostitution had probably been around as long as mankind itself, but this took a particular kind of cruelty and disregard for human life. Jason couldn't imagine that these children lasted long, which was probably why Sybil Grant had to bring more and more victims to the establishment. She seemed to have delivered a girl every few months or so.

"When was the last time you saw him?" Jason asked.

Alice slid upward so that her face was inches from his and whispered into his ear, "'E's 'ere now. Second door on the left from the stairs. That's Lucy's room."

Some part of Jason wanted to charge into that room and blow the man's testicles off, but he had to get what he'd come for and then get out safely and wait for the man to leave. Jason was in no doubt that Lord Cherry was someone he'd already met, so spotting him wouldn't be a problem, and it would be easier to apprehend him once he was outside and sufficiently far away from the Orchid to preclude Seth from coming to the rescue. Jason could easily handle one man, but not two, especially given Seth's size and obvious belligerence. Besides, it was possible that he was armed as well.

"Alice, has anyone died since you came here?"

Alice's eyes filled with tears. "Three girls."

"What did they die of?"

"One topped 'erself, one was beaten to death by Seth, and another died in childbirth. She were twelve."

"Dear God," Jason said under his breath. "Will you be all right?"

"I thought ye were going to 'elp me," Alice said accusingly.

"And I will, but I have to come back with reinforcements."

She nodded, but the hope had gone out of her eyes. She didn't believe him.

"Alice, I will come back."

"Ye 'ave a gun. Ye can take us all out of 'ere. The punters will do nothing to assist Miss Cherry. They care only about their own safety. Please," she wailed.

"I will come back. You have my word."

"Much good it will do me," Alice muttered. "I don't even know yer name."

"Jason. My name is Jason Redmond."

Alice nodded, but he didn't think she believed him.

Jason put on his coat and opened the door. The corridor was dim, lit by one sconce affixed to the far wall, the lack of light meant to protect the clients' privacy. He was halfway down the corridor when the door to Lucy's room opened and a man stepped out. Their eyes met, the spark of recognition igniting a flare of rage and disbelief in Jason. There was a moment of utter stillness, as if time had stopped and every sound faded into the vacuum as the two men stood frozen, unsure how to proceed. And then all hell broke loose.

Roy Nevins let out a roar of fury and charged, knocking Jason against the wall and punching him in the face. Jason felt momentarily stunned. His vision grew hazy, and he tasted blood, but he wasn't about to go down without a fight, not when Sybil Grant's killer was in his sights. Now it all made sense. Or at least a partial sort of sense. Jason would have liked to take a moment to slot everything he knew into place, but now wasn't the time.

As Nevins drew his arm back to administer the next blow, he left his midriff exposed, giving Jason the advantage he needed. Jason grabbed Nevins by the upper arms and drove his knee into the man's stomach hard, sending him staggering against the opposite wall. Nevins gasped, involuntarily bending over to minimize the pain as his arms went around his middle. Jason grabbed him by the throat with his left hand, pressing his thumb against the man's Adam's apple as he fumbled for his Colt with his right.

Having been a soldier, Jason had a well-honed survival instinct. He had mere moments before Roy Nevins would regroup and break free, and then he'd kill Jason, for although Jason had the advantage over him in size and was armed with a pistol, Roy Nevins was fighting for his life. Judge Grant was undoubtedly somehow involved, but it was Roy Nevins who must have killed Sybil Grant, possibly because she'd found the courage to stand up to him, or perhaps she'd been his lover, willing or otherwise.

Jason saw the glint of a knife as the dull light reflected off the blade. Strange that Roy Nevins felt the need to go around armed inside a brothel, but Jason didn't have time to ponder his rationale. He lowered the Colt from Nevins' chest and fired at his wrist. The shot sounded like a cannonball explosion in the small space, shattering the quiet of the corridor, splintering bone and tearing muscle.

The knife clattered to the floor as Roy Nevins let out a roar of pain and instinctively brought his injured arm to rest against his chest, protecting it with his good hand. Jason kicked the knife into the corner, where Nevins couldn't easily reach it. Miss Cherry came pounding up the stairs, but Jason was prepared. He had the gun trained on Roy's head, his finger on the trigger.

"Go downstairs and open the door," he commanded.

"As if I would," Miss Cherry countered.

"I have several bullets left, madam. First, I'll shoot your worthless son and then I'll shoot you."

He thought the threat might deter her long enough to consider her options, but she charged toward him with a roar, grabbing a heavy wooden candlestick off the hall table. Jason had no time to lose. Despite his wound, Roy Nevins still had plenty of fight left in him, and his mother was about to strike. What she lacked in advantage, she more than made up for in fury. If the two of them managed to overpower Jason, they'd bash his skull in.

Jason aimed and fired, the bullet perforating the woman's ample thigh. He didn't intend to kill her, only to slow her down. Miss Cherry opened her mouth in a moue of surprise before stopping mid-step, her knees buckling and the candlestick clattering to the floor. Blood bloomed on the mauve silk of her skirt, the ragged edges of the stain reminiscent of a scarlet carnation.

Miss Cherry moaned, her gaze fixed on her son, who stood frozen, blood dripping down the front of his shirt and staining the waistband of his trousers. His skin was pale and clammy, his eyes glazed with shock and pain, and his mouth partially open, as if in a silent scream. He raised his uninjured hand to indicate that he wasn't going to fight.

Jason stepped back but kept his Colt at the ready in case Seth decided to jump into the fray. He was a big man, and if he came up, he'd be armed, possibly with a pistol of his own, in which case, Jason would have no choice but to shoot to kill.

Glancing over at Nevins, Jason was relieved to see that the man was wise enough to know when he was beaten and any further attempt to disarm Jason would probably end in his death. As things stood, Roy Nevins wasn't long for this world, but where there's life, there's hope, and he no doubt still believed that he could talk his way out of his predicament. After all, all Jason had really seen was him coming out of a whore's bedroom. He had no definitive proof that Roy Nevins had been the one to kill Sybil Grant, nor would he attain it without a confession.

Jason sighed and turned toward Miss Cherry. As a doctor, he felt compelled to offer medical assistance, but he couldn't surrender his advantage. He needed to get to Joe and get these two into the carriage and over to Scotland Yard. Just as he moved toward the stairs, his gun now trained on Miss Cherry, who was in his way and could conceivably still put up a fight, Jason heard the splintering of the door and then the pounding of feet on the stairs. He braced for an encounter with Seth, but Daniel erupted into the corridor, followed by Constables Putney and Napier, and Joe. Taking quick stock of the situation, Daniel instructed the constables to cuff Roy Nevins and his mother, then look in the bedrooms in case someone was armed and decided to resort to violence.

Pandemonium ensued as several young girls and much older men were dragged into the corridor. The men looked disheveled and terrified, but the girls appeared rather pleased once they appraised the situation. They would all be questioned once the constables took the Nevinses away, but for now, Jason had to see to the wounded.

He put away his pistol and entered the nearest room, returning with a sheet that he tore into strips using his teeth. He handed several strips to Daniel, then turned his attention to Miss Cherry, who was lying on her back, her cuffed hands before her. She was deathly pale, her eyes firmly shut, but she was conscious, her chest heaving with panic and pain. The bleeding had slowed, so Jason dressed the wound and instructed the constables to find something to carry her on. Miss Cherry was in no condition to walk. Daniel had wrapped Roy's shattered wrist and made him a makeshift sling.

"What now?" Jason asked once the first aid had been administered.

"Now we wait until Constable Napier returns with the police wagon. Had I known you were going to start shooting, I'd have come better prepared," Daniel said with a grim smile.

"I had no idea I was going to come face to face with Nevins, did I?" Jason retorted.

He felt a little guilty for opening fire and wished he could have subdued mother and son by other means, but he'd made a decision and wasn't about to second-guess it. Had he chosen a more humane way, he might have been the one carried out to the police wagon with a sheet over his face, for he was under no illusions that he would have left the Orchid alive.

Jason turned to look at the girls and smiled when his gaze settled on Alice. She looked adorably smug, the dead-eyed glare of only a half hour ago replaced by excitement and satisfaction. And hope.

Chapter 33

Saturday, June 13

By the time Constable Napier returned with the wagon, faint streaks of light had appeared on the horizon, a new day dawning. After being thoroughly questioned, the girls had gone to bed and the clients had been allowed to leave. Daniel would have liked to arrest the punters one and all, but he had to focus on the masterminds of this drama. Besides, the men were so scared, they'd think twice about going to a place like this again. Although the more cynical part of him thought that nothing short of death would cure them. Whatever the appetite, there were always those who were willing to satisfy it, for a price.

Miss Cherry, now going by Mrs. Nevins, and her son were loaded into the wagon, but Seth had been wise enough to run off as soon as he heard a gunshot. He was likely responsible for more than one death and would face the gallows if arrested, but Daniel thought he might be able to track him down once the Nevinses had been interviewed. He was in no doubt that they'd be happy to blame Seth for everything they could if their cooperation might somehow minimize their own guilt.

Constable Napier jumped up on the bench, Daniel taking a seat next to him, while Constable Putney had to ride with Joe, since there was no room for him, and Daniel wouldn't dream of asking him to ride with the Nevinses, although they were surprisingly quiet. Daniel had expected to hear curses and proclamations of innocence, but mother and son were silent as the wagon pulled away from the curb.

Jason gazed out the window of the brougham, amazed by the ordinariness of the morning. The city was waking, the streets filling with produce wagons, shopkeepers on their way to open their premises, and elegant carriages filled with dandies returning home after a night of carousing. Street vendors and costermongers were already appearing on street corners, ready to start selling their wares to the passersby who might want a hot bun or an orange before starting their workday. And ragged children who worked as crossing sweeps, their eyes still gritty with sleep, stood at the ready, their twig brooms in hand.

Jason tried to think about the interviews ahead, but his mind kept returning to Alice and the other girls, who had looked small and frightened as the policemen turned to leave, appearing even more vulnerable in their wrappers and with their faces scrubbed clean of rouge.

"What will become of us?" one girl had asked, and Jason had been forced to admit that he didn't know.

The girls could remain at the Orchid for a few days at least. There was food enough to last them a while, and they would probably take or sell anything of value, but Jason had no idea where they would go afterward. It wasn't the police's responsibility to see them settled or to worry about their well-being. No matter what became of them, their childhoods had been stolen, and they would never forget what had been done to them. The stronger ones would rally, while the weaker ones might not make it to adulthood, choosing the oblivion of death over a life of fear and mistrust.

Jason had promised Alice that he would come back for her and take her to Andy, and she had reached up to cup his cheek, her gaze that of a grown woman and not a young girl as she thanked him. He wasn't at all sure where the children would go once reunited. Perhaps he could find some charity that would take them. He'd focus on that later, but for now, he needed to hear what the Nevinses had to say. It was important to interview them while they were still confused and feeling at a disadvantage. Once they'd had time to consider their situation, they might come up with a plausible story to explain their presence at the Orchid.

When they arrived at Scotland Yard, Daniel saw Superintendent Ransome jogging up the steps as if he couldn't wait to begin his day. Daniel and Jason met him just inside and relayed the evening's events. Ransome listened carefully and nodded his approval as he snuck a peek at Jason's bruised face.

"Well, now," he said, smiling that predatory smile. "At least you haven't hauled in Judge Grant."

"I've no doubt he's involved," Daniel replied. He meant to stand his ground. If Grant was guilty, he'd be going down, no matter his connections.

Ransome nodded. "If you have solid proof, Haze, he's all yours. Come find me after you've questioned the suspects," he called out over his shoulder as he headed to his office.

Daniel decided that before he did anything, he had to have a cup of tea and something to eat. He sent Constable Collins to find some breakfast and made tea for him and Jason in the small room the men used to eat their lunch. The tea was hot and sweet, and the bacon sandwiches Constable Collins brought back were thick and filling. Daniel and Jason left Constables Napier and Putney to enjoy their own well-deserved breakfast and went down to the cells where the Nevinses had been taken upon arrival.

Given that Mrs. Nevins was currently stretched out on a bunk in one of the cells, fast asleep after her ordeal, Daniel decided to start with Lord Cherry himself. He would be defiant and try to refute the charges against him, but Daniel had spent his time at the brothel wisely. He'd gone through the desk in the study at the back of the house, finding various invoices for food, spirits, and coal, all signed by R. Nevins. He'd also found Nevins' cheque book and what he believed to be a trunk of Sybil Grant's things. The man Andy had seen had definitely been Seth, the thug's vicious countenance enough to frighten the child out of his wits.

Roy Nevins shuffled into the room, his scowl twisting his face into something resembling a gargoyle.

"I've done nothing wrong," he seethed as he settled at the scarred wooden table.

Constable Collins stood behind him, baton at the ready, should Nevins try to fight his way out, since it would have been cruel to keep his shattered wrist in cuffs.

"That remains to be seen, Mr. Nevins," Daniel said.

Jason sat next to him. He looked tired and shaken by the night's events, but Daniel knew he wouldn't miss this for the world. He'd sent Joe home with a note for Katherine to reassure her that he was well and would tell her everything later.

Roy Nevins fixed Jason with a gaze that would have killed him had Nevins been able to load it with bullets. "Bastard," he hissed.

"You should talk," Jason retorted sarcastically. "I can't even begin to imagine how many criminal charges you're looking at."

Nevins looked defiant but didn't reply. Daniel took this opportunity to lay out the items he'd acquired at the brothel on the table before him, making sure they were well out of reach should Roy Nevins try to grab for anything with his good hand.

"There is enough evidence here to prove that you are the owner of the brothel known as the Orchid. Your signature appears at least a dozen times on invoices as well as the deed for the property. Plus we have statements from all the girls, who claim to have been led to believe they were going to be offered honest employment, then were forced into sexual slavery by you and your mother. They have also confirmed that the person who approached them at the Angel Inn was none other than Sybil Grant, who I assume you were blackmailing, since she'd have no reason to help you otherwise."

Daniel took a deep breath and continued. "You stand accused of entrapment, imprisonment, blackmail, and...murder," Daniel added, as if he'd forgotten that last offense. "I suggest you start talking. Your cooperation might earn you a reduced sentence."

Roy Nevins snorted at that. "What kind of fool do you take me for, Inspector?"

"The kind of fool that's likely to go to the gallows regardless," Daniel said. "You can tell us your side of the story, or you can let me present my case to the court as I see fit."

"I didn't kill anyone," Nevins exclaimed.

"No?" Jason asked conversationally. "You didn't kill Sybil Grant?"

"Her brother killed her," Nevins replied.

"Why?" Daniel asked. He didn't believe Nevins for a second.

Nevins paused, probably unsure whether it would serve him better to withhold the information or talk and see if he could twist the truth enough to cast doubt on his own guilt. "He found out what she was up to."

"And what was she up to?" Daniel asked.

"She was guilty of kidnapping and imprisonment. Not me."

"It was your establishment where underage girls were kept under lock and key and forced to service countless clients."

"I wasn't even there half the time. I didn't know what was going on. It's not illegal to run a brothel. There are hundreds of them in London. You going to take them all down?"

"I saw you coming out of Lucy's room," Jason said. "Lucy confirmed that you had forced yourself on her numerous times over the past few months."

"Didn't hear her complaining, did you?" Nevins asked, his mouth twisting into an ugly grin.

212

"I expect her complaining would have fallen on deaf ears," Daniel said. "Or would have earned her a beating. You did beat a girl to death, did you not?"

"That was Seth. He got carried away."

"We'll talk about Seth later," Daniel replied. "In the meantime, let's talk about you. Do you have anything to share with me besides pointless denials? Do you have any proof of your supposed innocence?"

"And who will believe me, Inspector? I had a taste of justice when I was fourteen. I remember it well and know exactly how it works for someone like me."

"What happened when you were fourteen?" Jason asked.

"Wouldn't you like to know?" Nevins snarled.

"I would, actually. I'd like to know what sort of experience turns a child into a monster."

Roy Nevins' face changed at that, drooping like melting wax. "My father was hanged. He was innocent, but the proof came too late to save him."

"Tell us," Daniel invited.

It was obvious Roy Nevins needed to talk about his father and the unfairness of his death, and perhaps this was the vulnerability Daniel could exploit to get him to answer their questions about his activities at the brothel. Nevins remained quiet for a long moment, then seemed to make up this mind.

"All right. If you really want to know. My father was valet to Lord Cummings. His lordship was a widower, his children grown and gone, and he was a bit of a recluse, so it was an easy job. My mother was a parlormaid in his lordship's household. That's how my parents met. It was a good life, and we were safe and comfortable until Cummings accused my father of stealing his diamond tiepin. My father never put a foot wrong in his life. He pleaded with the man, told him he never took the pin, but Cummings wouldn't listen. Had him taken up the same day. He was hanged for theft a fortnight later. There was no proof he'd taken the damn thing. The only evidence was that he could have had he wanted to. He had means and opportunity, and the motive was obvious. Greed."

"I'm sorry you lost your father," Daniel said. If Nevins was telling the truth, the case sounded flimsy indeed, but Nevins was probably striving for pity.

"The pin was found three days after he was hanged," Nevins said, his eyes misting with tears. "Lord Cummings had gone to see his physician the day before he accused my father. He'd dropped the pin when he undressed in the surgery. The maidservant found it beneath the records cabinet. It'd rolled all the way to the back and lay on its front, so was hard to see."

"What happened then?" Daniel asked. "Did you get any restitution?"

"Are you joking? Who'd give us restitution? Nothing was mentioned in the papers. They never bothered to clear his name, and my mother and I were turned out regardless, left with nothing, not even a decent character. We found lodgings in Seven Dials and did our best to scrape by." He stared at Daniel, his dark gaze accusing. "Oh, did I mention it was Judge Grant that passed the sentence? That's right. Sent him down on the flimsiest of evidence. Figured he must have done it."

"So how did you come to be employed by Judge Grant?" Jason asked. "You seem to have managed to turn the situation to your advantage."

Roy Nevins laughed, but there was no mirth in it, only derision. "My father taught me everything he knew about being a good valet. I'd learned at his side, but no one would hire me without a character, no one respectable, anyhow. I suppose it was sheer dumb luck, or maybe fate, that I found a place with a journalist. He needed a manservant, and I needed employment. He was a good man. Decent. And it was that decency that got him killed."

"Who was he?" Daniel asked, but he though he already knew.

"David Ellis. An investigative reporter, he called himself, and he dug up all sorts of muck on the rich and powerful, the men who abused their power. I'd look at his files when he was out. It was quite enlightening."

Nevins smiled at the memory. "But the best bit came when he uncovered dirt on Judge Grant. Seems His Honor had expensive tastes, so he was open to bribes, but only from a select few. He wouldn't have taken a bribe from my mum even if she'd had the money. She was too lowly for him to deal with. He took money from his cronies, noblemen, members of Parliament, and other lawmen who needed a problem to go away."

"I still don't see how you wound up in his employ," Jason said.

Roy Nevins looked thoughtful, as if he couldn't figure it out himself. "It was strange," he said at last, "but it was as if fate had its own plan for me. I was biding my time, trying to figure out how to best use the information against Judge Grant, when my employer suddenly dismissed me. It seemed he'd told his lady love what he'd discovered about her brother and she gave him the heave-ho. He couldn't understand it, especially not when he thought they were to be married," Nevins said dispassionately. "He was an impulsive man, so he gave up his lodgings and went off to the United States to report on their war. He thought it might cure him of what ailed him. The only thing it cured him of was life."

Nevins sighed heavily, as if he actually mourned the man, then went on. "So, now I was out of a job again, but I had leverage. I could blackmail Judge Grant with what I knew, or I could make his life a living hell," Nevins said. "As he had made mine. I went round to Half Moon Street and told Judge Grant what was what and told him he just got himself a new valet. He tried to have me thrown out, but not only did I show him what I had, I also told him I had left a copy with a friend and if anything happened to me, he'd take it directly to *The Times*, as Mr. Ellis should have."

Roy Nevins had a faraway look in his eyes, clearly recalling that act of daring. "I didn't want the job, but I wanted the judge in my pocket, and my pocket was soon bulging with notes, so I decided to invest in a business that would take care of me and my mother for the rest of our days.

"And then I found out about Miss Sybil's bastard. Well, that there was a bit of good fortune. I needed a respectable-looking damsel to help me out in my new enterprise. You'd be shocked to know the sort of money posh coves are willing to pay for little girls. It's sickening, really. Ma drew the line at girls under twelve, but there were plenty of country bumpkins coming to the big city who were between twelve and sixteen to make a go of the place."

"So, you forced Sybil Grant to procure girls for you once the older ones were no longer of use to you?" Jason asked, his disgust obvious.

Nevins nodded. "Every time Sybil grew a conscience, I told her I'd snuff her little girl if she refused to do what I asked. So she went along. She had to. And the judge couldn't do a thing about it. He was caught in a web of his own making. The only honorable thing he did was to cut ties with his son. Didn't want him implicated if the truth ever came out."

"What happened the night Sybil Grant died?" Daniel asked, surprised that Nevins had been so forthcoming. What he'd told them sounded like the truth.

"Everyone has a breaking point, Inspector, and the little lady had hers, I suppose. Sybil told her brother she didn't care to protect him any longer and wouldn't go along with the charade anymore. Said she didn't care if his name was dragged through the muck. He was done, and so was she. She was going to go to the police and tell all, including how I had threatened her brat. She told him he'd ruined her life, was responsible for David's death, and had stolen her child from her.

"Well, he went for her then. Tried to strangle her first, but then grabbed the letter opener that was on the nightstand and stabbed her in the neck. I heard it all from the corridor but saw no reason to intervene. If guilty of murder, he'd be in my power forever," Nevins said, smiling slyly. "And I could find a different broad to find me girls."

"Does Judge Grant know you know?" Jason asked.

"Of course he does. He was horrified after. Asked me to help him cover it up. And I did. Got rid of the bloodied clothes, the letter opener, and the book. It was my idea to plug up the keyhole and make you lot think the killer escaped from a locked room. You fell for it too. Not the sharpest tool in the box, are you, Inspector Haze?"

"Where are the book and the letter opener?" Daniel asked.

"In the Thames, that's where. But you don't need them, do you? You'll see me hang even if you can't prove a thing. Let me guess, Judge Grant will preside over my trial." His mouth twisted. "Would be fitting, I suppose."

Roy Nevins looked from Jason to Daniel, as if something he hadn't considered earlier had occurred to him. "How did you find out about the Orchid?"

"Andy tipped us off," Jason replied smugly.

Nevins shook his head. "I knew I should have put my foot down about that kid, but I figured I'd throw Sybil a bone and let her do something for the boy. I thought it'd keep her sweet. Should have known the stupid bitch would bring about my downfall, even from beyond the grave." Roy Nevins' face grew serious then. "What'll happen to my ma?"

"She'll be charged with a long list of offenses," Daniel replied. "Don't worry. You won't be dying alone. Take him down to the cells, Constable Collins." He suddenly felt completely exhausted and wanted only to go home, but he still had to make his report to Superintendent Ransome and interview Mrs. Nevins.

"Daniel, if you don't need me, I think I'll head on home," Jason said. "The wheels of justice will turn without me, and I'm too heartsick to hear any more."

"Thank you, Jason. I'll call on you later if I have any news."

Once Jason had left, Daniel went to see Ransome. He listened to what Daniel had to say carefully, never interrupting his narrative, then nodded.

"Commissioner Hawkins had suspected Grant might be taking bribes and worse. A few of his judgments have been questionable of late. Bring him in, Haze. And good work," Ransome said, a smile of genuine approval splitting his face. "Pass my thanks on to Lord Redmond. I doubt I'll be seeing him any time soon."

Daniel pushed his exhaustion away. He'd rest later. Now it was time to arrest Oliver Grant. His reckoning had come.

Chapter 34

Daniel faced Oliver Grant across the table, his nerves stretched to the breaking point. Not only was he tired, having been up since dawn of the previous day, but John Ransome had decided to join him for this interview. The purpose was twofold. If Oliver Grant were found guilty, John Ransome would take credit for bringing down one of London's most respected judges. And if Grant were found innocent, Ransome would take credit for clearing the name of one of London's most reputable judges and keeping Scotland Yard's image from being dragged through the gutter. Also, Ransome would never allow Daniel to forget that he'd saved his bacon, because if he charged Oliver Grant and the man got off regardless, Daniel would never work in London again, or anywhere in England, for that matter.

Oliver Grant looked impassive as he faced the two men. He had shaved that morning but hadn't done a particularly good job, nor were his clothes as immaculate as they had been when they'd met before. It seemed he relied on his valet for more than mere discretion.

"I'd like to speak to Commissioner Hawkins," Grant said, his gaze directed at John Ransome.

"I'm afraid he's unavailable at present," Ransome replied.

"And I presume he will remain unavailable for the duration of my stay here?" Oliver Grant asked sarcastically.

"You presume correctly, sir," Ransome said.

Oliver Grant nodded. "Can't say I'm surprised. He's not a man to risk tarnishing his reputation, even if nothing has been proven against me. So why have you brought me here, Superintendent Ransome?"

"Haze, you can do the honors," Ransome said magnanimously. "It's your case, after all."

Daniel outlined the case against Oliver Grant, who listened carefully, his arms loosely folded, his gaze infuriatingly calm. He cocked his head to the side as he considered the evidence.

"As a judge, I can assure you, Inspector, that you don't have a shred of physical evidence that will stand up in court. Everything you have is purely circumstantial, the so-called facts fed to you by a man who's fighting for his life and will say anything to avoid the hangman's noose."

"So, you deny all the allegations?" Ransome asked.

Daniel fully expected Oliver Grant to say that he did, but something in his demeanor shifted.

"No," he said.

Both Ransome and Daniel leaned forward in their eagerness to hear what Grant had to say.

"Commissioner Hawkins is very impressed with you," he said to John Ransome. "He thinks you're clever and tenacious and will go far if you don't allow yourself to become corrupted. I've no doubt that given enough time, you'll find the evidence you need convict me. There's always a trail, no matter how hard one tries to cover one's tracks."

"Are you admitting to your crimes?" Ransome asked, his surprise evident.

"When I first started out, I swore that I would dedicate my life to upholding the law, and I was zealous in my resolve. I had thought to cleanse this city of the criminal networks and their foot soldiers that seemed to be multiplying with every passing day, but I'm human, and my judgment is flawed. After my wife died, I made several unwise investments and lost a great deal of money. She had been my moral compass and my greatest ally, but I found myself alone, not only in my grief but in my folly."

"So you started taking bribes?" Daniel asked.

"It was preferable to developing a reputation for being someone who didn't pay his debts. I thought I was discreet, but I was no match for David Ellis, who saw himself as a crusader for justice and the mouthpiece of those who couldn't speak for themselves. Being that he was enamored of Sybil, I thought he might not go after me, and I was even prepared to overlook that her intended was nothing more than a glorified scandalmonger."

"But then he presented Sybil with the evidence of your corruption," Ransome said.

Oliver Grant nodded. "He did. I'm not sure what he hoped to accomplish, but Sybil couldn't believe the brother she'd looked up to her whole life could be capable of fraud, so she sent Mr. Ellis away, feeling she was unable to pledge herself to a man so willing to destroy someone who was dear to her. Ellis was so distraught, he took himself off to a war zone, the foolish man. Had he stayed, he'd have discovered she was carrying his child and they would have no doubt married, which would have left me free to deal with my own problems in my own way."

"And then Roy Nevins blackmailed you," Daniel said, eager to move the narrative along.

"Yes. He showed up on my doorstep one day, demanding to see me. We had a chat, at the end of which it was decided that I would dismiss my current valet and hire him. I never really had a choice. When Sybil told me she was pregnant, Nevins followed us to Southend to see what I was really up to, and it wasn't long before he had additional ammunition against us." Oliver Grant sighed, probably wishing he could turn back the clock and get rid of Nevins while it had still been feasible.

"Go on," Daniel prompted him.

"It was around this time that he set his mother up in a brothel. She might have been a good woman once, but life had not been kind to her, and neither had I when I sentenced her husband to hang. She opened the Orchid. At first, it was just another London brothel, but then Nevins got the notion of offering the clients young girls. There was an extra charge for a virgin, of course, and he charged the moon. There's a market for such a thing, sadly," Oliver Grant said, shaking his head as if he still couldn't believe it.

"And he needed someone who'd win the girls' trust?" Ransome asked. He was clearly disgusted but tried to keep his feelings in check.

"And who better than Sybil?" Oliver Grant replied. "They saw a refined young woman in need of a maidservant, and they trusted her instantly. Sybil had just lost David and her baby, and now she was forced to work for Nevins. She was broken inside and didn't think she deserved any happiness. She liked Captain McHenry more than anyone else since Ellis's death but refused his suit. She couldn't bear for him to find out the sins she was guilty of."

"What happened the night she died?" Daniel asked, wanting only to bring the interview to a close and send the man down to the cells.

"We argued. She told me she was done. She didn't care what happened to me or to her, but she wouldn't ruin the life of another innocent child. She said she hoped I'd be crucified for the part I had played in everything that happened because it had been my greed that had been at the root of it all. It had given Nevins ammunition against me."

"So you murdered her in your rage," Ransome said, nailing Oliver Grant with his steely gaze.

Oliver Grant nodded. "Yes. I completely lost control. It was the result of years of fear and helplessness in the face of Nevins' threats. I killed my sister and then I had Nevins help me cover it up. So, here it is, gentlemen. My confession. Even though I would have had a fair chance of walking free, I will set it down on paper and sign it because, to be honest, I don't think I can live with myself for the rest of my days knowing what I have done to my family."

"You know what that means, don't you?" John Ransome asked. "A guilty verdict is guaranteed."

"I will meet my end knowing that for the first time in a long while, I have done the right thing. I would ask one thing of you, though," he said, looking to Ransome.

"And what might that be?" Ransome asked.

"May I see my son? I would like a chance to explain before he reads about me in the papers."

Ransome nodded. "I will arrange a visit with your son before you are transferred to prison, where you will await trial."

"Thank you, Superintendent. And thank you, Inspector Haze. You proved to be cleverer than I had anticipated, you and that American of yours. Please give him my regards."

"I will be sure to do that," Daniel said, relieved that the case was finally over, and justice would be served.

Chapter 35

It was nearly noon by the time Daniel arrived at home, but it felt to him as if he'd already lived a whole day. All he wanted was to eat something and lie down for an hour or two. His eyes felt grainy from lack of sleep, and his stomach growled, the bacon sandwich he'd had hours ago long forgotten. He longed to tell Sarah about the arrests and John Ransome's praise, but the house was strangely quiet, the downstairs rooms empty.

Daniel took off his hat and coat and hung them up on the coatrack before taking himself to the kitchen, where Grace was peeling potatoes. Charlotte sat on a rug in the corner of the kitchen, her wooden blocks spread out before her. She looked up and smiled, and Daniel smiled back. He thought he'd pick Charlotte up, but she lost interest in him and went back to her game.

"Good day, Inspector," Grace said.

"Good day, Grace. Where is Mrs. Haze?"

"Mrs. Haze hasn't come down yet. I think she decided she needed a bit of a lie-in."

"Did you check on her?" Daniel asked.

"I was afraid to wake her, but I opened the door a crack and took a peek. She was sleeping like an angel."

"How long ago was that?"

"Oh, round ten, I think."

Daniel felt the first stirrings of unease. "I'll go see if Mrs. Haze wants to join me for luncheon."

"Of course, sir."

Daniel turned to leave, but Charlotte looked up and reached out to him. "Mama?" she asked.

224

"I'll go get Mama now," Daniel said. "You stay here with Grace, and I'll be right back."

Charlotte looked disappointed but didn't insist he take her along.

"It's time for your lunch anyway," Grace said as she scooped the child up and settled her in her highchair. "Some nice chicken fricassee with peas for you," Grace cooed. Charlotte didn't look impressed but opened her mouth all the same.

Leaving Charlotte to Grace and the fricassee, Daniel hurried from the kitchen and took the stairs two at a time, his stomach in knots as he approached the door to the bedroom. He'd never known Sarah to sleep this late, not even in the days after Felix's death when she could scarcely get out of bed. She had to be ill. Good thing she'd unlocked the door last night.

Daniel considered knocking but changed his mind. Opening the door softly, he peered into the room. Sarah was in bed, her face peaceful in repose. Her dark lashes were fanned against her pale cheeks, and there was a half-smile on her lips, as if she were having a lovely dream.

A wave of relief washed over Daniel. She was just tired, worn out by all her needless worrying. She needed time, that was all. Just as before, she would finally come around. He didn't disagree with Jason's supposition that some people were prone to melancholy, but Sarah certainly had reason to feel as she did. She just took longer than most to come to terms with the cruel realities life had subjected her to.

He tiptoed into the room and stood by the bed, watching Sarah sleep. She was so beautiful, so young, and they had years and years ahead of them in which to build a bridge to the future and possibly have more children. He knew they wouldn't replace the child they'd lost, but perhaps Sarah's heart would grow so full, her grief would finally lessen.

Despite his better judgment, Daniel reached out and took Sarah's hand. Perhaps it was inconsiderate, but he wanted her to wake. They would have luncheon together, and he would tell her about the case and the children they'd liberated from the brothel. She would be proud of him, and maybe even a little impressed. Daniel's daydream ended abruptly when he realized that Sarah's hand was cold and stiff. His gaze flew to her chest, praying he'd see it rise and fall, but all he saw was unnatural stillness.

"Sarah," he whispered desperately. "Sarah, wake up."

Daniel squeezed her hand, irrationally expecting her to wince and open her eyes. He wanted her to be angry with him and to admonish him for waking her, but there was no response. Sarah's face remained perfectly still, the little smile still in place.

"Sarah, please," Daniel begged. "Sarah!"

Finally letting go of her hand, Daniel hurried back to the kitchen. "Grace, quick. Fetch Jason Redmond." He took a few coins out of his pocket. "Take a cab. Tell him it's an emergency."

"What is it, sir?" Grace cried as she untied her apron. "Is it Mrs. Haze?"

Daniel nodded miserably. "Mrs. Haze is ill," he said, unable to utter the words that would make his worst nightmare a reality.

Chapter 36

Jason followed Grace into the house and ran up the stairs, his medical bag in hand. Grace had given him no indication of what was wrong with Sarah, only that she was ill, and Inspector Haze had sent for him. Jason knocked on the door and entered. He found Daniel on his knees by the bed, his head resting against Sarah's hand, which he held in his own. Jason approached slowly, taking a moment to disguise his shock. Sarah was no longer in need of a doctor, but Daniel was in need of a friend.

"Daniel," he said softly. "Daniel, what happened?"

Daniel finally looked up. His eyes were red-rimmed, his expression haunted. "I don't understand," he rasped. "Oh, Jason, I don't understand."

"May I?" Jason asked as he approached the bed.

Daniel struggled to his feet and moved aside. Jason gave Sarah a cursory examination but saw no signs of illness or violence. Rigor mortis had already set in, which meant that Sarah had been dead for at least six hours, but he thought closer to twelve. Jason looked around the room. There was nothing suspicious on the nightstand, nor did he see anything out of place. His gaze settled on the bottle of cod liver oil Sarah kept on her dressing table. There was a picture of a fish on the yellow label. Jason walked over and unscrewed the bottle, sniffing experimentally.

"Jason, what is it?" Daniel asked. He was still standing by the bed, looking lost, his gaze pleading. He needed an explanation, a reason his wife had been taken from him. "Was she ill, do you think? Did we miss something vital?"

"Daniel, this isn't cod liver oil," Jason said softly. "It's a tincture of laudanum." The bottle was almost empty, only about a tablespoon of liquid left at the very bottom.

"That was nearly full yesterday," Daniel said, his brow creasing with confusion. "At least I think it was. Oh, Jason, did she do away with herself?"

"It's possible that she took too much by accident. If she'd been taking it every day, there was already a quantity of it in her system."

Jason set the bottle down. He'd never know for certain if Sarah had intentionally ingested the entire contents of the bottle, but he was fairly sure she had. Lying to Daniel about what she was really taking, her inability to accept Felix's death, and her unwillingness to forgive herself for the part she'd played in the accident as well as the death of the man who'd run him down were all glaring signs. Sarah simply couldn't cope with the weight of her guilt, nor could she find a balance between the blessings life had bestowed on her and the tragedies. Sarah had been too emotionally fragile to find the strength to move forward, even for Charlotte's sake, and now her daughter was motherless, left with a father paralyzed by grief.

Jason approached Daniel and laid a hand on his shoulder, forcing Daniel to look at him. "You must grieve for Sarah, but then you must let her go, Daniel," Jason said. "Charlotte will need you."

Daniel nodded. "I hate to say it, but she's better off, Jason," Daniel said, his voice breaking. "At least she's finally at peace, and maybe she's with our boy. Maybe they're finally together." He looked away as tears spilled down his stubbled cheeks. "She'll want to be buried next to him at St. Catherine's."

"Would you like me to make the arrangements?" Jason asked.

"No, thank you. I will need something to focus on in the coming days. Dear Lord, Jason, how do I explain this to Charlotte? She's still so small."

"Just be there for her," Jason said. "Every day."

"Harriet will want to take her," Daniel said, his voice flat. "She'll say that I don't have the time or the gentleness needed to raise a little girl. But I won't let her. Charlotte stays with me," Daniel snapped. "She's all I have left."

"Daniel, have you eaten?" Jason asked, noting that Daniel was still wearing the clothes from last night.

Daniel shook his head. "I just got home. Oliver Grant has been charged with his sister's murder."

"That doesn't matter right now. You need to eat something, and then you must get some rest. I will stay here with Charlotte and Grace."

"I don't think I can move," Daniel said, his eyes pleading with Jason to understand. "The moment I walk out of the room, all this will become truly real, the days flowing into weeks, months, and years. I knew she wasn't happy, but she gave no indication that something was so seriously wrong. I thought she was angry, and sad, and frustrated with me for not understanding, but I never imagined…" Daniel's voice trailed off. "I thought she loved me, despite everything."

"She did love you, Daniel. Of that I'm sure," Jason said.

"Not enough. Never enough," Daniel replied. "If she loved me and Charlotte, she would have fought the darkness. She would have stayed with us."

With that, he turned away from the bed and walked out the door with the air of a man determined not to return.

Epilogue

August 1868

Jason set aside the newspaper he'd been reading. He'd come down early, unable to sleep. Thankfully, Mrs. Dodson was already up and had made him a pot of coffee and some breakfast.

It was only two days ago that he'd seen the news of Oliver Grant's execution. "Hanging *Hanging Grant*," the headline had screamed. Roy Nevins and Cheryl Nevins had been hanged on the same day, as well as Seth Dooly, the three having been found guilty of entrapment, imprisonment, extortion, child prostitution, blackmail, and, in Seth Dooly's case, murder. It was a fitting end to a sad story that would have repercussions for the victims for decades to come.

After the story finally broke, there had been much outrage and impassioned speeches about the plight of orphaned children and the corruption of London's judges, but the only story that really interested Jason was the fate of the girls rescued from the Orchid. There were ten girls in total, ranging in age from twelve to sixteen, and Andy, who wouldn't be parted from his sister. As an act of goodwill, Commissioner Hawkins had vowed to see the girls safe. His idea of safety was to place them in a home for fallen women, where they would learn valuable skills and eventually move on to a life in service. Jason couldn't help but wonder what would become of them, but there wasn't much he could do to influence the outcome short of taking them in himself.

Just as he couldn't influence Daniel, whose grief had turned into simmering anger against the woman who'd given up on him and their daughter. Perhaps Daniel found it easier to be angry than heartbroken. Jason could certainly understand that, but Daniel's refusal to even mention Sarah's name was a bit extreme. Having returned from Birch Hill after the funeral, Daniel had thrown himself into work and caring for Charlotte and had recently been credited with breaking up a drug-smuggling ring. Several opium dens had been shut down, but no doubt twice as many had sprung up since. Criminality in London was like the mythical Hydra: Cut off one head, and several more appear in its place.

Jason was startled out of his reverie by the arrival of Dodson, who looked resigned rather than annoyed.

"Constable Napier," Dodson intoned as if announcing the royal consort.

"Thank you, Dodson. I can see him," Jason replied, smiling at Constable Napier, who was hovering at Dodson's shoulder. "How can I help, Constable?"

"There's a body, sir," Constable Napier announced. "At Highgate Cemetery."

"I would think there are many bodies," Jason replied with a heavy sigh since he already knew precisely what was to come.

"A body of a young man was found inside a tomb when it was opened up to receive a recently departed viscount. There are no signs of violence, but the tomb was locked from the outside, so Inspector Haze suspects foul play."

"Right," Jason replied, debating whether he'd need his medical bag. He decided not to bother. "Lead the way, Constable Napier," he said as he pushed to his feet. Despite his pity for the victim, he felt a sense of urgency. A new case was about to begin.

The End

Please turn the page for an excerpt from

Murder in Highgate

A Redmond and Haze Mystery Book 9

Notes

I hope you've enjoyed this installment of the Redmond and Haze mysteries and will forgive me for killing off a beloved character. It wasn't an easy decision, and I will miss Sarah as much as you will.

I'd love to hear your thoughts. I can be found at irina.shapiro@yahoo.com, www.irinashapiroauthor.com, or https://www.facebook.com/IrinaShapiro2/.

If you would like to join my Victorian mysteries mailing list, please use this link.

https://landing.mailerlite.com/webforms/landing/u9d9o2

An Excerpt from Murder in Highgate

A Redmond and Haze Mystery Book 9

Prologue

The morning was misty and cool, the leaves dripping tears of dew onto the weathered gravestones. The cemetery was quiet. Even the birds dared not sing as the cortege moved down the lane, led by a hearse pulled by two magnificent horses decked out in ebony plumes. The black hearse was decorated with a gold and silver pattern that gave it a regal appearance. The mahogany casket, visible through the glass windows, was smothered in white lilies that gave off a sickening miasma that wafted over the mourners closest to the hearse. Two undertakers, their top hats trailing black ribbons, walked behind the hearse, closely followed by the weeping widow and her son, Neville Cunningham, the new Viscount of Ashford.

The late viscount's daughters walked behind their mother and brother, followed by at least forty mourners, the ladies swathed in yards of black satin and lace, the men wearing their most somber suits, black armbands encircling their sleeves. A train of carriages stood by the main gates, ready to collect the mourners after the entombment, the drivers waiting silently out of respect for the departed instead of chatting and dicing as they normally would to pass the time.

The procession finally reached the family vault. It was fairly new, compared to some of the other vaults in Highgate, and extravagantly large, built of pink granite with two columns flanking the entrance and a peaked roof, reminiscent of a Greek temple. Only three generations of Cunninghams were buried in the vault thus far. Those who had come before rested in Scotland, where they had been born and wished to be buried, the family tombs there less ostentatious and more in keeping with the landscape.

The hearse came to a dignified stop before the vault, and Gregory Fielding, the director of Fielding and Sons Undertakers, broke away from the procession and went to unlock the doors. The funeral service had been performed at St. Paul's Cathedral, no less, so now the only thing left was to transfer the coffin to the vault and wait for the mourners to depart.

Gregory Fielding took out the key the new viscount had given him and unlocked the double doors. Sullen morning light penetrated the interior of the vault as the doors swung open. Fielding's breath caught in his throat, his heart pounding with shock at the sight that greeted him. There, hung from a noose suspended from a hook in the ceiling, swung the body of a young man, his face white, the blue eyes staring in death. Gregory Fielding had seen many a dead body since joining his father in the family business at the age of ten and knew right away that the man had been a victim of murder, but just then, the cause of death wasn't the issue.

The funeral procession had stopped just outside the vault, the family ready to see the late Viscount Ashford laid to rest in the family mausoleum. They would be shocked and distressed, and possibly refuse to pay the balance of the fee, blaming the undertakers for this unprecedented fiasco, but there was nothing Gregory Fielding could do. The police had to be summoned and the body taken away before he could proceed with the entombment. He only hoped the family wouldn't publicly blame him for this grotesque display and spread the word to their social circle, therefore putting a kibosh on new and lucrative business.

Gregory Fielding backed away and quickly shut the door to protect the ladies' sensibilities before requesting a quiet word with the viscount, who turned as white as the corpse inside when informed of the problem. Fielding sighed heavily and dispatched one of his sons to fetch a constable. This was going to be a very long morning.

Chapter 1

Tuesday, September 15, 1868

Summoned by Constable Napier, Jason Redmond hurried up the steps of Scotland Yard and made his way directly to Inspector Haze's office, where he found Daniel looking broodily into space, his black notebook open on the desk and an empty pewter mug before him. Daniel was dressed in his usual manner, in a dark gray tweed suit, a white shirt, and a black tie, his round spectacles perched on his nose and his short beard neatly trimmed. The only concession to mourning was the black armband, which he'd been wearing since the unexpected death of his wife three months before.

"Ah, Jason, I'm glad you're here," Daniel said when Jason entered the room.

Jason removed his hat, set down his Gladstone bag, and settled into the guest chair. "What exactly happened?"

The only thing he'd been told by the constable who'd come to fetch him at St. George's Hospital, where he'd just come out of the operating theater after removing a gall bladder, was that he was needed urgently at Scotland Yard. As the young constable had so eloquently put it, "Some daft cove 'ad the temerity to 'ang 'is foolish self in a viscount's tomb, and lucky for 'im, 'e's dead or the Viscount Ashford would 'a murdered 'im with 'is bare 'ands, and make no mistake 'bout that, yer lordship."

Jason preferred to go simply by Dr. Redmond when volunteering his services as a pathologist at Scotland Yard, but everyone was aware of his noble rank and still used the proper address, out of respect as well as habit.

"What a debacle this morning," Daniel said with an exasperated sigh. "One would think the poor undertakers had hung a body in the Ashford vault for their own amusement. Neville Cunningham, the new viscount, was livid, blaming everyone from the London Cemetery Company to the Commissioner of Police for allowing such an unseemly display to disrupt his father's funeral. Of course, his rage was more than justified," Daniel said with a shake of his head.

"The undertaker sent for a constable, who, when he finally appeared, immediately took off for Division N to alert the desk sergeant. The desk sergeant wisely decided that this was a matter for Scotland Yard, given the exalted rank of the family involved. He sent a runner here, who had to wait at least a quarter of an hour to be seen by Superintendent Ransome, who was in a meeting with the commissioner and didn't realize the severity of the situation until Commissioner Hawkins went puce in the face upon hearing the news and advised him to send an inspector, crime scene photographer, and several constables to Highgate forthwith or Ransome would be speaking in falsetto because the commissioner would have his bollocks for lunch if he so much as put a foot wrong."

"Sounds like an eventful morning," Jason said with a smile. "Where is the body? I assume you had no choice but to move it, given the exalted rank of the family."

"It took more than three hours for the late viscount to finally assume his final resting place, so yes, we had no choice but to move the body as soon as the photographs were taken and the victim was cut down. He awaits your pleasure in the mortuary."

"Were you able to examine the crime scene properly?"

"I was given about ten minutes, since the Viscount Ashford wasn't about to delay the proceedings by a minute longer than he had to. Had it been just him, he might have been persuaded, but when the body was carried out, the widow burst into hysterics all over again, and the two young ladies, the viscount's sisters, got the vapors and had to be taken back to the carriage to recover. I was ordered to leave and take 'that damned nuisance of a corpse' with me," Daniel said.

"Tell me about the victim," Jason invited. He liked to know as much as possible about the crime before beginning the postmortem.

"The body is that of a young male. Early twenties, I'd say. There are no signs of violence that I could see."

"Are you sure this wasn't a suicide?" Jason asked.

"Quite," Daniel replied. "I've seen a number of individuals who had died by hanging, and they presented very differently from our man."

"How so?"

"Unless their hands were tied behind their back, there are usually scratch marks and bruising on the neck, and their facial expression is nothing like the almost peaceful countenance of our victim. Likewise, there was nothing the man could have stood on as he placed the noose around his neck, and the noose was fairly high up. The vault was locked from the outside, so unless he had help, he couldn't have done it to himself."

"Is he in any way related to the late viscount?" Jason asked. "It was well known that the Viscount of Ashford would be laid to rest this morning, so this display may have been intentional."

"None of the mourners knew who he was, and believe me, I checked. I had the two constables carry the body past the funeral attendees, his face exposed, to see if anyone might recognize him, but no one knew who the man was, and I noticed nothing that would lead me to suspect that someone was hiding anything beyond the natural unpleasantness of being faced with a dead body. I also interviewed as many of the mourners as would speak to me after the viscount was finally entombed."

"And did many of them agree to speak to you?"

"None of the women would stop, but most of the men paused long enough on their way back to their carriages to assure me that they hadn't recognized the man and were deeply shocked by what had taken place."

"How difficult is it to get into the vault?" Jason asked.

"One would need a key. There were no signs of forced entry, and no evidence of a struggle inside. Whoever this person was, he walked right in. You can examine the crime scene once the photographs have been developed. Norm Gillespie promised to bring them by in an hour or two."

"Did you notice anything else when examining the vault? Anything that stood out?"

Daniel shook his head. "The only thing I noticed was that the hinges were well oiled, and the interior of the vault was cleaner than I would expect. The floor in particular surprised me, as it looked as if it might have been recently washed. However, this is the viscount's family vault, so I expect the undertaker had made it his business to prepare it for the interment. No widow wants to see her husband laid to rest in a vault thick with cobwebs and swirling with dust motes."

"Well, let's see what the postmortem tells us," Jason said, pushing to his feet. He was ready to begin.

Daniel pulled out his watch and checked the time. "Would three hours be enough? Superintendent Ransome wants a report as soon as possible. Given that the commissioner is now involved, there's pressure from above to see this case solved quickly and efficiently."

"I'll do my best to have the results in a few hours," Jason promised. "Would you like to attend the postmortem?"

Daniel gave him an incredulous look. He never attended postmortems, having discovered early on that he didn't have the stomach for them. "Let's reconvene here once you're finished," Daniel said.

"Very well," Jason replied, and headed to the mortuary, located on the basement level, just down the corridor from the holding cells.

Chapter 2

Jason hung his coat and hat on a coatrack, set down his bag, and donned the leather apron and linen cap he wore during autopsies. The corpse was laid out on a granite slab, still fully dressed. Jason had expressly requested in the past that the victims be left exactly as they had been found, since there could be telltale stains or secretions on their clothes that might help him narrow down the cause of death as well as identify the method of murder if it wasn't immediately obvious.

Standing back, Jason began by studying the deceased. At first glance, he appeared to be in his early twenties, with longer-than-fashionable fair wavy hair, a neat goatee, and unblemished skin. No one had bothered to close the eyes, and they appeared to be staring at the ceiling, the blue irises still as bright as they must have been in life. The young man must have shaved shortly before he was killed, since there was no stubble on his cheeks or jawline.

His hands were clean and surprisingly soft with neatly trimmed and buffed nails. Jason reached for a magnifying glass and examined each finger carefully, peering beneath the nails to determine if there might be skin cells or traces of blood. He found none, so he moved on to the clothes. The garments were of good quality, the shoes almost new, and the hat that had been set aside when the body was brought in was neatly brushed. The cravat that was wrinkled and soiled with what looked like dried dirt must have been pristine before coming in contact with the rope, which lay coiled on a nearby chair in case Jason needed to examine it. He would take a look at it after he was finished with the postmortem.

The clothes were clean, the cuffs of the shirt crisp and white, with expensive-looking onyx cufflinks still in place. The soles of the shoes bore stains consistent with walking through the streets of London as well as a cemetery, where the paths were graveled, with bits of grass sprouting between the stones, but there were no traces of blood or any other organic matter besides that which one might step into while out about town. On a table in the corner stood a small cardboard box containing the deceased's pitifully few belongings. Jason decided to examine them before beginning the autopsy in the hope that they might tell him something of the man he was about to eviscerate.

There was a leather purse of good quality containing nearly five quid in coins of various denominations, a brass key that was probably to the man's front door or rooms in a lodging house, and a clean handkerchief. There was also a pocket watch. Jason reached for the magnifying glass again and examined the watch carefully for an inscription not visible to the naked eye or some sort of identifying mark. There was nothing distinctive about the watch, nor did Jason think it was particularly expensive. He was no expert, but based on experience, he decided that this was the sort of timepiece any clerk could afford, so it wouldn't be readily identified as having been crafted by a watchmaker of distinction.

He then checked all the pockets before undressing the corpse, in case something had been overlooked, but there was nothing. Ready to begin, Jason removed the shoes and socks and was surprised by how dainty the man's feet were, the nails as carefully buffed as those on the hands. There was a faint smell of lavender soap as well as a hint of expensive cologne. This was a man who had paid attention to detail and taken personal hygiene seriously, unlike many of the corpses and patients Jason had had to deal with in the past, who made him grateful for the linen mask he usually wore during surgeries and postmortems to minimize the smell.

Setting aside the shoes and socks, Jason untied the cravat and examined the neck thoroughly before removing the coat and trousers, leaving the man in just his shirt and underclothes. Jason gently touched the face, looking down at the body.

"Who were you? And what happened to you?" he asked the silent corpse, a wave of pity for the young man washing over him.

Then, bracing himself for what lay ahead, he went to remove the rest of the clothes and begin the more invasive part of the process.

Chapter 3

It was nearly three in the afternoon by the time Jason finished the postmortem. He covered the remains with a sheet, leaving only the face exposed, then cleaned up the mortuary, thoroughly washed his hands with carbolic, and removed the apron and cap. Grabbing his things, Jason left the mortuary and headed to Daniel's office on the ground floor. He hoped the deceased would be identified and receive a proper burial rather than be dumped into a pauper's grave with not even a wooden cross to mark the victim's final resting place.

"Well?" Daniel asked when he spotted Jason in the doorway. "Was it murder?"

"Without a doubt," Jason replied. "Let's speak to Ransome."

Superintendent Ransome looked up eagerly from the paperwork he'd been perusing, his eyes glinting with something akin to derision. "You seem to get all the best cases, Haze," he said as the two men settled before him after shutting the door on the busy station. Daniel had been the only detective on hand when the runner from Division N had arrived that morning, and Ransome, who hadn't looked nearly as calm then as he did now, had dispatched Daniel to Highgate Cemetery with all due haste.

"If you mean the most complicated, then I suppose I do, sir," Daniel replied acerbically.

Daniel admired and respected the superintendent, but he also resented his lack of support and the naked ambition Ransome never bothered to conceal from those working beneath him. John Ransome meant to be commissioner one day, and he would be, not through luck or useful social connections, but through the dogged pursuit of his goals. Ransome liked to be kept abreast of every intriguing case that came into Scotland Yard and made sure to give a statement to the press in person, getting his photograph in the papers with irritating frequency. This tactic ensured that he received credit when the case was solved.

If the case hit a dead end, as they sometimes did, he was quick to lay blame at the investigating detective's door, therefore absolving himself of any responsibility and reassuring the public that their safety was his number one priority and always would be. Ransome was not only driven but good-looking, which made him popular with the ladies who saw his photograph in their husbands' newspapers, and with the men who were drawn to ambitious, smooth-talking officials in whom they could place their trust.

Ransome chuckled. "Complicated, yes, but also career-making," he said. "No one remembers the copper who cuffed a thief or a smuggler, but they remember the man who cracked a puzzling murder case with few clues to go on. And speaking of clues, what have you got for us, Lord Redmond? Is it safe to say the victim died by hanging?"

"No, sir," Jason replied.

"Sorry?" Ransome asked, looking disappointed.

"The victim died by asphyxiation, but there are no signs of strangulation and no extensive bruising to the neck, the sort you would get if the individual were alive at the time of the hanging and was bucking and jerking as the breath was choked from the body. There are no scratches on the neck, and the nails are not broken or chipped as they would be if the victim had clawed at the rope. Likewise, there's no bulging of the eyes or pallor localized to the areas of compression. Neither urine nor feces had been evacuated at the time of death, and the hyoid bone is still intact. Also, there are no defensive wounds that I can see, so there doesn't appear to have been a struggle."

"How would you explain that?" Ransome asked.

"Aconite poisoning presents as asphyxiation but leaves no discernable traces in the body. When the victim ingests a small amount, they might experience stomach pains, nausea, vomiting, diarrhea, and irregular heartbeat. If a large dose is taken, death is almost instantaneous. The poison causes paralysis of the heart and the respiratory system. The victim suffered none of the physical symptoms before death occurred, so it had to have been a considerable dose."

"How can you tell?" Daniel asked.

"The stomach still contained the remains of the last meal, which would no longer be there had the victim vomited. And there were no traces of either vomit or excrement on the victim's clothing, hands, mouth, or rectum. However, the victim did ingest strong spirits shortly before death. Brandy, most likely," Jason said. It was difficult to tell, since the alcohol had almost certainly been infused with the poison.

"If the root of aconite had been soaked in the contents, the concentration of poison would be extremely high. Death would have been quick and virtually painless. Since there are no witnesses, I have no way of knowing what symptoms occurred just before death, but the few facts I possess support the theory that the victim had ingested aconite or some other highly toxic poison."

"So, he was poisoned, then strung up to make his death look like a hanging?" Ransome asked.

"Yes, I believe so. But there's more," Jason added, his gaze fixed on Superintendent Ransome so as not to miss his reaction. "He is a she."

"What?" Ransome and Daniel cried in unison.

"The victim was a woman."

"But he wore a goatee," Daniel protested.

"Attached with some sort of adhesive, probably the kind used in theatrical productions."

"Are you quite certain?" Ransome asked, still unable to accept Jason's pronouncement.

"I think I can tell the difference between a man and a woman, sir," Jason replied, enjoying Ransome's reaction more than he should.

"Good God! How was she able to pull it off?"

"As you already know, she wore a fake goatee, her breasts were tightly bound, and she had inserted a balled-up wad of cloth into her drawers to simulate the male organ, should someone look too closely at her groin. She also wore no corset, so her waist wasn't cinched in, allowing the clothes to hang more naturally off her frame. She wasn't tall or broad for a man, but she was of slightly more than average height for a woman, and her arms and legs were firm, which leads me to believe that she had spent a considerable amount of time on her feet and had probably worked with her hands in some capacity, although it wasn't manual labor because her hands were neither calloused nor reddened."

"Why was she dressed as a man?" Ransome exclaimed.

"The better question is, what was she doing in Highgate Cemetery in the middle of the night, and who murdered her and locked her in a vault?" Jason asked.

"Could she have been murdered elsewhere?" Daniel asked.

"It's possible," Jason replied, having considered the possibility. "She'd been dead for twelve to fifteen hours at the start of the postmortem. Had she been killed elsewhere, the body could have been transported to the cemetery and taken to the vault. No one would have been there to witness the final act, given that it would have been in the dead of night. However, neither the clothes nor the shoes show any signs of the victim being dragged or dropped."

"Extraordinary," Ransome muttered, shaking his head. "And utterly pointless."

"How do you mean, sir?" Daniel asked.

"Well, what's the point of this charade? If someone wished to kill this woman, they could have simply done so. A poison could be administered anywhere, even in the middle of a crowded restaurant. If it can't be traced definitively during a postmortem, then the poisoner is safe in pretending their companion simply became ill and died. Why go to all the trouble of either transporting the body to the cemetery or luring the victim there and then making it look like a hanging? The gates would be locked, so the murderer would have to get in somehow, drag the body all the way to the Ashford vault, then prepare the noose and suspend the body. That's a lot of physical effort, and as you have pointed out, Lord Redmond, there's no evidence the body had been dragged. And if they meant to make it look like a suicide, why lock the door from the outside?"

"Even if the door had been left unlocked, no surgeon would mistake this death for a suicide. The victim was dead by the time she was hanged. She couldn't have done it herself."

"She might have had an accomplice," Ransome pointed out.

"Yes, she could have, but that still doesn't explain the need to hang the body once it was already dead."

"Perhaps the display was meant to implicate someone," Ransome mused. "Someone connected to the viscount's family, or the viscount himself."

"None of the mourners were able to identify the deceased," Daniel said. "I watched them carefully as the body was carried past, and I didn't notice even a spark of recognition. The victim was a stranger to them all."

"Some people are good at hiding their emotions," Ransome said, "and if someone knew the body was in the vault, they would hardly be surprised, so perhaps you shouldn't be so quick to discount an Ashford connection, Inspector Haze," he added, taunting Daniel.

"I intend to question the family, sir," Daniel replied, his tone controlled, "but I could hardly insist on an extensive interview during the funeral beyond the obvious question of whether anyone could identify the deceased."

John Ransome inclined his head in an uncharacteristic show of acknowledgement. "No, you couldn't," he said. "It wouldn't do to behave in an insensitive manner. We don't want any complaints made to the commissioner. Talk to the family as soon as it's seemly."

"Yes, sir," Daniel replied.

"Well, I for one would dearly like to know what the purpose of this morning's display was," John Ransome said, turning to Jason.

"Whatever it was, it was a terrible waste of a young life," Jason replied. "Did you find anything in the vault or just outside?" he asked, turning to Daniel. "A vial, a cup, or even a flask?"

"No," Daniel said. "We found nothing out of the ordinary except several cheroot stubs, but those were still fresh and belonged to the mourners, who were smoking to pass the time."

"Lord Redmond, had the woman been sexually interfered with?" Ransome asked.

"There were no signs of assault or sexual activity."

"Was she a virgin, then?" Ransome asked.

"The victim's hymen had been broken, but the hymen is not always a reliable proof of virginity."

"Last I heard, it was," Ransome countered.

Jason didn't reply. He had no way of knowing if the woman had been sexually active without visible proof, so he wasn't willing to commit himself either way.

"Might she have been sodomized?" Ransome persisted.

"I found no evidence of anal penetration or any semen in the rectum."

"And was she in good health prior to death?" Daniel asked, clearly uncomfortable with the images Jason's reply had conjured up.

"She was in excellent health. She did have a slight curvature of the spine, but it wasn't enough to be noticeable or cause her any real discomfort. And the forefinger and thumb of her right hand were a bit calloused. It could be from holding an instrument of some sort."

"So, you believe she did some sort of physical work?" Daniel asked.

"She might have been a devoted letter writer, for all I know," Jason replied. "Without knowing something of her life, I can't really tell."

"What sort of profession would account for such callouses?" Ransome asked.

"Someone who wields a knife, like a cook, or a paintbrush."

"Was there anything beneath her fingernails, like traces of food or paint?" Daniel asked.

Jason shook his head. "No. Her hands had been scrubbed clean."

"And we have nothing that would help us to identify her?" Ransome asked, turning to Daniel.

"Not at the moment, sir. There was nothing distinctive about the watch or the cufflinks."

"Lord Redmond, did the young woman have any distinguishing marks?" Ransome asked.

"She had a birthmark on her neck, just here," Jason pointed to the left side of his own neck, "and a small scar on the palm of her left hand, right below the thumb. I left the woman's face uncovered and made sure no scars from the postmortem are visible. I think you should ask Mr. Gillespie to take some photographs of her face for the purpose of identification."

Ransome nodded. "Excellent idea, my lord. In fact, if we don't have any leads by tomorrow, I think we should appeal to the public and have the photographs of her face, both as a man and a woman, printed in the papers. Someone is bound to recognize her."

"Yes, that would probably yield results," Jason agreed.

Seeing photographs of a deceased person wasn't pleasant, but most people wouldn't find it shocking or gruesome. Many families invited photographers into their homes to take photographs of their dead so they could remember them once they were buried. Some even went as far as to ask the photographer to pose the departed with the family, as if they were still alive. Jason found the practice morbid in the extreme, but he could understand the need to have one last memory of a loved one, especially when the deceased was a child, or a baby whose face would be forever lost to time without that one piece of tangible proof that they had existed at all.

The woman on the slab was someone's child, and it was very possible that her parents were still alive and hoping for word of her.

"I will check with the other stations in case anyone fitting the victim's description has been reported missing," Daniel said. "Although it's probably too soon for her loved ones to realize she's gone. If she was seen yesterday, they might not report her disappearance for several days yet. Still, it's worth a try."

"Do that," Ransome replied, his tone indicating that the meeting was at an end. "Thank you for your assistance, your lordship," he added, smiling at Jason in an ingratiating way before turning his attention to a stack of papers on his desk, effectively dismissing them.

Jason and Daniel walked out of Ransome's office together. "I'm giving a lecture at the Royal College of Surgeons from four to six, but I can come by after, if you'll be at home," Jason offered.

"Given that I have virtually nothing to go on in this case, I think it's safe to assume I'll be there," Daniel replied sourly. "I'll see you this evening."